FALLING FOR YOUR FAKE FIANCÉ

A SWEET ROMANTIC COMEDY

EMMA ST. CLAIR

To Rob, my always

CHAPTER ONE

Thayden

"GO OVER IT AGAIN," I demand, leaning my elbows on my massive mahogany desk. The wood surface is completely bare, since I swept the contents onto the floor after reading the clause my father added to his will.

Scott pushes his black glasses up his hawkish nose, blinking rapidly. "I've read it twice. Unless there's a message in invisible ink, it says what I told you: if you want to keep the firm, you have three months to get married and must stay married for at least one year. Otherwise ..."

"The Walker Firm goes to Duke." My lip curls as I say his name.

"Yes."

I groan. Yeah, that's what I thought it said. I was just hoping Scott might see something different. Like, a bold

JUST KIDDING! somewhere in the middle. But my dad was never one for joking.

Humor? Not a chance. Making a joke of my life? Sure.

I'm a lawyer and shouldn't need another lawyer to read through a simple contract. But my vision turned red the moment I got past the second paragraph. I was ready to light the thing on fire, right here at my desk when Scott, one of only three people I legitimately like at the firm, walked in. He tried to back out, seeing the rage on my face and the contents of my desk on the floor, but I forced him to stay and pick through my father's will with me.

Maybe for most guys, this document wouldn't carry with it the sound of a death knell. Would it be unwelcome? Of course. I don't know any guy who wants to have their father meddle in their love life, much less place a binding contract about their livelihood on their marital status.

But, me? I'm the last guy alive any woman should want to marry. And I had zero intentions of getting married. Ever.

Oh, you want reasons? Maybe you should sit down for this. We could be here a while.

Forget that. I'll keep it short and sweet, narrowing it down to the top two.

Reasons why Thayden Walker is Unmarriable:

Reason #1 - I've been around the block. And back. Then, around the neighborhood. I've heard that the kind of women who want to settle down aren't too keen on that.

Don't think I'm proud of this, either.

Maybe there was a time I didn't think much of my casual dating. Now, at thirty-three ... I guess I've matured into a different way of thinking. I haven't really dated or kissed or *anything*-ed a woman in over a year. Unfortunately, the past doesn't just vanish. It's a dog at my heels. Only, I'm the dog in this scenario.

Girls want to marry princes, not canines.

Reason #2 - (and this is the biggie) I don't want to get married.

Partly to save women from a guy like me (See? I can be thoughtful!) but also because I can't imagine finding a woman that I'd want to wake up to every morning. I should know.

Not once have I been sorry to say goodbye to a woman. I've never missed anyone, never longed for something more serious, more committed. No woman—other than my mother and my housekeeper—has set foot inside my home. I'm happy living alone. Well, alone save for my almost two-hundred-pound dog. He's all the company I need.

Which leaves me in the no-man's-land somewhere between playboy and monk. I don't want to date casually the way I've done in the past. But I also don't want to settle down. That isn't going to change just because my dead daddy says I have to.

This is like one last trick pulled from his supersized bag of dirty tricks. When he died, I thought there might be some relief for me, from the control he had over almost every aspect of my life. But even now, he's pressing that thumb down on my life. And, of course, he wrote Duke in as motivation. Dad knew how much I hated his good buddy, a partner that I avoid as often as I can.

"And Duke knows?"

Scott sighs. "It says that he's been made aware."

"Because Dad knew Duke would fight me if I tried to find a way out."

Courts hate inheritance clauses like this. A judge might throw the whole thing out. But Duke could fight me for months. Years. And he would. Even if he lost in the end, he would do it just to drain my time and resources.

I bet Duke has already turned his office down the hall into a war room, assembling a team to look at this same document, planning how he'll fight me. I'm sure he's salivating at the prospect of taking the Walker Firm from me. He probably wouldn't even change the name, keeping it as Walker just to rub it in my face.

"I need a loophole," I tell Scott. "A good one. You're good at those. Find one."

I give Scott my harshest look. Too bad I'm better at charming people than scaring them.

Scott stares back at me helplessly. I may not run this law firm—yet, thanks to this ridiculous clause—but he's still below me, hoping to make partner one day. So, he has to cater to my whims, however impossible.

"I doubt that there's anything in here—"

"Find something." My growly voice sends Scott scurrying out the door.

I call my mother the moment he's gone. "What was he thinking?" I say, in lieu of hello.

Mom sighs. I suspected that she knew, but that bone-weary sound confirms it. Disappointment is such an ugly feeling. Is it too much to ask that my own mother wasn't aware of this plan?

"He loved you," she says, her tone pleading, already defending the man who's getting a good laugh from the grave.

"This isn't love," I manage to grind out, my teeth clenching.

She sighs. "Love takes many forms."

"Love doesn't hold things over people's heads until they obey. Love isn't a puppet master making his wooden son dance."

Love wouldn't put a stipulation in its will forcing

4

someone to get married if they want to take over the family firm. Love wouldn't still be haunting me after death.

But that's exactly what my father has done. For years, he manipulated, orchestrated, and pretended like he was the mob boss and I was his neighborhood to control.

I should be grieving, not feeling a building resentment. It's only been a few weeks since he died.

Mom sniffs. "Don't say things like that about him, Thayden. It's not right."

If you can't speak ill of the dead, when *can* you speak ill of them? Seems like the perfect time to me. And everything I've said is true. I know Mom is hurting, but how can she keep taking his side? It feels like such an affront.

But Mom sticks to this party line. *His* party line. She always has, even now.

"Plenty of people marry for reasons other than love. Why couldn't you find a nice girl and just decide to take the plunge? Marriage isn't so bad." She laughs a little.

"I don't want to get married," I say. "Not ever. And definitely not because Daddy says so."

Her voice brightens. Always an optimist, my mother.

"Well, it's unconventional, but you could find a woman to be your wife in name. Separate bedrooms, separate bank accounts. Who knows? Maybe you'd end up falling in love over time."

I'm not touching that last part with a ten-foot pole. Sure, I'll fall for a woman I'm forced to marry. Sounds reasonable and realistic.

"Wife in name only. Right. I'll get on that ASAP. Should be easy to find someone willing to pretend to marry me."

"You'd have to *actually* marry her, but it shouldn't be hard to find someone willing. I could make a few calls ..."

"Really, Mom? I'm surprised at you, willing to defile the

sanctity of marriage. And also, it sounds like you're pretty familiar with this document Dad drew up. Thanks for the heads-up."

She's quiet for a moment. Too long.

"I love you," Mom says, finally.

She sounds miserable, and my gut twists. I know Mom means well. But is it bad that I question the veracity of that statement? Because love doesn't look like standing by as your husband spends his life terrorizing your son. Never physically, mind you. I firmly believe Mom would have left at the first sign of violence.

He may never have struck me, but the wounds my father left are buried much deeper. Just as painful, or maybe more since they don't fade like bruises. Invisible, unless you know where to look. And Mom clearly doesn't know where to look.

She has always been kind to me. A bright beacon of cheer. Unlike Dad, she's a good person. But with one fatal flaw: him. I thought maybe we could have a different relationship now that he's gone. I shouldn't be surprised that even in death, he's driving a wedge between us.

"I just want you to be happy," Mom says. "And yes, I would love for you to settle down. Maybe you could start out with an arrangement and it could blossom into something—"

"I love you, Mom."

My words are true. Even if I'm saying them to stop her from spouting nonsense about faking a marriage.

That's the sting of it. I *do* love her. And in a messed-up way, I even loved Dad. I know I cared far more than I should have about his opinions, even if I resisted them. My eyes burn with the fresh reminder that he's gone. I *did* love him, despite it all, though I'm not convinced he ever loved me.

But I don't have time to dawdle or pick apart that thought. Because now, Mom is playing matchmaker.

"I know this very sweet woman, the daughter of a friend. She's an incredible cook. Has a little bit of a shopping addiction, and some debt." She laughs a little. "But who doesn't have debt these days?"

"Mm-hm. Any other eligible bachelorettes you want to send my way? Maybe ones without a terrible credit score, looking to cash in?"

She hesitates. "There's another woman I met recently. No debt that I know of. And other than the face tattoo—"

"You're recommending I marry someone with a face tattoo?"

"Looks are only skin-deep."

I laugh. "In this case, literally."

"Thayden."

"Mom."

For a moment, we're both silent. And then, we're laughing. Nothing about this is funny. And I mean, nothing.

Dad is dead. He's trying to force me to get married rather than passing on the family business I've worked for my whole life. And Mom is suggesting that I fake marry someone with a face tattoo. Which has to be a joke.

"I better go, Mom. Need to start the hunt for a suitable wife. Do you think Craigslist is a good place to start? Maybe Facebook Marketplace?"

"Thayden James Walker!"

"Love you, Mom!"

And on that note, I disconnect that call. I have work to do and a wife to find, one willing to marry an unmarriable man.

CHAPTER TWO

Delilah

I BLINK AT MY SUPERVISOR—'SCUSE me, about to be *former* supervisor—hoping my big blue eyes might make a difference. They used to. But I've gotten rusty at using what Mama called my *feminine wiles*.

I hate that I'm even *trying*. When I escaped to Austin at eighteen with the scholarship money I earned in the pageant circuit, I cut that skill set off. Shut it down. Cold turkey. It was the start of my new life and called for a new Delilah Hart.

No more doe eyes. No more glancing up through my lashes and ducking my chin bashfully. No soft giggles at just the right moment. No mirroring someone else's body language.

None of the same skill set that I share with a common con man. I'm out of the game. No more games. But at this moment, when I'm losing a job I *need*, I am desperate enough to use the things I learned at my mama's knee. Unfortunately, just like that scholarship money, which dried up years ago, my charm appears to be gone.

"I'm sorry, Delilah," Kevin says. "Not as many people are paying for doggy daycare. We're cutting back on our staff."

I get it. I do. The fact that anyone pays for doggy daycare to begin with baffles me. I think about prices in increments of my favorite Starbucks drinks. And as expensive as those are, one day at the Puppy Palace would be about seven grande peppermint mochas.

Kevin is still talking while I nod like I'm listening. What I'm really doing is scrambling like an egg in a hot pan. I need rent money. Gas money. Forget hair and nails and clothes money. That dried up a year ago, swiftly followed by food-that-has-any-nutritional-value money.

I'm flat broke, and worse, wading through a landfill of student debt. Scholarship money only gets you so far when you choose an out-of-state school like the University of Texas. My escape from my trailer park in Alabama has cost me a bundle.

Currently, I am a few hundred dollars from being homeless. My friends would never allow that, of course, so they can't know. I'm going to have to confess this week, at least a little, because we're meeting to discuss renewing our lease. My financial situation was already a stretch. Now? I'm sunk.

"I'm happy to put in a good word for you somewhere else," Kevin says. "You've been an excellent employee."

Right. Because shoveling dog poo out of kennels is such a demanding job. Actually, I wonder if I could say on my resume that I have experience in waste management. It sounds fancier than minimum-wage poop scooper and dog walker.

Kevin licks his lips, his tongue brushing against his handlebar mustache in a way that makes me feel icky. Ickier than I feel even looking at his dirty stache. Don't get me wrong—I love facial hair on a man. But it takes the right kind of hair and the right kind of man.

Two strikes there, Kevin. Two strikes.

"Look, how about I take you out for dinner after work? We can brainstorm ideas for your future employment."

Oh, Kevin. You just had to, didn't you? Maybe my feminine wiles aren't so rusty after all. But I wanted to keep my job, not get a date. I can't decide if I overshot or undershot.

Kevin must see the *no* written on my face because he backpedals faster than a Baptist walking into a dance hall.

"Actually, I forgot tonight won't work. But you've got my number if you ever want to—oh! My phone is ringing! See you later." Kevin scurries off.

I turn back to the kennels, where no one ever hits on me. Drools on me, yes. Jumps on me? Also yes. But they don't talk back, and they love me for more than my face.

They love me for the dog treats I keep in my back pockets.

"Don't you, boy?"

I've saved my favorite dog for last. Apollo is a massive Great Dane who makes me feel like a pocket person since his deep gray, regal face almost reaches my shoulder. He can lick the underside of my chin without doing more than tipping up his head.

Thankfully, he keeps his kisses reserved to that one area. I've seen his whole tongue hanging out, and that thing could drench my face in one swipe.

"Are you ready for a walk? Me too, big guy."

I clip the lead to his collar while he waits like the well-mannered dog that he is.

"Yes, you are. Your owner has done a good job with you. Yes, he has."

I don't know that the owner is a he, but it's a game I play, guessing about the owners based on the name, breed, and manners of a dog. I start the game as I walk Apollo around the edge of our property. October is fall, not summer, but Austin hasn't gotten the memo. It's still humid as all get-out, and I tie my hair up into a messy knot while Apollo lifts his leg on a bush.

Apollo is the kind of name a guy would choose. A cultured guy, educated. He didn't go with Zeus, a more common name from mythology. Maybe he knows his mythology.

Apollo always struck me as a god-of-all-trades, being associated with music, poetry, archery, light, and truth. He was also considered the most beautiful, which this dog certainly is.

"Is your owner handsome too, big guy?"

I picture a man with short, dark hair. Maybe a five o'clock shadow. Khaki pants, a button-down shirt, open at the throat to show off nice collarbones. I'm a total sucker for a good set of clavicles.

Apollo nudges me. "Right. Sorry. I shouldn't be focused on your owner, but on you. You're probably much more handsome. Much more well-behaved. Though a well-trained dog means a good man." He jerks the lead a little, almost making me stumble. "No pulling. Don't make me take back my compliments, big guy."

I alternate my doggy conversations between effusive baby talk and actual human conversation. The dogs I walk know all my secrets. More even than my friends. It's not that I don't trust my four besties. They pretty much changed my life. But when you grow up like I did, you learn to hold your cards close.

"Whoa, boy."

Apollo jerks again, and before I can correct him, he takes off with a sharp bark toward the fence and a dark-haired man on the other side.

The laws of physics I barely remember from high school suddenly come into play as Apollo's leash snaps taut. Something about force and immovable objects definitely applies, I think, as my arm jerks halfway out of the socket and my feet leave the ground.

For a brief and almost magical moment, I'm airborne. I feel the law of gravity distinctly as I hit the ground with an *oomph*, all the air whooshing out of my lungs.

As Apollo drags me, I literally cannot breathe. My ribs won't move. My lungs won't expand or contract. I'm going to suffocate right here, as Apollo yanks me across dry grass and gravel.

I need to let go of the leash to stop the horse of a dog from dragging me, but I've looped the end around my wrist. And without my breath, I can't think straight.

"Apollo!" a deep, male voice calls.

I'm aware of movement, and the man Apollo's running toward half climbs and half vaults himself over the fence.

I was right, I think. *He does have dark hair.*

I close my eyes as gravel digs into my skin. Thankfully, Apollo stops running. But I'm a scraped-up mess and still cannot get air.

"Why didn't you just drop the leash?"

The voice is close, and my eyes fly open. Why does he sound so handsome, yet so irritated? I'm the almost-dead one here. If anyone gets to be irritated, it's me. Also … why does he sound *familiar*?

The man manages to free my hand from the leash just as Apollo's giant paw and the full force of his almost two hundred pounds crushes my right breast.

Goodness gracious! I will never be able to nurse a child. My breast will not come back from this. It's going to shrivel up and fall off my body. I'll be a one-boobed wonder.

I open my mouth to scream as I curl my hand over my injured breast. No sound comes out but I'm finally able to take a gasping breath.

I'm not dying! I can breathe again! Whether I'll have one or two functional breasts remains to be seen.

It takes my brain a moment to catch up to reality. I'm lying on the ground, my shirt pulled halfway up my torso. I can feel the scratches and scrapes from gravel on my bare back. Everything hurts, but most especially the sharp pain radiating from my boob.

I think there's dirt in my mouth. I'm working just to breathe.

And though I can't make out the features of the man leaning over me because the sun is so bright behind him, I know he's handsome. I just know it. From the glimpse I had of him over the fence and also from the deep timbre of his voice, which made me think of maple syrup dripping low and slow off a stack of pancakes.

Something niggles at my mind, because again, he sounds familiar. Normally, I never meet the owners, and I think I'd remember a voice this sexy.

I squint up at him just as Apollo decides to help by sticking his tongue into my mouth.

I almost wish I had died from lack of air. Because there are few things as disgusting as the tongue of a Great Dane inside your mouth. It's the most action I've seen in over a year, and I am NOT here for it.

"Apollo, no! I'm sorry, Delilah."

Strong hands pull me upright with a gentleness that's jarring compared to the sheer violence of the last two minutes.

Sputtering, I wipe my mouth with the back of my hand, trying to dislodge the slime Apollo left in his wake.

"I'm fine. I think. Wait! How do you—"

In my new seated position, I can see the man's face, not just a man-shaped silhouette framed by sunlight. And it's a face I definitely didn't expect or want to see here.

"You!"

Thayden Freaking Walker chuckles, that stupid dimple I don't care a lick about popping out. How can someone get so much mileage out of just one dimple? Gracious, what if he'd had TWO? I definitely wouldn't be able to maintain my distaste for the gorgeous specimen of man before me.

Lucifer, I should call him. Because even the devil disguises himself as an angel of light. And this man is definitely wrapped up in a beautiful package.

"It's me," Thayden says, as he starts to brush off my cheek.

I slap his hand away. I'm not sure I want to know what is on my face. But I know that I do not need more of his touch. No, sir, I do not.

I realize my shirt is still yanked up, exposing a heck of a lot of skin that's now scraped up. I jerk down the hem before Thayden gets any more of an eyeful.

"Are you all right? I'm so sorry! I came to pick up Apollo and I guess he saw me through the fence."

Forget all my nice imaginings of Apollo's owner. His dog is certainly more well-mannered than this man. Thayden's first words when we met a few months ago were so over-the-top that I left a nice handprint on his face. Not that it seemed to put him off in the slightest, based on the smile he's giving me.

"This big guy is yours?" I refuse to think more highly of Thayden because I love his dog. I *refuse*.

Thayden smiles down at the oversized gray beast, who is lying next to us, seeming to smile with his eyes, tongue lolling out. I narrow my eyes at him.

Oh, no you don't, Apollo. I've seen 101 Dalmatians. *And I am not about to be set up by a dog. Nuh-uh. Stick to planning which tree to water next, buddy. Because you are not playing matchmaker with me and your donkey's butt of a human.*

"Delilah?"

I forgot how lovely it sounds when Thayden says my name. Not that it's been so long since I've seen him. A few weeks ago he was my date when his buddy, Gavin, married my friend, Zoey.

Being Thayden's date was not by choice. I agreed as a tradeoff favor for Zoey. Thayden would get a date with me if he agreed to fly Zoey out to Gavin's ranch on his private jet. His *private jet*. Because the dimple is not enough to work with, the man clearly comes from money too.

Not that I care about money, per se. I'm no gold digger. I simply want enough to cover my rent, pay off my mountain of debt, and maybe have someone other than me cut my hair.

When you have your own plane, that's excessive. The kind of wealth Mama would have been telling me to latch on to and never let go. All the more reason to steer clear. Plus, he ditched me at the wedding right after the ceremony. The nerve!!

I know, I know. I can't have it both ways. If I didn't want to go with him in the first place, I should have been fine if he left. But I'm a complicated woman, especially where Thayden is concerned, and I sure minded being ditched.

"Is your, um, chest okay?" he asks.

I realize I'm still clutching my breast, which thankfully is feeling a little less tender. I'm gonna have one heck of a bruise though.

"My chest is fantastic, thank you very much."

Well, that didn't come out right. I see the start of a grin, and Thayden's eyes flicker. I can almost hear him winding up to make some smart remark about my cleavage.

I poke his chest with my finger. "Don't you say a word."

"What would I possibly say?" He's full-on smirking now, and dang, if his chest didn't feel nice and firm underneath my fingertip.

"Uh-huh. I'm onto you, buddy."

I stand, straightening out my Puppy Palace polo and brushing off the worn khaki pants that make up my uniform. At least for today.

Which reminds me. I take Apollo's big head in my hands as he stands, shaking off and looking as innocent as they come.

"I'm going to miss you, big guy. Even after that stunt. No one filmed it, so it's like it didn't happen. Right? All's forgiven. But you can try it on your owner any time you want. In fact, try it as often as you'd like. Good boy."

I pat him on the head, scratch his floppy ears, and accept one more lick underneath my chin. Of course now, his manners are impeccably restored. How convenient.

"You should probably come back through with me to check him out, but you can take him home," I tell Thayden, bordering somewhere between coolly professional and Antarctic levels of deep freeze.

"Okay," Thayden says, falling into step beside me. "But why are you going to miss him? He'll be back tomorrow.

Unless they kick him out for atrocious behavior and mauling an innocent woman."

I have to laugh. Even though it feels like the wrong kind of signal to send. I don't want to encourage the charmer.

"Today's my last day," I say, trying to get used to my new reality. Which might include living under a bridge.

"Really? Why?"

Because I got fired, you big dope. And maybe I don't want to talk about it.

"Delilah!"

Kevin has the worst timing. "Yep. I was just escorting Mr. Walker in."

He glares, that stupid mustache twitching. "Owners aren't allowed out back. It's an insurance liability," he says in a snippy tone, glancing between me and Thayden.

"I climbed the fence," Thayden says. "It's not Delilah's fault."

I can tell that Kevin does not like the familiarity with which Thayden says my name. Even though I already turned Kevin down earlier with my eyes. But somehow he's taking personal offense to this. And who always loses in this kind of scenario? The woman. Of course.

"If I hadn't already let you go, I'd have to do so now," Kevin says, with a pitying look I'd like to punch off his face. Or maybe I'd just give that mustache a good yank.

"I said it was my fault," Thayden says, his tone a little sharper. "Apollo saw me and ran, knocking her off her feet. I climbed over the fence to help."

"Right," Kevin says, in the ultimate brushoff.

Which I would normally enjoy when it comes to Thayden, a man who seems all too used to getting what he wants. But in this situation, I'm the big loser. Fired, assaulted by a canine, and now reprimanded for something I didn't even do.

"I'll walk you out, Delilah," Kevin continues. And suddenly I'm being treated like an employee who has been fired with cause, not just let go because of slow business.

"I don't need you to walk me anywhere, Kevin. Plus, I have an hour left on the clock."

Kevin's look of pity deepens to where I'm almost feeling sorry for myself.

"I'm sorry, but given the situation, I think it's best you leave now."

"The situation?!" My voice is a shrill screech, nothing like the soft Southern drawl Mama helped me perfect as one more tool in my toolbox. I sound more like a banshee.

Thayden's strong hand wraps around my arm, and I swear that's the only thing keeping me from launching myself at Kevin right here.

"*I'll* walk you out, Delilah," Thayden says, his voice like sexy steel. "Because I'd love to discuss having you work privately for me. Since I plan to take my business elsewhere after today. Come on."

Well, now. I may not *like* Thayden, but he sure is useful in a pinch.

Kevin's mouth opens and closes a few times, but Thayden is already leading me toward the back doors. There's a brief pause at the front desk while Thayden checks Apollo out and loudly cancels his membership for personal reasons. Which he explains are the "idiots running this place."

I have to bite my lip to hide my grin. Can't show too much of my hand to Thayden. He might get the wrong idea. Heck, I think I'm beginning to get the wrong idea. Lots of very, *very* wrong ideas.

I wait for Thayden, even though I don't need to. Partly, it's because his hand around my arm feels nice but also because Kevin has joined us inside and looks incredibly irritated. So, sue me if I don't mind him suffering a bit.

We walk out front together, Apollo trotting alongside Thayden. I try to wiggle away and head to my scooter, but Thayden isn't discouraged and keeps my arm in his grip. Not tightly, but just firm enough to make my stomach do a standing backflip.

"*This* is your ride?" he asks, staring at Annabel Lee like he wishes he could stuff her in a trash compactor. "What happened to your car?"

I'm not about to tell Thayden that I sold it for the money. Especially considering I barely got enough to purchase Annabel Lee, aka my new ride. I slide on the helmet and brush my hair over my shoulders.

"I like her better." Even I can hear the defensiveness in my tone. With the crazy Texas drivers and the insane Texas heat, I'm not sure how anyone could enjoy a scooter more than a reliable, air-conditioned car. Especially when my hair looks like a discarded bird's nest every time I get where I'm going.

"Her?" His lips twitch. "Does she have a name too?"

"Maybe." And I'm not about to tell him. Who knows what Thayden would think about me naming my scooter after a dark and romantic Poe poem.

Thankfully, Thayden moves on.

"I wasn't joking," he says. "I'd like to hire you."

I close my eyes for a moment. Wishing he'd asked me on a date instead. That, I could say no to. Easily. Or ... mostly easily.

But offering a job to a woman who has none is like holding out a big old cake in front of someone on a low-carb diet. And I'd know. Because Mama insisted I stay carb-free from the moment I started developing curves. As if removing sugar from my diet would keep my A cups from sprouting into C cups. In case you were wondering, it did not.

"Hire me to do what?"

Thayden smiles, and it's devastating. I have to look away lest I be turned to dust by the force of it.

"I need someone to take care of Apollo while I'm at work. Seeing as how I just fired my doggy daycare."

"Apollo, huh. So, I wouldn't have to see *you*?"

There's a brief pause wherein my unbelievably rude words sink in. I can't believe I said them.

Thayden's face goes from shocked to amused, and he lets out a bark of laughter. Even Apollo gives him a look.

"I should be offended, but somehow, this just feels like par for the course with you."

"To clarify, it would just be me and Apollo? Alone?"

"Unless you want my company. Because I'm sure I could sneak home for lunch breaks, or—"

I hold up a hand, cutting him off before he can get out whatever has his eyes flashing with mischief. I swear, it's like this man's mission is to torture me. And based on the rapid beating of my heart, the more primal, less logical part of me loves it. That part of me needs to have a come-to-Jesus meeting.

"I'll be fine with just your dog."

Thayden looks much too pleased. This must be some kind of trap. Oh no. Maybe it's not too late to take it back. Kind of like the five-second rule, except for stupid words, not half a sandwich you drop on the floor.

"Perfect. I'm excited to have you."

He says it like I'm his guest, not his soon-to-be employee.

I hop on Annabel Lee and fire her up. Which sounds a little like starting up a remote-control car or something.

"How should I contact you?" Thayden asks.

Giving him my number feels like giving up somehow. Like he's won whatever game we're playing.

"You can get it from Gavin," I tell him.

"You can't just give it to me now?"

"Nope."

"Playing hard to get?"

"I don't play games. I *am* hard to get. Bye, handsome," I call. Thayden's brows shoot up, and a grin stretches over his face. "And goodbye to you too, Thayden."

I wait until I see understanding hit him. But it's not so satisfying when he laughs, rather than being offended that I called his dog, not him, handsome. In truth, they're both pretty spectacular. But I prefer Apollo, even after today's incident.

Thayden is still laughing, and I hit the gas, putt-putting away on Annabel Lee and leaving the man and the dog behind me.

CHAPTER THREE

Delilah

OF COURSE, the very first question I'm asked when I get home is, "How was work?"

Sam smiles from the couch, where she's in work mode with her laptop balanced on her knees and a bag of sour gummy octopus next to her. She lifts her blue light glasses to the top of her head and pops another octopus in her mouth before offering me the bag.

I don't like sour candy, not even a little bit, but I stuff the thing in my mouth anyway to give me a moment to consider my answer. By the time I manage to choke it down, my eye is twitching, and I've composed an answer that's half true.

"I got mauled by a dog and rescued by a handsome rogue. So, basically, normal." I shrug.

Sam laughs, but I don't miss the way her eyes light up. I

should have known better than to even hint at a man around her. Rookie mistake.

She sets the laptop aside and clasps her hands. "Tell me more about this rogue."

"Who has a rogue?" Abby appears out of nowhere, leaping over the back of the couch and snagging the bag of octopi. Octopuses? Whatever.

"Hey!" Sam grabs the bag. "That's my reward stash. I write another chapter, I get another octopus."

"How's the book coming?" I ask.

Sam narrows her eyes at me. "Nope. Back to the rogue. Details, please."

Now I've backed myself into a corner. All of my roommates can be pushy and nosy. But none so much as Sam, who is publicly known as Dr. Love. We are all like her little relationship guinea pigs. Anything that happens to us is fair game to go in the book she's been writing.

"Fine. There was an incident at work with one of the owners."

"I love incidents," Abby says, stealing another octopus from Sam. "Was he hot?"

"As sin. And before you ask, no. I did not give him my number."

"Boo!" both Sam and Abby say.

Abby holds up a finger. "But did he ask for it?"

"Maybe."

"You little heartbreaker. You're like the Fort Knox of women. Whoever gets past your security is going to be one lucky dude." Abby twirls the end of her purple hair around a finger.

A mental image of Thayden, grinning with that stupid dimple pops up in my mind. *Get behind me, Lucifer!* I tell him.

But he just winks and blows me a kiss. Even in my own mind, the man does what he wants.

"You okay, D?" Sam asks.

"Hmm?"

"You've got a funny look on your face. And you're fanning yourself."

I am, indeed. I drop my hands to my lap. Seeing Thayden today has reduced me to an overheated, overimaginative mess of nerves. That man shouldn't get any of my mental space.

Bu-bye! I visualize kicking his behind out of my head. But, like playing whack-a-mole, his smirking face keeps popping right back up.

"Delilah? You sure you're okay?"

I hop up from the couch and force a stretch, yawning for full effect. "I'm exhausted. Gonna veg for a while and head to bed. Where's Harpy?"

"Probably throwing a giant tire over her head or something," Abby says with an eye roll.

"Or squatting ten thousand pounds." Sam drops her glasses back in place.

"Yuck." The three of us are all on the same page when it comes to the gym, which is Harper's workplace and second home. "See y'all."

I'm almost to my room and mentally patting myself on the back. I made it through that conversation without confessing that Thayden was the rogue or dropping the bomb about getting fired. Score!

"Don't forget! Lunch the day after tomorrow to discuss our dire roommate situation!" Abby calls.

Ugh. That lunch is like a giant doomsday clock in my head for multiple reasons. I pass Zoey's old room, the empty space only adding to my sense of dread.

The five of us had planned to live together one more year in this little house ... until Zoey got married. Abby will probably be next, marrying Zoey's twin, Zane. And we've been waiting for Sam's boyfriend to put a ring on it for months.

We can't afford this place without all five of us. Heck, I can hardly afford it *with* the five of us. And my roomies are dropping like flies into serious relationships, which puts a serious kink in our living arrangements.

Only Harper and I are perpetually single. Go, us! But she has a great job training elite athletes, so I'm the only one single *and* broke.

While they're all moving forward, I'm not moving anywhere but in circles around a drain. And I've got two days to figure out how to tell my best friends that I'm not only flat broke, but jobless.

Unless I take Thayden up on his offer. But do I really need to give the man any more space in my life? I feel like I tried to slam the door on him and he keeps on wedging his foot inside.

I flop down on my bed, ready to lose myself in YouTube for a little while. Only, worry has me fidgety and unfocused. Despite kicking the man out of my head, thoughts keep going right back to Thayden.

I do love his dog. Definitely not the man. He's a rake. A rogue. A modern woman might refer to him as a canoe for feminine wash. But I'll stick with Shakespeare. Thayden is a scoundrel and a knave.

But working for him might tide me over. Maybe he could recommend me to some of his high-class friends. That could keep me from having to explain the full extent of my dire financial situation to my very best friends in the world. Women who, each in their own way, are making it. While I'm simply floundering, balancing on that thin wire hoping my smile is enough to see me through to the other side.

And what's on the other side? a persistent voice in my head wants to know.

My dream job is out of reach. Being a professor would require more schooling and more debt. The pay is peanuts. I'd be sending off checks to loan companies at my retirement party. Not to mention the fact that no one in my department ever took me seriously. I think it's the accent. Or my looks, which served me well in pageants, but not so much in academia. Every step of that journey would be a battle.

Thayden's job would be like patching a leaky tire. It'll hold me for a little while ... but I need a full replacement, not a patch.

Shaking off my worries and frustration, I tune into my favorite booktubers and makeup tutorial videos. Judge away, but as much as I love reading, sometimes a good YouTube binge does my soul good.

Thirty or three hundred minutes later, I'm as zen as I get. Maybe TOO zen, which is why I accidentally answer a call from an unknown number.

"Hello?" I say, my finger hovering over the screen in case it's a telemarketer.

Worse, it's Thayden.

"You answered," he says, not even bothering with the usual telephone pleasantries.

"I didn't mean to," I say honestly. This man makes me forget all my manners.

He laughs, and my stupid mouth thinks that's a signal to grin. *Oh no, it is not.* I bite down on my lip, hard. *That'll teach you, mouth.*

"No big plans this evening? It sounds quiet."

"And you sound like you're fishing for personal information," I snap. "Now, if you're not calling about the job you offered me earlier, we best hang up now."

"Business over pleasure. Okay. How would you like to start tomorrow?"

"Slow your roll, buddy. Why don't you let me know a bit more about what you expect me to do and what you consider a fair wage. I need to be sure you're not planning to lock me in some basement."

Now, why does that idea have me fanning my pajama shirt away from my body? It most definitely should not have that effect.

"Unfortunately for us both, I don't have a basement."

Thayden's chuckle is low and dark, as though my thoughts are projecting right to him. There's a whole bunch of butterflies trying to take flight in my belly without permission for takeoff.

"Come by tomorrow morning. I'll feed you breakfast, show you around my place, tell you what I expect and what I'll pay. If you don't trust me to be a gentleman, Gavin will vouch for me. Plus, Apollo will be there to chaperone."

He had me at breakfast, but I don't want him to know that. Honestly, as much as the man drives me up a wall, I suspect that underneath the charmer, there's a decent man. Thayden is Gavin's family lawyer, both for him and his sweet parents. Anyone that Gavin's mama loves can't be half bad.

And that's what scares me.

The knave? I can deal with. A knight in shining armor would have me swooning.

"Why don't you just tell me what you're paying now and save us both some time? I realize that the word no doesn't seem to be one you hear often, but trust me when I say I'm more than happy to keep saying it to you."

Thayden laughs again. Why does he keep doing that?

And why do I like it so much?

"I hope you do. I love a good challenge. But you won't say no to what I'm offering. Trust me. I'll send you the address. See you in the morning!"

And before I can get another word in, he has hung up on me. My phone buzzes with a text. It's Thayden, giving me his address.

Being nosy, I plug it into Google Maps. And though his neighborhood isn't in the fancypants area that Gavin and Zoey call home, it's in a fabulous—and expensive—location, right near the center of town.

I do the Google street view—because what was that invented for if not to better stalk people?—and my jaw flaps when I see the place.

Somehow, I would imagine Thayden in some sleek, modern monstrosity that's all glass and steel. Expensive and ostentatious and ugly as sin. But I never would have expected the adorable, craftsman-style bungalow that's a lot like ours, only in better shape, even if a little smaller.

It's a mint-green color with white trim and a wide front porch. Hanging baskets along the front hold bougainvillea, the deep pink petals cascading over the sides.

And, wait—is that Thayden?

He is in the very corner of the photo, shirtless and looking good enough to eat. Apollo sits nearby, watching Thayden water the front lawn. It's just Thayden's luck that he'd be out front when the little car goes by to take the images. And just my luck that it's blurry when I try to zoom in on his bare torso.

I click my phone off and clutch it to my chest. I cannot be softened up like a stick of butter on a summer afternoon by the man's house. But bougainvillea! My favorite flower!

He must have a woman already, and I hate the thought.

Stabby, burning hate. Because truly, what man would think to get hanging baskets with that particular flower? None, I tell you.

Except the man of my dreams.

Sure, call me fickle and shallow. But I believe the fabric of a person can be known by their stitching. That is, the small parts helping to make up the whole quilt.

Thayden has an amazingly well-trained, handsome dog and my favorite flower hanging on his porch. Two good stitches.

But only two!!

They don't make up for the smart mouth, the playboy reputation, and the pride that stretches halfway from here to my home state of Alabama—no, *further*. I bet his pride doesn't stop 'til it dips its cocky toes in the Atlantic Ocean.

I flip off the light and lie awake, staring at the familiar ceiling. My stomach growls, empty, and my mind is full of things I don't want to think about: my joblessness, my debt, and Thayden.

Just one more look, I think, unlocking my phone to stare at the blurry image taken from the Google-mobile of a roguishly handsome man and his not-quite-but-almost-as-handsome dog.

From: DatingGrandpaGosling@DrLove.advice
To: DrLove@DrLove.advice

Dear Dr. Love,

I'm dating the nicest guy. So nice he's … *too* nice. It's like dating a church librarian crossed with a grandpa.

I mean, he doesn't LOOK like a grandpa. He looks like Ryan Gosling. But there's just no spark. Hard to imagine with someone who looks like Ryan Gosling. THAT'S how nice he is. If he were a flavor, he'd be diet vanilla. If he were a color, it would be beige. If he were a temperature, it would be tepid bathwater.

He's so nice that I can't imagine having The Talk. What if he cries? I mean, picture Ryan Gosling crying because of you!

Wow. Actually … I feel like maybe I could work with that. Anyway, can you give me ideas to let him down easy?

Sincerely,

Dating Grandpa Gosling

————

From: DrLove@DrLove.advice
To: DatingGrandpaGosling@DrLove.advice

Dear Dating Grandpa Gosling,

Wow. If I met a guy who looked like Ryan Gosling and was as nice as my grandpa, I'd put a ring on that SO FAST.

But I get it—sometimes we just don't click with people. I get it.

My advice? Don't drag it out. Be kind, but be honest, and do it before things go too far.

And then, you should probably email me about a writing

job. For real—you need to be working with words if you aren't already.

Give me a call! And feel free to pass my number along to Grandpa Gosling too.

Sincerely,

Dr. Love

CHAPTER FOUR

Delilah

I HOPED Thayden's house would look worse in real life. As though the low-quality image on Google would be a step up somehow from the real thing. But as I park Annabel Lee at the curb and shake my hair out from the helmet, I find myself stamping my foot in a petulant show of irritation.

It looks even better! There aren't two but FOUR hanging baskets draped heavy with deep pink flowers, like he's got some kind of secret greenhouse, breeding bougainvilleas in the back.

What if he does? Be still, my heart.

I can hear Apollo barking inside, that deep woof that's practically bone-shaking.

I wave, though I can't see him yet, and call out as I make my way up the sidewalk. "Simmer down, sugar! It's only me!"

The deep blue door practically flies open, and there is that man. Smiling so smugly that he practically withers the grass with all that smugness.

And he's wearing pajamas! A white T-shirt clings to his chest and his cotton pants are patterned with sheep. It's the most informal I've seen him, and he looks frustratingly adorable. I want to cover him in a trench coat or something.

"I didn't know we were already at the point of using pet names," Thayden says. "But you can call me sugar anytime."

I breeze by and into the house. "Oh, I'm sorry. I meant the dog. Didn't I, sugar?"

I let Apollo give me his signature polite lick under the chin and scratch his velvety ears, silently apologizing. Poor guy doesn't know he's being used as a pawn in this game of tug-of-war Thayden and I seem intent on playing. I'm determined not to be the one pulled over the line and into the mud pit.

Delilah Hart doesn't lose.

That's one phrase Mama drilled into my head, even if it's not true. I lost plenty, even if I won big. And the current state of my life is definitely on the losery side.

But with Thayden? No. I won't let the man win.

"I'll try not to be too offended," Thayden says, closing the door.

"Well, whom did you think I was here to see? You?"

"*Whom?*"

I give him what Mama would have called the hairy eyeball. "English lit major. I may speak Southern, but I do like my grammar and correct word choice."

And if it matters, I'm Team Oxford comma all the way. But I doubt Thayden knows, uses, or cares for my ride-or-die punctuation.

Thayden smiles, shaking his head, like I'm some mystery

he can't figure out. "Okay, then. I'll do my best to stay on my grammatical toes. Now, I'm glad you and Apollo get along swimmingly, but he's not the one promising you bacon."

"Bacon, you say?"

"And grits."

"Hm. White or yellow?"

This shouldn't be a question. But every time I've ordered grits in an Austin eatery, they're yellow, and I don't mean from butter. I may not have the stereotypical Southern palate, but I do have a certain standard when it comes to breakfast, and yellow cornmeal, aka polenta, does not belong on a breakfast plate.

Thayden scoffs, his lip curled in a way that draws my eyes where I don't want them to be—that luscious mouth of his.

"What do you take me for? A hipster gastropub? *White*."

I have to slap a hand over my mouth to stop the laugh that bursts out of me. That doesn't hide the sound though, and I'm rewarded with the widest, most brilliant smile.

Fail! Total fail. Control yourself, Miss Hart!

"Don't hold a laugh that beautiful in. Not on my account. Come on. Let me feed you."

He casually turns and heads deeper into his house, but I don't follow right away. My feet are planted firmly on the refinished hardwoods like I'm about to sprout roots. Because following this man, spending any more time with him, especially in a house so perfect that it makes my heart ache with longing—well, it seems like a very bad idea. Especially with him throwing out lines about my beautiful laugh and offering me bacon and grits.

"Don't let your biscuits get cold!"

Biscuits?!

Probably from a can, I tell myself. The thought is desperate. Even if they're from a can, no man has ever made me biscuits. Heck, I don't make biscuits. Cookies are the only thing I can make without burning.

Apollo nudges my hand with his big, cool nose. I glare down at Thayden's co-conspirator.

"He's good, isn't he? Tell me, how many women has he made breakfast for in that kitchen, huh?"

Apollo just nudges me, this time with the top of his head, like he's trying to scratch an itch using my body. I have to sidestep, which gets my feet moving toward the kitchen. He really is Thayden's partner in crime.

I wonder if there's a doggy obedience school teaching the art of using your pup to win over women. Knowing this world, probably. And if there is, I'd lay down money on Thayden attending.

I walk slowly, taking in the details of Thayden's house, which are as surprising as the outside. Rather than a gut job, this home looks carefully, lovingly, expensively restored. From the original floors I noticed when I came in, to the built-in bookshelves surrounding a large fireplace, to the thick casings around the windows and crown molding.

The furnishings consist of dark woods, fabrics in shades of blue. Everything looks expensive, but the kind of expensive that you can enjoy. Not like museum fancy. And somehow not pretentious.

The smell of bacon and buttered biscuits and coffee hits me as I walk through the arched doorway to the dining room and open kitchen. My shriveled-up stomach rumbles, sensing an actual meal nearby. I press a hand to it, willing it not to shame me.

It's obvious immediately that Thayden did make the biscuits because flour is everywhere. I didn't notice when he answered the door, but it dusts the chest of his shirt and there's a little on his cheek as he turns to smile at me.

"Do you like the house?"

"Is that a question?"

All this added temptation has me feeling snippy. He has to know the house is amazing. Just like he knows—or *believes*—he's God's gift to women.

"Yes. I'm asking you if you like the house."

I sniff, glancing around at the kitchen with its gray-painted cabinets, wide marble island, and deep sink. This room, unlike the rest, looks like it was completely over-hauled, though it still fits with the house's original style.

It currently looks like a bakery exploded in here, but that just adds to the charm. The sink is piled high with dishes. And the aforementioned flour is all over the counters and floor. Why does it make me like him even more, and also make me angrier, that he left things as-is, rather than trying to clean up the room for me?

Lived-in. That's the thing I love most about this house, what it says from the porch to the flour-dusted kitchen floors. It's like a beating heart, alive and warm.

And it's totally spinning my thoughts in circles because it's another surprising stitch in the fabric of the too-hand-some man in front of me.

"It's nice," I say. Honestly, it's more of a grumble.

"Nice? Okayyyy. Tough crowd. Hopefully, this is more than nice."

Thayden nods to a stool at the island and slides a plate toward me.

Oh, it's more than nice. There's bacon, just the right amount of crisp and piled recklessly high, as though a package of good bacon doesn't cost seven dollars. Grits, steaming and creamy with butter pooling in the center. A flaky, buttermilk biscuit the size of my fist is arranged behind scrambled eggs with cheese.

Because the man seems bent on overachieving, he pushes a bowl of sliced fruit toward me. Not like the fruit salad Mama used to serve with apples, oranges, and too-ripe bananas, but *fancy* fruit. Pineapple. Strawberries. Kiwi. Mango.

My eyes are stinging as I look down at more food than I usually eat in a day. I'm starved, but not just for the calories and the taste of this luxury. I am starved for someone who will take care of me like this.

And that's the most dangerous thing of all. Because I don't want it to be Thayden. Why does it have to be him?

"How do you take your coffee?" Thayden asks, and I'm thankful his back is to me so I can swipe away the single tear that managed its jailbreak.

"Or do you like tea? Water? Juice? Mimosas?"

He turns and gives me a wicked grin, flashing that dimple, and thankfully, I've pulled myself together enough to respond.

"Coffee is perfect. Cream and sugar."

"Lots of cream? Lots of sugar? Or just a taste?"

"You don't have to complicate it. It's coffee, for heaven's sake!"

I'm immediately ashamed by my reaction. The man offered me a job. Made me a breakfast that I can't even bring myself to eat, and I'm biting his head off like a grumpy T. rex.

With my gaze trained on my lap, I take a few deep breaths. Thayden doesn't speak, just fixes my coffee and sets it in front of me, like I didn't snap at him for no reason. A cold nose nudges my fingers and then Apollo's head shoves all the way into my lap, barely fitting between my thighs and the counter.

"Guess it's a good thing you at least like my dog," Thayden says, taking the barstool next to mine.

He's quiet, and I'm quiet. We sit in silence for a few long moments, not eating and not speaking. What must he think of me?

"I'm sorry for snapping at you," I say, finally. "I just—I am …"

There isn't a good explanation for my bad behavior. I'm not even sure why I'm so resistant to him. Maybe because when we met, I pigeonholed him as a charmer and a ladies' man. Now, he's trying to rewrite that image, and my brain is not ready to let him. He jumbles up my insides something fierce. I thought he was one way, but now I'm seeing a different man. At least, I think.

The jaded part of me—which, to be clear, makes up eighty percent or more—is suspicious of his charm. I've seen my fair share of men like him moving in and out of Mama's bed. Not one could be trusted. Not one stayed.

"Hey," Thayden says softly, brushing the hair back from my shoulder with a touch lighter than a bird feather. "Just eat before your food gets cold. You need to make your judgment on my grits while they're hot."

It's his teasing tone that frees me up to move again. Giving Apollo a final pat, I lift my fork, reminding myself to use my manners. From the first bite, I'm tempted to shovel everything in as fast as possible before it disappears like some kind of food mirage.

"Is he bothering you?" Thayden asks, nodding toward Apollo. "I've worked with him on not begging. He thinks if he stays quiet and *small*, he can get away with this."

I smile. "Does he think he's a lap dog?"

"Oh yeah. I try not to let him on the couch. Or, uh, the

bed. But since it's just me and him at night, I usually give in."

Huh. Just Thayden and Apollo at night. So, he's not a womanizer? Or is that just what he wants me to think?

I give him a sideways glance while I chew my biscuit, which is one of the best I've ever had.

"I had you pegged as a man who didn't lack for … night-time company. What with the ridiculous amount of flirting and all."

Thayden takes a sip of coffee, not meeting my eyes. "In the past, I've not been lonely," he says, finally, the words coming slow and careful.

The words, though vague, send a shudder through me. It's unfair, really, because this man isn't mine. And even if he were, we all have our pasts. But somehow the idea of Thayden with another woman—other *women*, plural—makes me feel hurt and small. I'm reminded how surprisingly sheltered I've been, how naive to so many experiences. Like serious boyfriends. Falling in love. Having someone make me breakfast.

Thayden spins on his stool, resting one forearm on the counter and leaning close. The air in the room has been sucked out. Maybe all of it is trapped in the big breath I'm holding in.

"Things have changed for me in the past year. *I've* changed. I'm not saying I'm some great man, or that I regret all my past. I never cheated or lied about my intentions, but I also never brought a woman to my home."

So many words to process, and so hard to think with a mouthful of perfectly cooked grits and a man who smells tastier than bacon sitting much too close to me.

I swallow, measuring out my words. For the first time all

morning, I'm careful in what I say. "You don't owe me an explanation, Thayden. For your past or your present."

He doesn't know how it made my heart constrict to know that I'm the first woman who's been in this kitchen. What does that even *mean*?

The man has always been a flirt, but it didn't ever feel real. Like, he wasn't pursuing *me*, just doing what came natural. Or chasing the unattainable when I didn't fall for him the first time we met.

"I do owe it to you though. When I first met you, I offended you so much that you slapped my face and punched me in the gut."

"I did do that, didn't I?" I can't help the pleased smile that takes over my face. I regret nothing. Thayden made some kind of remark to me and Zoey about a two-for-one special. I'd slap him again. The comment still gets my blood boiling. But honestly, I've heard nothing like that again. Flirting, yes. Nothing even remotely close to that crass joke.

"You did."

Thayden smiles, and I have to pick up my coffee mug to have some kind of shield. A small, caffeinated buffer.

"And then I forced you to be my date for Gavin's wedding."

"That you did. Though I'm not sure the terms were equal, considering you flew Zoey to Gavin's ranch in order to win that one measly date with me."

"Worth it," he says.

I take another sip of coffee. "Was it? Because as I recall, you bolted out of there early. Left me high and dry and dateless."

I know I can't resent the man for making me date him, then be mad when he ditches me. I can't want to hate him and also revel in the fact that I'm the first woman he's made breakfast for in this house.

If he's even to be believed.

And that's the thing with someone so charming. How do you *know*?

My trust issues have their own zip code. But especially when it comes to men, and even more especially when it comes to charming men. My mama used that charm to con people, and taught me to wield my charm as well. Even knowing better, she fell for her own tricks when it came to men. If there's one life lesson I learned from childhood, it's to watch out for a pretty face and a golden tongue.

Thayden? He's like the poster child for both.

"Delilah, about the wedding—"

A door closes, and Thayden's eyes widen before a woman calls, "Hello? Thayden, dear?"

My eyes narrow, but her voice and tone don't sound like a girlfriend. She talks like … a mother.

"My mom."

Thayden closes his eyes for a moment, like he's saying a silent prayer. He opens them a moment later, slight panic visible in his green gaze. "I'm sorry. I had no idea she was coming, and I'm just … sorry."

In twenty-four hours I've gone from halfway hating Thayden to being rescued and hired by him. Now I'm eating his home-cooked breakfast, having deep talks, and meeting his mama.

"It's fine," I say, but I'm not so sure I believe it.

CHAPTER FIVE

Delilah

HEELS CLACK their way through the house, and Apollo darts out of the kitchen, wagging his tail. A moment later, a beautiful woman with a sleek head of dark hair threaded with gray appears in the wide doorway, then stops.

If she had pearls, she'd be clutching them. Instead, her fingers close around a diamond pendant that has to be at least three carats. I try not to stare at it.

"You're beautiful," she breathes, her eyes glancing over me before coming to rest on Thayden, who sighs with deep resignation. "Thayden, she's beautiful."

When Thayden stands, I find myself getting to my feet as well, smiling and hoping that the flush in my cheeks isn't too noticeable. I smooth down my skirt, making sure it isn't tucked into the bike shorts underneath. I started wearing the shorts when I learned the hard way what happens to skirts on a scooter.

"Hello, Mom," he says, brushing a kiss over her cheek. She hardly seems to notice but has gone back to studying me with grass-green eyes the same color as his.

I'm used to being on display, being looked over and judged like a calf at a livestock show, but up close and personal with Thayden's mama, it's a little odd. Mostly because I suspect she has the wrong idea about who I am. I also suddenly feel out of place, the disparity between my wealth and theirs, my background and theirs, coming into sharp focus. I can often forget my trailer-park roots and the shame I carry from being Mama's little lackey, but it rears up at the worst times.

Thayden puts a careful arm around my shoulders, looking like he's afraid I might bite him. Sensible man. Because I just might.

"Mom, this is Delilah. Delilah, my mother, Elizabeth."

I fix a smile on my face that's at least halfway genuine and hold out my hand. "It's a pleasure to meet you, ma'am."

She takes my hand in both of hers, squeezing. An emotion that seems far too expressive given our situation fills her eyes.

Okay, she definitely seems to have the wrong idea. Breakfast in a man's house usually implies a sleeping-over kind of situation. Which this definitely is not.

I'm about to clear up any confusion, when she lets me go and turns to Thayden.

"How did you find someone so quickly? I mean, under the circumstances. You didn't take much time."

Huh. Okay, maybe she *does* understand that I'm Apollo's new canine babysitter. Thayden did just fire the doggy daycare yesterday. Does that mean he talks to her daily about his life stuff? Because that's really ... sweet.

"Where did you meet her?" his mother asks, when still neither of us has spoken.

Thayden glances between us, looking embarrassed. Maybe because he should be embarrassed by his behavior when we met. "Actually, um, we—"

I don't let him finish. "We met through mutual friends, then ran into each other again at doggy daycare," I say.

Her eyes warm and she slides onto a stool, patting the one next to her.

"Thayden, fix me a cup of coffee, please."

"Yes, Mom. But you should know—"

"Hush, dear. Delilah was about to tell me about your recent run-in. I am all ears."

With a sigh, Thayden fixes a mug of coffee and a small bowl of fruit for his mom. I think it says something about the man that he knows his mama well enough to know how she takes her coffee.

Apollo sets his heavy head in my lap and looks up at me with deep brown eyes. I begin to rub his soft ears.

"So," Elizabeth says, "tell me everything. Start at the beginning."

I glance at Thayden, still unsure. She mentioned finding someone quickly, so she must know why I'm here. Yet, she seems far too invested in Thayden's dog caretaker. Something feels off, but then, he apologized for her, so maybe this is par for the course.

"I have to finish getting ready for work," Thayden says. "Will you two be safe?"

Elizabeth laughs, patting my shoulder. "What kind of question is that?"

Yeah, what kind of question is that? His mother seems a

bit emotional, though that's a thing between moms and sons, isn't it? Nosy, overbearing, and perfectly normal. At least, from what I've gathered from TV and movies. I try not to use my own experience as any baseline for normalcy.

"It's fine," I assure Thayden. "Don't you worry your pretty little head. Go on and get ready."

Thayden's lips twitch, and I realize too late that I shouldn't ever refer to him as pretty, even if it's an expression. If anything, the man is hot, but hot as sin, which is to say off-limits. He gives off a vibe that's like an Open 24 Hours sign, but all I see is neon lights flashing Do Not Enter.

Even if he has been completely different this morning. Thoughtful. Kind. Less flirtatious and more genuine. Like he took off the normal mask he wears and let me peek underneath. He needs to put that mask back on before I get any untoward ideas.

Thayden disappears upstairs, and his mom blinks at me, then looks down at Apollo, giving him a quick pat.

"He seems really taken with you," Elizabeth says, sounding a little choked up.

I stare down at Apollo. Is he like her honorary grandson? Does she *have* grandchildren? I realize I know very little about Thayden, like if he has any siblings or other family. This is the perfect opportunity to get the dirt.

Apollo snuggles closer. "He's very sweet. Do you have any other children? Grandchildren?"

Elizabeth sucks in a breath, and her wide green eyes meet mine. "No. Thayden's an only child. Which makes this big guy my only granddog." She laughs, but it seems to be more of a cover for the emotions she's battling. "You're already thinking about children?" She gives me a sly sideways glance.

"Me? Oh, no. I mean, not yet. I'd want to get settled first. I love kids though."

"How wonderful." She sniffs.

"I would love to know more about Thayden, since we don't know each other well." I give her my best smile. "You know, all the stories I can tease him about. Has he always been so charming?"

She smiles, laughing a little. "Always. The boy could talk his way out of about anything. From time-out at school to parking tickets."

"I'll bet."

"How did he talk *you* into it? I mean, if you don't mind me asking."

Money. Pure and simple. Which makes me feel somehow like I'm a terrible person.

I glance down at Apollo, who seems all too pleased with the attention I'm giving his ears. Meanwhile, I'm thankful for the distraction he provides. I'd prefer not to get into the details of my pitiful financial and occupational situation.

"Well, I'd just lost my job, actually. I was feeling a bit desperate. Thayden swooped in, a veritable Prince Charming, and here I am."

Okay, so maybe I embellished a bit for the sake of his mama. Who, clearly, adores her son. It makes me a little weepy too, to be honest. I'm not sure Mama ever cared this much about me, except as it related to my ability to line her pockets.

"So, it's just about the money, then?"

Elizabeth seems oddly disappointed, though I can see the effort she's making to pretend she's not.

What else would it be about?

"I mean, for sure, I need the money. But I really do like him," I say, moving to scratch Apollo's neck. "Ideally, it will turn into more."

More business. More high-end clients. Less worry about whether or not I can pay rent.

"I mean, we haven't talked specifics yet, so we'll see. The timing couldn't have been better. I'm grateful Thayden is giving me the opportunity."

I'm surprised at how true the words are. It scares me a little bit, to be honest. My view of Thayden has shifted sideways a little too much today. What with the house, the serving me breakfast, the bonding-with-his-mother thing. If I don't watch out, this man could undo me. He already is.

He's a charmer, I remind myself. *It's all an act. And you've seen what charming men can do. Be Fort Knox! Not an open-all-night convenience store.*

"Sounds like it's mutually beneficial. Tell me again how you met? Through which friend?"

"Gavin. He married one of my good friends, Zoey. I was Thayden's date to the wedding. Even though we didn't quite hit it off at first."

Elizabeth's eyes soften, and she's about to ask another question when Thayden breezes back into the room. He is a vision in a suit.

"What do you mean, we didn't hit it off?" he asks, adjusting his tie as he grins. "I seem to remember us hitting it off very well. Emphasis on the *hitting.*"

I toss him a glare with no heat behind it. At least, not the angry kind. "Only because you were hitting on me."

"Such a flirt," his mother admonishes. "But that's all changing now, isn't it?"

She sniffs again, and I swear, this woman must be the most emotional person I've ever met. I glance between the two of them.

Thayden clears his throat. "Mom, really, we don't need to—"

"Hush." Elizabeth waves dismissively, then puts her hand over mine. "It's been so hard, losing his father so suddenly. Things between him and Thayden were so complicated. But he loved you very much," she says, turning back to Thayden.

He lost his father? It must have been recent, which might explain his mother's delicate state. And there is clearly a story there. *Complicated* usually translates to lots of pain and heartache.

Oh, no. My caretaking instincts do not need to activate. Thayden does not need me to give him a hug or bake him cookies. He doesn't need a shoulder to cry on—at least, not *my* shoulder. But I already feel more of my walls crumbling.

I wonder if he likes chocolate chip or iced sugar cookies? Maybe snickerdoodles?

Thayden shifts, fiddling with his cuff links and refusing to look at me. "Mom," he says, his voice pleading. "Could we not?"

In typical mom fashion, she ignores him. "I know he would be so proud of you. He always was, even if he didn't express it well."

Thayden looks like a dam, about to spring a leak. A solid wall, but with a tiny crack starting to form from all the pressure behind it. I reach out and put a hand on his arm.

It's not much of a connection through his suit jacket and his shirt underneath. Maybe Thayden still is a charmer, but losing his daddy? He gets a dose of grace for that.

"I better go," he says, his eyes fixed on my hand.

I get a sense of the muscles bunching underneath all the layers of fabric. Goodness! The man certainly must know his way around a gym. I drop my hand before I do something unbecoming to a lady, like measure the thickness of his bicep between my fingers.

Thayden brushes his mother's cheek with a kiss, and

before I can stop him, he does the same to me. It's barely a whisper of his lips on my skin. It shouldn't have the effect of caffeine mainlined into my bloodstream. But, oh boy, it does.

I narrow my eyes at him, and catch half a smirk as he walks away. It's a bit subdued compared to his usual devilish grin, but no less handsome.

Apollo trails after him, giving a low whine, and Thayden pauses to scratch his ears and receive a lick. Thayden is much taller than me, so he actually has to stoop a little for this giant dog. I can't help but smile.

"You be good today for Delilah. She'll take good care of you, okay?" His eyes cut to me. "Have a good day. Don't worry about the kitchen. I'll deal with it later."

Because my manners decide to make a sudden appearance, I find myself saying, "You made breakfast. Cleaning up is the least I can do."

Dang it. There I go. Agreeing to more than I should because the man has eyes like a field I'd like to lie down in and a smile that could charm the stripes off a zebra. Not to mention he's sweet to his mama and just lost his daddy.

Is one morning all it takes to win me over? Maybe I'll find something incriminating later when I'm snooping, because I one hundred percent *will* be snooping later.

Maybe he embezzles money from old ladies. Doubtful, given his sweetness with his mama.

Or maybe there's a whole room dedicated to magic tricks. That might do it. Though I could totally imagine Thayden in a silky black cape and top hat.

I'd let him saw me in half any day of the week.

No! I most certainly will not!

I realize he's leaving while I'm daydreaming about being a sexy magician's assistant. We never even discussed pay or where Apollo's leash is.

"We need to talk!" I call as Thayden disappears from sight.

"How about over dinner? I'll call you!"

The door slams shut before I can tell him that we most certainly are not. Dinner? Not on your life. I need to see this man less, not more. He is not good for my health or my heart.

"I should go too," Elizabeth says, surprising me with a genuine hug. "Maybe we could meet up later this week for lunch? Or shopping?"

She brushes a hand over my hair as she stands, looking so excited that I don't have the heart to say no. Especially when the slightest bit of maternal affection has me borderline weepy.

Now who's the emotional one? Oh, right. *Me.*

"You don't need to do that. I'm just the hired help."

Her jaw sets and her eyes blaze. "Don't think of yourself that way, dear. I know I won't. And, if I'm right, neither will my son. Not for long."

That's just what I'm afraid of. And this morning, I've seen how easy it is to feel more for him too. I'm already halfway there.

CHAPTER SIX

Thayden

AN HOUR LATER, I'm still coming down from a high after my breakfast with Delilah. (I'm choosing to forget the part where my mother showed up. I'm also choosing to ignore her phone calls and texts.) There is something about being with that woman that sends energy pinging through my body.

All of which crashes spectacularly the moment Duke shows up in my office.

"Hello, son."

The only thing more irritating than his smug face is the fact that he insists on calling me *son* or *boy*. We'll be sitting at the same table in court next week, as I had to pick up my father's caseload, but Duke needs to make sure I know he doesn't see me as an equal.

"Ready for the big case?"

Every single word out of his mouth rubs me like coarse-grit sandpaper. And I know that's his intent—I can see it in the curl of his thin lips and the light in his eyes. The best thing I can do is ignore him.

Why do I struggle so much with the application of that knowledge?

"Been ready. Are you?" The words sound like a challenge.

He laughs, his big belly shaking with it. Now, I feel like the small person he thinks I am. That's what I get for taking his bait. He walks the perimeter of my office, as though measuring it with his steps. A visual reminder to me that his office, right next to my father's old one, is larger than mine.

"How about that other thing?"

"What other thing?" I shuffle some papers and folders on my desk, wanting to appear busy to get him out of here.

Duke stops right in front of my desk, toying with the pens in my cup holder. I resist the urge to smack his hand. He really brings out the worst in me.

"The marriage thing."

My breath leaves my chest with a low wheeze. I'm going to blame Delilah for the fact that I stepped right on this bear trap. It should have been front of mind, especially since my mom clearly thinks Delilah is my fake fiancée. I am not ready to face the wailing and gnashing of teeth when I tell Mom the truth.

Finally locating my self-control, I don't rip Duke's head off, instead giving him a wry smile. "Aw, Duke. You're worried about me. How sweet."

He chuckles again. "I know you didn't want to settle down, but getting married doesn't mean you have to wear the ball and chain."

And … yuck. I don't know how someone like Duke manages to find women to cheat with, but he does. Frequently, according to the rumors. He's overweight, balding, and has the kind of character I wouldn't touch with a ten-foot pole. I would feel sorry for his wife, but she is almost as miserable a person as he is. A total snob with a sharp tongue and a roving eye of her own.

As if wanting to make sure I get his point, Duke slips the wedding band off his finger. "Just be sure to get this loose enough."

Is that what his morality is like? Something you just slip on and slip off?

I feel dirty just for having him standing near me. My father may have been awful to me, but Duke is in a whole different class. I can't imagine Dad ever cheating on Mom. The best thing I can say about my father is that he doted on Mom. He and Duke worked well together but couldn't have been more different.

And yet, your father is giving this *man the firm if you don't get married.* I cannot even fathom his decision to do so.

My phone buzzes. My mother again, but Duke doesn't need to know that. I hold up the phone, screen facing me.

"Loved our little talk, but duty calls."

"I'll be seeing you soon." His words hang in the air, the threat in them like stale cigar smoke. I need an industrial cleaning of my office now. No—one of those home exorcisms, where someone comes and burns sage and rubs essential oil on everything. Maybe when Scott finds a loophole, I'll fire Duke, then have the whole firm saged and cleansed.

"Hello, Mother."

"Thayden!"

After having Duke stain my presence, Mom's voice is refreshingly bright. I chuckle.

"I just love Delilah. She is perfect for you!"

The funny thing is that I don't even disagree with her. Though that doesn't mean I've changed my stance on marriage. I'd like to *date* Delilah. She intrigues me in a way no other woman has.

She doesn't fawn over me or say what she thinks I want to hear. She isn't manipulating me, and doesn't have an agenda, other than telling me no. Plus, she's gorgeous. Her hair is the color of a jar of honey with the sun shining behind it, and blue eyes like the sky on the best kind of lazy summer day. Even in her doggy daycare uniform, I couldn't take my eyes off her. Grass-stained khaki pants have never looked so good on a woman.

But it's more than the physical attraction that I may have noticed first. I wasn't lying when I told her she was the first woman in my house. Other than my mom, that is. She's the first woman I wanted to invite inside, and the house finally felt *whole* with her in it.

And is it so wrong that it feels so right when Delilah gives me a hard time? I could listen to her insult me all day long.

I'm hoping to wear Delilah down, turning her *no*s into a resounding *YES*. Marriage talk would send her sprinting for the hill country.

Even if I ever did decide to get married, it wouldn't be on my father's timeline. The fact that he's trying to force this only makes me want it less.

"I'm glad you like her. You should know—"

"Like her? I *love* her." Mom sniffs, and I know she's crying, or just on the cusp.

Why does this make me feel guilty? None of this is *my* fault.

"Calm down. Delilah is Apollo's dog walker. Not my fake fiancée. So, let's dial it back a notch."

My mother's screech could be heard from a space station. "*What?* No. No, no, no. That can't be! She was so ..." Mom trails off and I can almost hear her thinking back through the conversation they had.

"Yes. I hired her to watch Apollo while I'm at work. Take him for walks, pick up his poop—"

"Thayden, *honestly*. Do you have to be so crass?"

I can't help smiling at her outrage. She raised me. Does she not remember how crass boys can be?

"But why was she there so early? And you were in your pajamas! Did she not—was she not—?"

Mom sputters over how to phrase what she's thinking, and I decide to help her out. The last thing I need right now is to hear my mother talk about sex.

"Delilah did not spend the night, if that's what you're trying so graciously to ask. I invited her to breakfast so I could give her the details of the job. Which I never ended up doing because an unexpected guest came by."

"Oh."

"Yes. *Oh.*"

Her voice sounds watery, like her tears have leaked down into her throat. "But, Thayden, I *like* her."

Me too. I definitely can't admit that now, or Mom will be all over me. I hate disappointing her, but she needs to get it through her head that I'm not marrying Delilah. Or anyone.

"I asked her to go shopping with me," she whines. "I was looking forward to it."

"You still can. You'll just be shopping with my dog walker, not my fake fiancée."

"But why couldn't she be?"

Mom's voice has shifted from disappointed to determined and stubborn. Which is not a good thing. My mother can be just as hardheaded and focused as I am when I want something.

"No."

"I like her. You seem taken with her. She mentioned needing the money. It's win, win."

"No, Mom. I don't want to get married. And I don't want to scare Delilah off with our family drama."

"What about the company? Are you just going to let all your hard work go to waste?"

"I'm finding a way around it."

Mom's sigh is bone-deep. And though I can't do this, I hate disappointing her. This morning, she'd been so excited. It was the happiest I've seen her since Dad died. I drag a hand through my hair, tempted to give it a good yank.

"Your father wasn't the only one who wants to see you happy."

"Forcing me to get married or lose our family legacy isn't looking out for my happiness. It's manipulation. A desire for power and control."

Mom sighs again. "Your father wasn't a villain."

"Correction. He wasn't a villain to everyone. Just me. Good fathers who love their sons don't try to force them into a fake marriage."

"But it doesn't have to be fake. I saw the way you looked at Delilah this morning. Maybe something could blossom over time—"

"I'd like to ask Delilah on a date. I'm not going to ask her to fake marry me."

"Wonderful! You could date her, and then in a few months—"

"I'm not going to change my stance on marriage, Mom. Let it go."

Mom is silent for a moment or two. So much hangs between us. History, memories, my father's ghost.

"You know, if you don't go after what you want because it's what your father wanted too, you aren't winning."

"It's not a game."

"I know."

Now, we're both quiet. It's a rare moment, and I resist the urge to make a joke and break up the tension. She's right. I know Mom's right. And that infuriates me. Because I know that I am still making decisions because of *him*.

I need to find out what I want apart from what my father wanted. I also shouldn't avoid things just because of him. His opinion is like a tick, and I need to dig it out.

"Thayden?"

"Yes?"

"What will you do if you aren't going to get married?" she asks.

"You know, continue to live my life as a happy and fulfilled single man with a great dog and a wonderful mother."

She chuckles a little. "No, I mean, about the Walker Firm?"

Mom likes Duke about as much as I do. And though my grandfather started the company, it was my dad who took it to the next level, making us a serious name in Austin. Mom sacrificed so much while Dad was building this little family empire, almost single-handedly parenting me in the early years. She's woven into the fabric of the firm as much as Dad was.

"I'm having Scott look for loopholes in Dad's will."

"Scott?"

"One of the lawyers here at the firm. Great at contracts. Don't worry. We'll find something."

"Hm. Scott, great at contracts. Okay." Mom sounds like she's taking notes, which is adorable.

"Well, I still think you should consider Delilah. Not as a fake fiancée. But a real wife."

Normally, when people discuss me getting married, I get that feeling like someone just walked across my grave. Today, though, I don't *hate* the idea. Not that I'm suddenly open to it, but I don't shudder or sneer at the idea. Maybe because I've found a woman who makes me feel something more.

Enough to make me want to get married? Nope. Still a hard pass.

"I'll talk with you later," Mom says, sounding totally distracted. She's probably moving on to think about more pressing things, like how much tickets for her next fundraiser should cost per plate.

"Bye, Mother."

I've only just set the phone down when it buzzes again. A text this time.

Delilah: Where is Apollo's leash?

I smile. Just seeing her name on the screen shouldn't have that effect on me. But it does.

Thayden: You haven't found it yet when you were searching through my drawers?

It's just a guess, but I think a pretty good one. The next response takes a little longer. I bite my lip as I wait.

Delilah: Do you have security cameras set up in here? Are you watching me right now? Which finger am I holding up?

I laugh. Maybe louder and longer than I've laughed in months. It should bother me that she's in my house, looking through my things. I somehow don't mind the idea of her snooping at all. There's nothing I can think of that I wouldn't want her seeing.

Honestly, I'd kind of love to come home and find her sitting on my couch, dressed in my clothes, eating my food.

Thayden: No. I was making a joke. Are you really going through my drawers?
Delilah: What's the deal with this moisturizer? I mean, it smells nice and all, but a whole cabinet full?
Delilah: Are you some kind of hoarder?
Thayden: I have a skin condition.
Delilah: I'M SO SORRY
Thayden: Just kidding! I happen to like it. Especially if you think it smells nice.
Delilah: Jerk.
Delilah: But why so much? You can't possibly use them all by the expiration dates. Don't tell me—you're one of those extreme couponing people.
Thayden: Nope. They discontinued it. I bought every one in every store I could find.
Delilah: How enterprising of you. Again—the leash??
Thayden: It's in the laundry room off the kitchen. The drawer next to the sink.
Thayden: Didn't check that one yet?
Delilah: I was more focused on the interesting parts of your house.
Thayden: Like …?
Delilah: A lady has to keep some secrets for herself.
Thayden: But you get to go through my things and learn all of my secrets?
Delilah: Where does Apollo like to walk?
Thayden: He'll go anywhere you take him. Just watch out for men in suits.

Delilah: Um … explain, pls.

Thayden: Business suits, firemen suits, mailman suits—you get the idea.

Delilah: You mean UNIFORMS?

Thayden: Suits, uniforms. Either way.

Delilah: Got it. Will do our best to avoid men.

You'd better.

I refuse to type that out and send it. Delilah already knows that I'm interested. No need for her to understand how much.

The phone goes still, and I watch until my screen goes black, then unlock my phone and reread the whole thread, smiling until my cheeks cramp.

CHAPTER SEVEN

Delilah

I THOUGHT MAYBE WALKING the neighborhood with Apollo would release other things along with endorphins. Like the ridiculous, crush-like feelings bubbling up in me for the man I thought I hated.

So far, the only thing I'm releasing is sweat. Buckets of it. Whoever said ladies only glow never lived in the South. Or knew actual ladies.

When we get back to his house, it's early afternoon, and Apollo drinks sloppily out of his water bowl, flooding the laundry room, and then collapses on the cool tile floor in there. He's snoring in moments.

Which leaves me alone in Thayden's house, bored. So far, I've cleaned up the mess from breakfast, walked Apollo twice, and poked my nose into every drawer and cabinet and closet in the whole house.

When Thayden mentioned looking in his drawers earlier, my heart stopped dead in my chest. I really thought for a moment he had hidden cameras in here, and my skin crawled with worry. But apparently, it was just obvious to him that I am that kind of person. He didn't seem to mind, and I'm not at all sure what that says about *him*.

Mama used to say that if curiosity killed the cat, I wouldn't make it past kittenhood. Once at my friend Lily's birthday party, her mom found me coming out of their attic.

"Why are you up here?" she had asked, looking shocked when I emerged from the attic stairs I discovered tucked away in an upstairs closet.

"I wanted to see what y'all have."

I was six.

My curiosity hasn't dimmed any, and despite how it may sound, I do have *some* limits. I didn't go into the files in the wooden file cabinet in his room, though it was unlocked. (Yes, I checked.)

I did not un-make his bed and create snow angels on what I imagine to be a ridiculously out-of-my-league thread count.

I also did not go into the pull-down attic.

(I'm saving that for tomorrow. Also, I wasn't tall enough to reach the chain to pull without dragging a chair into the hallway.)

Honestly, the whole being-nosy bit didn't take long. Considering the man's family has a private jet, his house is surprisingly modest. Not cheap—I mean, it's in a great location right in the heart of Austin, certainly not cheap in this inflated market, but he could afford something much larger and newer.

The main floor consists of the living room, dining room, kitchen, a half bath tucked under the stairs, and a laundry room which is the only part of the house that doesn't appear original. Upstairs is tiny, with two bedrooms connected by a Jack-and-Jill bathroom. The bathroom, like the kitchen, had more of an extensive gut job, with a large soaker tub taking up most of the small space.

In short, I'm in love with the man's house. It's a cozy, inviting bungalow full of character. Not in a million years the kind of house I would have imagined Thayden choosing. He's more of a mystery to me than he was before snooping.

Though comfortable and homey, there were few personal effects. Only one framed photograph of Thayden and his mother. I did find a few interesting things, like the cabinet full—and I do mean *full*—of lotion. His explanation about it being discontinued makes sense though. And I was relieved, because to be honest, I considered searching *lotion fetish*, and did not know what I might find.

Mama once stocked up on a CoverGirl lip color that got discontinued, and I remember feeling like it was an all-important quest as we went to every CVS, Walgreens, Target, and Walmart in the county looking for the remnants. This is one of my favorite childhood memories with Mama, which says something about my childhood. And my relationship with my mother.

I could—and probably should—go home. I mean, we didn't discuss what Thayden expects, but it's probably not a full-time nanny. Honestly, though, I love being in his space.

I grab a copy of *A Midsummer Night's Dream* from his bookshelf, pleased that he has my favorite Shakespeare play, and flop down on the couch. I smile a few pages in when Hermia says, "The more I hate, the more he follows me."

"I feel that, sister," I mutter. "Thayden is the same way."

Apollo lumbers in at the sound of my voice and flops down next to the couch. He rolls over on his back, gangling legs up in the air. I give him a nice, soft belly rub, and he thanks me by sneezing in my face.

"Thanks, big guy," I say.

With one hand still on Apollo's belly, I set down the play and shoot Thayden a text.

Delilah: We neglected to discuss the terms of my employment this morning. How long am I supposed to stay here?
Thayden: As long as you want. Apollo is VERY needy.

At that moment, Apollo lets out a snore that would put a grown man to shame.

Delilah: Your DOG is needy? Or you are?
Thayden: Both.
Thayden: Seriously, stay as long as you like or leave whenever. I like imagining you in my house.

Okay, that has me hiding my face under a pillow and squealing. I cannot be excited about Thayden's flirting. I can't. But I am.

Thayden: Did you finish going through all the rooms? Find anything else you want to ask about?

I blush, even though only Apollo is around to see my face, and he's still snoring. Because I *did* find one thing that I definitely *can't* ask him about ... in his underwear drawer.

No, I'm NOT a perv. Everyone knows that the underwear drawer is designed to hold special things, *secret* things, not just underwear. That's why I looked. Not to see what Thayden has on under his suit. I'm not that kind of girl.

Okay, maybe I'm a *little* bit that kind of girl. Just because

I'm curious. Not like I'm picturing him or anything. I'm not. (Not right this second, anyway.) For the record, and in case I ever need to use this detail to identify his body, he wears Calvin Klein boxer briefs in only black and gray.

Anyway, the point is: I found something, I'm just not sure what.

Behind all the Calvin Kleins, there are ten sealed and unmarked envelopes. They're just the regular white letter size. Sealed tight (not that I picked a little at the edges just to be sure) and light enough that I would guess they only have one piece of paper in them.

Who are they from? Why ten? Why hasn't he opened them? Or did Thayden write and seal them? Could they be love letters to some long-lost woman?

That last idea, which came to me as I was stuffing them back in the drawer, didn't sit well with me. It doesn't take a genius to figure out that I'm jealous, but I'm pointedly ignoring this feeling. I'm also choosing to believe that whatever they are, they're not love letters. Nope.

Thayden: Your silence has me worried.
Thayden: Should I be worried?
Delilah: I've mostly been hanging out with your dog, who is, as you pointed out earlier, very NEEDY.
Thayden: He's not the only one.

Okay, THAT text has me putting down the phone so I can regulate my breathing. A few months ago—no, even yesterday—this kind of comment would have had me all narrow-eyed and ready to smack Thayden.

That was before he made me breakfast. Before I met his sweet mama. Before I fell for his dog and his house. Before I knew his daddy, with whom he had a *complicated* relationship, recently died.

Now? I'm hungry for all the flirty remarks, and I've gone from hating Thayden to hating myself just a tiny bit.

Thayden: I'll be done around six and pick you up. Dress casually.
Delilah: For …?
Thayden: Dinner, remember? Where we'll discuss the terms of your employment.

The idea of dinner with him gives me a little thrill. Which, like a kitchen fire, needs to be snuffed immediately.

He's feeding you lines, D. Just lines. And you know what we do with lines? We cut 'em. We do not take the bait. No matter how shiny.

Cut. The. Line.

Delilah: I'd like to get a contract, please.
Thayden: You don't trust me?
Delilah: You're a lawyer. No one trusts lawyers.
Thayden: Who do you think draws up contracts? LAWYERS. Also, I'm a lawyer.
Delilah: Exactly.
Thayden: Ouch. I thought Southern girls were supposed to be sweet.
Delilah: Southern girls are as sweet as iced tea, but as sharp as a sticker bush.
Thayden: Good to know. Text me your address so I can pick you up. 6:30?

Dinner with Thayden. I shiver and rub my arms, like that will stave off the goose bumps. More bad signs. I somehow know it will be more than just talking about a contract. He could just leave a piece of paper here for me to sign. Then I could avoid seeing him, which was per our verbal agreement.

Delilah: Why don't you just drop off the contract after work?

I bite my lip, not so secretly hoping he'll say no.

Thayden: We might need to discuss the terms. Plus, dinner sounds more fun.

That's what I'm afraid of.

He keeps right on texting, clearly trying to make an airtight case on why I need to have dinner with him tonight.

Thayden: Plus you have to eat. And I'd like to know how Apollo is doing. I have a lot of questions about how his day went. I'm a little overprotective of my loved ones.

I love a man who loves his dog, and one who's protective of his people. What would it be like to have that same protectiveness extended to me?

"Argh!" I shout, tossing the throw pillow I'd just had over my face.

Apollo startles and gets to his feet, jogging over to the pillow and sniffing it, like he's trying to see how it offended me.

Thayden has moved too quickly from being an infuriating man and a clear HECK NO, to being something else entirely. He's at least moved up the sliding scale to tolerable and a confusing OKAY, MAYBE.

Delilah: Fine. But only because of Apollo.

Thayden: Of course. I know you wouldn't agree to dinner just for ME.

He's fishing for compliments, hoping I'll disagree. It would be so easy to keep this banter going all dang day. Sadly, it's better than the conversations I've had on my last few dates. Which were ... how long ago? Far too long ago and very unmemorable.

Cut the line, D.

When I don't answer right away, he sends one more text.

Thayden: I've got a meeting now, but I'll see you at 6:30. And I'll make sure to get you a contract ASAP.

Before I leave, I take Apollo for one more walk, wishing I'd dressed like Harper in athletic gear for all this outside time. It feels like God put a glass dome down on top of the city, trapping the wet heat.

The sweat dripping down my back makes all the little scratches and scrapes from being dragged by Apollo itchy. Was that only yesterday? Most of them were pretty shallow and will heal up just fine. For now, I'm a sweaty, itchy mess.

At a corner, Apollo stops to smell a signpost that's clearly popular with the canine crowd. I pull my shirt away from my body, trying to get some air up in here. I'll definitely need a shower before our date.

Our DINNER. Not our date. It is not a date.

Is it?

To be super-duper, extra clear, I text Thayden as I'm walking back up his driveway.

Delilah: Tonight is NOT a date. It's dinner. But not a DATE.

He doesn't respond though, which makes my stomach feel like it is now housing one of those butterfly exhibits they have in science museums.

I almost drop the leash when Thayden's mother pops out of a dark car I hadn't seen parked along the front curb next to my scooter.

"Delilah! I was hoping you'd be here!"

"Hello, Elizabeth!"

Apollo wags his tail as she hurries over, giving me a hug. I know I'm being stiff, but she surprised me. I'm just hoping she doesn't have any matchmaking plans. Because I'm having a hard enough time resisting the man himself, without his mama on board too.

Exactly how close are Thayden and Elizabeth? I wonder if I should expect her to pop in like this any time I'm here. I mean, the woman is sweet, though a bit excitable. I remind myself that her husband just died, and soften a bit as we walk up to the house together.

"I just came from Thayden's office with your contract," she says, giving me a brilliant smile once we're in the kitchen.

"That was fast," I tell her, refilling Apollo's water bowl in the laundry room. The big dog is very clean overall, not hairy or stinky, but when he drinks water, it's another story. Those flappy lips and massive tongue send water all over the place.

Elizabeth takes the stool where she sat for breakfast and slides what looks like a graduate student's thesis across the smooth counter. I sit next to her and begin to flip through the typed document, which is so full of legalese that I feel sweat prickling at my hairline, despite the blast of cold air from the vent overhead.

"Um, wow. Thayden was … thorough. I thought he wanted to talk to me tonight?"

"Tonight?" She blinks at me.

"Thayden and I are having dinner to discuss the terms."

"Right. Of course. I'm sure he would rather talk about something else over dinner." She grins. Yep. A mama with a matchmaking plan.

I shove that thought away. I need to focus on the very official legal document before me.

"Should I be concerned that I have no idea what this thing is saying?"

"You know lawyers." She rolls her eyes, then pats my hand. "Most of it's just mumbo jumbo. You know. But he said he wanted to make sure you were *protected*."

My mind flashes back to our conversation earlier, how Thayden said he gets overprotective of the ones he loves. I don't want to think too deeply about this. Then again, yeah, I really do.

Remember when you hated this guy, D?

Sort of …

THAT WAS YESTERDAY.

Oh. Right.

"Huh."

Overprotective is right. This document is over-*something* for sure. I'm flipping through, seeing phrases like dissolution of persons and properties heretofore-legalese-blah-blah.

There is no way I'm going to get through this. I think my eyes have already crossed and come back around the other side.

Elizabeth leans closer and she smells like an English garden. The floral scent calms me, but only a little.

"I put a few sticky notes inside where you need to sign."

"I mean, shouldn't I read it first? It's just … so much."

She pats my shoulder. "You could always have your lawyer look over it. They usually charge by the hour and it couldn't be much more than a hundred and fifty dollars an hour or so. A few hours, and you could feel secure."

Right. For a woman wearing this kind of jewelry, whose son has a private jet, that sum is just chump change. I don't even want to know the number of peppermint mochas that would be. Even one hour at one hundred fifty would be crippling.

I smile and neatly stack the papers. "I'll definitely take a look."

More like, I'll have Zoey take a look. She's a serious business person, even if not a lawyer. Maybe Sam could do it. She had to sign a contract for her Dr. Love book deal. I can't remember if she hired someone or if her agent handled that.

"Good for you. I like a woman who looks at the fine print. Especially with how much money is involved. It would be life-changing. Now, should we plan our upcoming shopping spree?"

Just how much money is involved? It seems tacky to ask, but she brought it up, so I clear my throat and dive in.

"Where does it talk about money? Thayden never said how much he was paying me. I kind of just verbally agreed." I laugh nervously, hating this money talk almost as much as I hate reading lawyer-speak.

"You're too sweet." Elizabeth flips to a page near the end. "As you can see, it's *very* generous."

The numbers make my jaw drop.

"A hundred thousand dollars for a YEAR? That's insane!" I shove the contract toward her and stand, running my sweaty palms over my skirt as I begin to pace. "No. I can't do this. It's too much."

Elizabeth only laughs. "Do you have any idea what Thayden makes? Or what our family is worth?"

I shake my head slowly. I mean, I know about the plane

and that he has a fancy car and this house in a prime location, but I hadn't exactly googled him, other than the map
search to see his house. Maybe I should have. That seems
like a logical first step, one normally taking place *before*
looking into the man's underwear drawer.

I sink back down on my stool, trying to remember
breathing exercises Harper taught me. They're not working.

"This is nothing to him. And he's paying someone for
their trust as well. He trusts you. I know Thayden, and he
wouldn't just let anyone in his home." She laughs. "You
should see what he pays his housekeeper."

I can only imagine. But one hundred thousand dollars???
I knew—I *know*—how out of my league and class and income
bracket Thayden and his mama are. Until this conversation
though, it didn't bother me.

Now, I'm faced with that hungry desperation that comes
with being poor, and the shame that goes along with it. I'm
back in our trailer, seeing so many things I want that Mama
and I can't afford. Not just clothes that don't come from a
secondhand store, but things like college. A future. A home
one day that isn't a trailer where I don't ever quite feel
safe.

The only nice things I had were for the pageants, and
most of those, Mama either bartered for or possibly stole. I
never quite knew and knew better than to ask. And those
weren't things I wanted. They were part of what I knew was
my *job*.

"It's a salary, dear. I know you're used to less. But this is
not unheard of. We pay for discretion and for a job well done.
There's a nondisclosure in there too." She waves a hand,
diamonds flashing. "But have your lawyer look at it. I'm sure
he'll find it to be solid."

She pushes the papers back toward me, but a pen has

materialized out of nowhere, sitting right on top. Is his mother a magician? Or a genie?

My fingers twitch. A hundred thousand dollars would pay off the bulk of my student loans, plus allow me some wiggle room to live on. Maybe buy something other than ramen and fruit from the clearance bin. I stare down at the papers, almost tasting the freedom that they contain.

But it *does* feel like a trick. Because it can't be that easy, can it?

Elizabeth is rooting around in her purse, seemingly unconcerned about whether I sign or not.

My gut is telling me to have someone take a more thorough look at this contract. And my desperation is ready to prick my finger and sign in my own blood.

"I've got to make a quick call, dear. I'm just going to run upstairs for a moment."

Elizabeth leaves me alone with the contract, and a weight presses down on my shoulders the longer I stare at the papers. This would allow me to really start over. Without the student loans hanging over me, I wouldn't have worry dive-bombing me like a blue jay protecting its nest. I would stop feeling like the only unsuccessful one of my friends. I wouldn't have to think about possibly running home to Mama with my tail between my legs, which has gone from a worst-case scenario to more like a sure thing.

But what about Thayden?

Already, my resolve regarding my feelings is starting to crack, and it's the *first day*. How am I possibly going to resist him over time? Signing this contract feels like I'm admitting defeat.

I pick up the pen, and flip to the first sticky note.

I take a few slow breaths, trying to think calmly and rationally. But the part of me terrified for my future is fueled by something much more primal. It's that animal instinct to scurry into the cave for safety.

This money is a nice, warm cave, and I'm tired of being outside in the cold and dark.

I scrawl my signature once, twice, three, four, five times. I lose count by the end.

Then I put the pen on top with shaking hands, leave the contract on the counter, and head home without saying goodbye to Elizabeth, feeling a relief about my finances mixed with a stone of dread in my belly that I've just signed a deal with a charming devil.

From: BFF911@DrLove.advice
To: DrLove@DrLove.advice

Dear Dr. Love,
I've done a lot of dating, but haven't found a guy worth getting serious with. Until now.
The issue? My best friend called dibs. But yesterday, he asked ME out. I'm not sure what to do. He's the kind of guy I could see a future with, but I don't want to lose my friend over a guy.
Help! Do I choose my BFF or the BF?
-BFF 911

———

From: DrLove@DrLove.advice
To: BFF911@DrLove.advice

Dear BFF 911,
Now that we're in the 21st century, could we just make dibs not a thing?
Honestly, I get Girl Code and Bro Code, but staking a claim on potential isn't fair, especially when there is something ACTUAL brewing between you.
I don't know your friend and how she'd react, but I would sit down for a heart-to-heart. I don't want to choose guys over my friends and yet, when we commit to marry someone, we WILL do that. Our spouse will come first, even though we still keep our friendships.
If you really see a future with this guy, it's at least worth talking to your friend about it. And maybe also mention that we need to end this whole dibs debacle.

-Dr. Love

CHAPTER EIGHT

Delilah

"ARE you sure that's what you want to wear?" Harper asks.

"Positive."

Harper raises one dark brow, giving my jeans, pink Converse, and casual white top a look. I glance in the mirror next to our front door, cringing a little. My face is makeup-free. My hair is in a ponytail. I can't remember the last time I looked so ... casual.

I know if Harper is questioning me, it must be bad. I love the girl, but if it doesn't wick away moisture, she isn't wearing it.

But tonight, bad is good. I'm going to dinner with Thayden. Dinner. Not a date.

Not. A. Date.

My casual outfit is the period on the end of that statement. No date clothes, no date. My logic is sound.

"Chase, does this outfit scream Not a Date to you?"

Harper's best friend eyes me from his spot on the couch, then nods. "If you're trying to keep him in the friend zone, this is a good look."

Is that what I want? Friend zone? Is Thayden even a friend? I think of him more as a pinball, dropped into my life and knocking into every corner. And yeah, maybe he's making some lights flash and bells ring but that means nothing. Not a thing.

You don't want Thayden to like you. This isn't a date.

Harper flops down next to Chase, smacking him in the stomach. "Rude!"

"Ow! What? I'm not being insulting—you look great, Delilah. I'm just saying her clothes scream casual. Not like a first date."

Harper smacks him again.

"Do I need to separate y'all?" I ask, trying to hide my smile.

These two might be best friends, but the attraction between them is hot enough that they're violating a number of fire codes every time they're together. Even if Harper won't acknowledge it. It's a shame too, because they'd be the perfect couple.

When I allow myself to dream about love, it's like that, with a friend. No surprises, no wondering how you might get along. It would be solid and steady, something I could trust. Because trust is my currency, and the coins are rare, totally out of circulation.

"Apologize," Harper says, poking Chase in the ribs.

He laughs and twists away from her on the couch, grabbing her wrists in the process even as she tries to kick him.

"Ow! Fine! I'm sorry, D! I wasn't trying to be a jerk."

I wave a hand. "I got you, Chase. No need for apologies. I appreciate a man's point of view. You can stop attacking each other now."

The doorbell rings.

Suddenly, I can't face Thayden. I can't. I feel more exposed than if I were under a big yellow spotlight on stage with ten layers of makeup. Harper jumps to her feet, obviously seeing my panic.

"Chase, get the door," she calls, hooking an arm through mine.

Harper drags me down the hall to her bedroom and slams the door behind us.

Once we're alone, she takes me by the shoulders and begins a massage that feels like being manhandled by a prison guard.

"Breathe, D. In … and out. In … and out. That's it."

"Ow," I say.

She lightens up her massage. It still hurts, but I don't complain. "What's going on in that pretty head of yours?"

Wow. I must be bad if I'm getting girl talk from Harper. I'm not sure I've ever heard her tone of voice so soft.

"It's just … I'm afraid I might like Thayden." Saying it out loud only confirms the truth of it. I like the last man in the world I want to like.

Her eyes widen. "The jerk, Thayden? The one you've gone on and on about hating? The one who ditched you at Zoey's wedding? The one you've insisted you're *not* going on a date with tonight?"

I nod, wishing I didn't feel the prickle of tears at the backs of my eyes.

"Okay. You like him, but you don't *want* to like him?"

I nod again, biting my lip. "Is that stupid?"

81

"Nope. The question though, is this: is he a bad guy? I mean, I'm debating which Delilah to encourage here. The one who might like him, or the one who doesn't want to."

I think of the first time I met Thayden, and how he reminded me of the men who talked their way into Mama's bed, only to disappear. Good-looking, sweet-talking men.

When they lit out for greener (or younger or more wealthy) pastures, as they always did, it was usually with some of Mama's money and a piece of her heart.

Sometimes they left more than that behind. Bruises. Bad memories. Broken windows.

I close my eyes, picturing Thayden this morning in his kitchen. He might be a flirt and a ladies' man (or, if he's to be believed, a *former* ladies' man), but he is not like those men I grew up knowing to avoid, the ones that had me pushing a dresser up against my door at night, *just in case.*

"I'm not sure," I say.

Harper studies me for a moment. "I know I'm no Sam with all the smart advice. But here's my suggestion. You'll go out with him tonight. Get to know him better. Call it a date or call it a dinner, but it's a trial run. A risk assessment. Is he worth thinking about in a romantic way or not?"

That actually makes a whole lot of sense. I wish Harper could have the same sense when it comes to Chase. She stops her painful massage to stare deeply into my eyes.

"Can you enjoy your dinner without feeling any pressure?"

That sounds relieving, honestly. "I think so."

Harper's eyes narrow, and when she speaks again, she has her training voice on. The one she uses when she's running boot camps or bossing elite athletes around in the gym. I've only heard it a few times, but I know why it's effective, and why she's one of the most sought-after trainers in Austin. The gym and I aren't really what you'd call friends. More ... distant acquaintances who barely like each other.

"Can. You. Do. It?"

I nod more vigorously. "Yes, ma'am."

Harper rolls her eyes, gives my shoulders a last painful squeeze, and throws open her door. "Then, get out there, tiger. And whatever you do, don't go easy on the man."

The problem, though, is that I'm pretty sure Thayden loves it when I *don't* go easy on him. Which is only going to make things more interesting. Or harder. Depending on how tonight goes.

When I walk back out into the living room with my go-time face on, Chase is laughing at something that Thayden has said. Neither one is looking, so I get to check out Thayden with him being none the wiser.

The man should invest in cloning technology. Because he would be a billionaire if he could replicate those cheekbones, that lightly bearded jaw, the broad shoulders stretching out his button-down shirt. Even his forearms, visible by the way he's casually rolled up his sleeves, are hot. The man is perfection.

Especially when he sees me, and his green eyes light up with a sparkle that makes my heart bang against my ribs. It is a toddler I've put in time-out, and it wants me to open the bedroom door.

Thayden's gaze stays on my face as he gives me a wide smile. "I wasn't sure if you changed your mind and ran off."

I stop a few feet away, feigning a confidence I definitely do not feel. The man has turned my steely resolve into a cooked spaghetti noodle. "I thought about it."

His grin widens, and it's like a weapon. One with a laser

sight pointed straight at the center of my chest. The dimple appears, and I'm dead.

"You knew it would be futile, huh? Because I would have tracked you like a bloodhound."

"So, you agree that you're a dog," I say, putting my hands on my hips.

Harper has joined Chase and the two of their heads are ping-ponging back and forth like we're a table tennis match to the death.

Thayden throws his head back and laughs. "You got me, D. I don't deserve you. But I sure do like you."

My cheeks flush. "This isn't a date, remember?"

"Forgive me if I'm dreaming and scheming of how I can turn it into more." He holds out his arm, waiting for me to step forward and take it.

Mercy! The charm of this man could make a basket of venomous snakes fall in love. But I don't get the sense that it's false. It's flirtatious, but he's sincere.

At least, I *think* he is. But maybe I'm just a cobra, being tricked into putting away her venom by a sweet song.

I step forward and take Thayden's arm. Before he can lead me out the front door and to what is likely my demise, I remember my manners.

"Thayden, you met Chase, but this is Harper, one of my best friends and roommates."

Thayden extends the hand that doesn't have my arm, and I can see that even Harpy isn't immune to his charms. She smiles, a real one, and even though Thayden isn't being the least bit flirtatious, Chase frowns down at their clasped hands as they shake.

"Good to meet you, Harper. I think I've seen you around my gym. Don't you train some of the guys at Grit? The big dogs, if I remember correctly."

"I do."

"That's impressive," Thayden says.

"Delilah has my number if you ever want to step things up."

"As D knows, I like a challenge," Thayden says. "I may have to take you up on that."

Chase moves closer to Harper, so close that she glares up at him and tries to step away before he hooks an arm around her waist. I try not to laugh.

"Yes, she is impressive," Chase says, his voice low and threatening. Harper looks like she's about to toss him across the living room.

"Are you ready?" Thayden asks me.

No. "Yep."

I call my goodbyes to Chase and Harper and let Thayden lead me out the door. A fancy red sports car is parked by the curb, the one he was driving the day I met him. It gives me an idea.

I turn to Thayden and flutter my lashes. "Do you mind if I drive?"

He blinks at me. "I, uh—"

"Wonderful!"

I begin to drag him over to where I've parked Annabel Lee. I can feel his resistance, but he lets me lead him over. I pull my hand free to dig for my keys.

"I've only got one helmet. Do you want it?"

"Nope. Better cover the most valuable and beautiful of the two of us."

I swat at his shoulder. "Now, you just stop with the sweet talking, mister. It's not going to work on me."

Thayden grins as I strap on my helmet, and dang, if he doesn't seem to like me just as much with the silly thing on.

"What will work on you? Mind throwing a man a bone here?"

"Why, yes. I do very much mind. A real man doesn't need a cheat sheet. Now hop on and hold on."

I settle into the seat, chiding myself for flirting with the last man I should be flirting with. But when he settles in close behind me, SO close behind me, I gasp.

My idea to torture the fancy man by making him ride on my dinky scooter (sorry, Annabel Lee, but you know it's true) has backfired. This is going to torture *me*. His chest presses up against my back and his arms snake around my waist in a way that is not just platonic. Not at all. And then he leans his lips close. Of course I have the kind of helmet that leaves my ears exposed, so his breath skates over my skin.

"This was a great idea. Thanks for suggesting the scooter. It's much better ... for the environment."

The environment. His personal environment, maybe. To fight off the shivers working their way through my body despite the heat, I take off. Annabel Lee's tiny engine strains with the weight of two people.

Meanwhile, the man who is temptation personified just laughs, and I can feel that laugh moving through my body where he's pressed up against me. The vibration of it knocks something loose inside me that I don't think I'm going to be able to put back easily.

I realize a few blocks away that I don't know where we're going. I turn my head slightly, and, of course, Thayden is RIGHT THERE. The helmet is the only thing that keeps our lips from brushing. Maybe I'll start wearing it whenever he's around. That wouldn't be weird at all.

"Where to?" I immediately face front again. Because

keeping my eyes on the road is safer for more than one reason.

"You know Mozart's Coffee?"

"I do."

"Head there."

I didn't want this to be a date, but I'm disappointed. I mean, Mozart's is great and all, right on the water with great coffee. But I'm starved. That's the only reason I'm disappointed. *The only one.*

I swear, Annabel Lee barely makes it up the hill to the overflow parking lot across the street from Mozart's. The engine sputters and groans as I coax her.

"Come on, baby. That's a good girl. You got this."

Between the excess weight and the hills, I might have taken a few years off her life with this ride. Serves me right for trying to mess with Thayden. Now, my body is humming after spending twenty minutes with his warm chest pressed up against my back.

"So," I say, as we begin the walk down the hill and across the road toward Mozart's, "you love coffee?"

Thayden gives me a smile that could melt a dish of ice cream into a puddle instantly. "I do. Do you?"

"I'm human. So, yes. And you know that already from this morning."

If my tone sounds a little snippy, it's the hunger. I haven't eaten since my big breakfast this morning. My stomach, which had been used to existing on meager portions for months, is angry. And Thayden is getting the brunt of my hanger.

I start across the wooden deck to Mozart's, but Thayden gently takes my arm, pulling me away.

"I like coffee," he says, "but we aren't having coffee for dinner. I'm not a savage."

"Oh. That's fine too."

Thayden leads me toward Abel's, a restaurant I've admired every time I joined Zoey for coffee next door. It juts out over the water, just where Lake Austin begins. I can't help the giddy excitement that's bubbling up inside me. I'm so distracted that I hold Thayden's arm all the way inside the restaurant until we reach the table and he lets me go to pull out my chair.

It's then I remember I'm supposed to be resisting this man and his manners. Or, maybe I need to do what Harper suggests and just see where this goes.

Thayden sits next to me rather than across the table. Our legs brush and I glare at him.

"I'm sitting here for the view," he says, pointing toward the windows looking out over the water.

"Of course. The view."

Thayden may have pointed at the lake, but his gaze is trained on me. I focus on the menu.

I'd like one of everything, please, and put a rush on it.

"It all sounds so good," I say. "What's your favorite thing in the menu?"

"I usually come here for brunch. Not sure about the dinner menu, but everything I've had has been great," Thayden says.

I hum a noncommittal response.

"We could split an appetizer? Or get several, depending on your hunger level." When my stomach makes a very unladylike noise, he laughs. "Two appetizers it is. Ever tried alligator?"

"Nope. And I don't plan to start tonight. I do love calamari. And basically everything else. Just no gator, please."

The waiter arrives, and though I've never been one to like

it when a man exerts control or acts domineering, it doesn't feel that way when Thayden orders for us. Maybe because as he does so, he glances at me for confirmation. It feels ... nice. Like being taken care of. It's totally foreign, and I find myself shifting in my seat.

I'm surprised when Thayden orders water. "No wine or beer? You strike me as the type to enjoy a good libation."

Thayden chuckles. "Have I mentioned I could listen to you talk all day? The accent *and* the big words I have to look up later. Your vocabulary is sexy."

My mouth opens and closes, my sexy vocabulary having left the building. Maybe the state.

Thayden just grins. "I'm cutting back on the alcohol. Not cutting it out, just drinking less."

I stare at my menu, partly because my stomach is still shouting angrily at me, and partly because I cannot keep looking at Thayden. He's too handsome. Too winsome. Too good at saying all the right things.

"I'm making some other changes too," he says, and I know he means his dating life, which we briefly touched on this morning, and I'd love to never touch again.

"What motivated the changes?" I can't help my curiosity.

The waiter brings our drinks, and Thayden downs half his water before answering. "It's kind of about my dad, kind of just about me."

I swallow past the lump forming in my throat and finally look at Thayden. He's staring out over the water, his expression free from all the usual charm. Too bad for me, he's just as handsome and alluring this way, all serious and broody. I'm like the poster child for daddy issues and wannabe-daddy issues and step-daddy issues, so I get this on a very deep level.

"That's why I had to leave the wedding," Thayden says, still not looking at me.

Oh. OH. My stomach plummets, and I'm suddenly aware of all the mean thoughts I've had about him ditching me. "That's when he ... died?"

Thayden nods. "Heart attack. Sudden and immediate." Sighing, he runs a hand over his face before continuing. "My dad always tried to control me. When I was under their roof, it was with money or gifts. I could have a car ... if I ran for student council. A nicer car if I won. I'd get a trip to Europe if I took the daughter of his business partner to prom. He'd pay for college—*if* I went to the school he wanted."

Maybe that kind of money wasn't in the equation for me growing up, but if there's something I understand perfectly, it's that level of control. I place my hand on top of Thayden's. He looks down in surprise, then at my face, searching like he expects to find a trick.

"I can see how that would be difficult," I say.

He nods, then looks away again. "I played his game for years, but hated myself for it. I thought it would end when I finished law school. Despite my desire to do the opposite of what he wanted, sometimes our goals aligned. I went to work at the family firm. Only, without any special treatment. Which would have been fine, except what I got was harder treatment. Then, I tried playing against him, which didn't turn out so well either."

I know his daddy is gone and it's wrong to think badly of the man. But I want to throttle him because I can feel the pain radiating off Thayden. It's not just about the job or the hoops to jump through. Thayden's daddy withheld his love, dangling it on strings and attached to conditions. It burns me up.

I squeeze his hand. Our eyes meet and it lights a fuse. A

line of pure flame stretches between us, making my cheeks flush and my heart race.

Our waiter arrives with the food, and I pull my hand away, trying to compose myself. Thayden laughs as the waiter disappears.

"Sorry. I think I might have taken us a little too deep."

"Nothing wrong with a little depth," I say lightly, not sure about that at all.

I'm grateful as Thayden smoothly steers the conversation into safer topics, asking about my major, my time in college, my friends. Thankfully, nothing about my family or childhood.

The food is delicious, and despite myself, I have a great time. Thayden is funny, sweet, and easy to be around. When I stop trying to talk myself out of it, I genuinely enjoy his company. If I'm being honest, I'd even let him kiss me at the end of the night.

Okay, maybe I *want* him to kiss me at the end of the night. Every time our legs brush under the table, I catch my breath. When he passes me an extra napkin and his finger-tips graze my wrist, my skin erupts in goose bumps. I keep finding myself leaning closer, angling toward him like he's one of those high-powered magnets and I'm a flimsy piece of tinfoil.

Don't even get me started on his mouth, which should be illegal to own or operate without a special permit. When he speaks, my eyes can't seem to stop their downward trajectory to those luscious lips.

Yeah ... I'd totally let him kiss me.

To sum up, this non-date is totally smoking every real date I've had in my life.

Before I know it, we're polishing off English toffee cake with coffee ice cream. For the record, every meal should be finished with this dessert. Even breakfast. But I honestly hate that this is the end.

The waiter brings the check while I'm weighing the pros and cons of licking my plate clean. I decide it would be uncouth, and instead swipe a finger through the remainder of the icing. Because licking your finger is much more ladylike than licking your plate—etiquette 101.

"I thought you'd fight me on the bill, especially considering your insistence that this isn't a date," Thayden says with a grin. "You fight me on everything else. I'm not sure if it's refreshing, or if I should be worried."

I'm not about to tell him that I could barely cover this dinner, and if I did, I couldn't afford rent. I shrug. "Don't get too comfortable. A girl's gotta know when to pick her battles."

"I do like battling you. I also like this temporary peace treaty too." Thayden stands, holding out his hand to me. I take it, not missing the way his thumb strokes the back of my hand. At the door, his hand finds the small of my back and ushers me through. I wish I'd worn a low-backed dress so I could feel his palm on my skin.

The air is less sticky now that the sun's down, and strings of lights flicker in the trees outside. Thayden takes my arm and links it through the crook of his. We're not walking, we're strolling along the wooden deck, the silence between us as comfortable as my most worn-in pair of jeans.

I let Thayden lead me toward the outside seating area of Mozart's, where music filters out into the air. People are gathered around picnic tables, chatting while drinking coffee or working on laptops.

Thayden scans the tables, but there are none open. I bite my lip, not ready for him to lead me back toward the parking lot and Annabel Lee. He and I seem to be in sync, because he leads me to the railing looking out over the water.

We lean against the railing, facing each other. The Christmas lights are burned out on the branches directly above us, leaving us in a pool of shadow. The air is electric, and I wouldn't be surprised if the lights suddenly flickered to life, powered by the energy between us.

I shiver as Thayden lightly brushes a strand of my hair back from my face. He trails his hand down the length of my ponytail, his knuckles grazing the skin of my neck.

"Cold?" he asks, mouth upturned because it's anything but cool.

I shake my head slowly, feeling the draw of his presence in the way that my body wants to shift closer, closer, closer. The inches separating us are painful, a chasm made up of pure attraction.

I *hate* those inches.

"Too bad," Thayden says. "I'd offer you my jacket."

"You don't have a jacket."

I shove his chest lightly, the urge to touch him greater than my self-control to resist. My hand doesn't want to come back—the wanton hussy—and instead, I press my palm flat against the center of his chest, just inches from his heart, which is beating as erratically as my own.

Thayden grins before he speaks. "I don't have a jacket, but I have myself."

The man is so smooth.

So smooth that before I can even blink, his arms are around my waist and his lips meet mine in a kiss that is sigh-soft.

It's a brush, a question, maybe even a plea.

And yet it's also charged and electric, a lightning strike sending 300 million volts through me, causing a rolling blackout of every other function of my body until there is only *this*, only Thayden's lips and mine.

Gradually, I become aware of other sensations. The scrape of his beard against my cheek, gritty and delicious. The grip of his hands as they span my waist, like he's measuring to see if he can completely encircle it. My own hand, caught between us, feels the flex of muscle beneath the soft cotton of his shirt.

I shudder, my legs shaky and unsteady as a baby deer. Thayden's hold on me tightens, tugging me closer. My pinky finger catches on the opening of his shirt, ripping the button clean off. Thayden doesn't react, as though he knows the moment we pull apart, the magic of this moment will disappear in the air like fairy dust.

Not that I considered it (too much), but I assumed that Thayden would kiss like a man plundering, a kiss full of control and force.

But this ...

He is soft, his pace languid and sure. He draws me along, the movements like a trail of breadcrumbs meant for me to follow. And, hoo boy! I am hot on that trail.

Hot.

On.

It.

Thayden is a tease—that's what he is. Because though the kiss keeps rolling on, it's barely a step past chaste. Featherlight, soft. Lips barely parted. It's a baby kiss. A prologue. And I want to skip to the end.

As always with Thayden, I want to shake the man. This sweet kiss is not enough. I'm frustrated with the slow pace and I'm angry at myself for wanting him to speed up, for wanting this at all.

It's the anger that finally acts as the disruption, enabling me to disconnect and unplug, yanking my lips away in a move that should sound like a crack of thunder, but instead is silent. I shove him back.

I do and I don't want him to go. So, when his hands tighten on my waist, letting me move back inches, but no more, relief soothes the ache.

"I don't kiss on the first date," I say.

I would glare, but I can't seem to fully control my face. I'm slack-jawed and stupid, surprised that words even came out in a coordinated sentence.

"That's okay. You said nothing about your policy for kissing at dinners."

The smile on his face is so smug, so self-satisfied, so handsome, that I just want to thread my fingers in his hair and kiss it right off his face. I want to go to battle with my lips, to conquer him, to make him cry uncle and wave a white flag of surrender.

Other men I've dated, however few, never made me feel this way. I *liked* them. They *liked* me. Boring, vanilla nothingness.

Meanwhile, Thayden and I are like two people drag racing on a two-lane road, whipping around corners too fast, ignoring oncoming traffic and steep drop-offs on either side. We're vying for position, jockeying to get ahead. It's nerve-racking and exhilarating and the stakes seem way too high.

Harper said to give him a chance, to see how I feel, but my feelings for this man are anything but simple. I won't even know how to answer if she asks how tonight went. I am terrified and worked up and I don't even know what else. *Confused.*

Yes, that.

I am somewhere between wanting to slap him and ordering monogrammed onesies for our unborn children.

His phone rings, a welcome intrusion. Thayden steps back, grimacing as he lets me go, his hands falling away. I press my back against the tree, needing an anchor, needing space.

"Ordinarily, I wouldn't take this, but it's my mother."

He answers the phone while I curl my fingers into the rough bark of the tree, remembering the scrape of his stubble on my cheeks as though it's a distant memory, one I'll only ever relive in my mind.

"Hello, Mom," he says, flicking his eyes up to me. There's a pause. "Yes, I'm with her. You WHAT?!"

He's silent for a moment, eyes squeezed closed and his free hand pinching the bridge of his nose. "No. The thought does *not* count. This is something *he* would have done. I can't even—I have to go."

He disconnects the call, breathing heavy like he just stepped out of a boxing ring. I watch the rise and fall of his shoulders. He slides the phone in his pocket and turns, not to me, but to the water. With both hands, he clutches the railing.

"Did you sign a contract today?"

Dread pools in my belly. "Y-yes."

"Did you read it?"

I'm suddenly five years old, and I've spilled milk fixing myself cereal while Mama slept off a hangover. I feel stupid and small, and there are few things I hate more. We just shared the most perfect kiss of my life and now the beauty of it has been ripped away.

"Not fully. Your mama said it was from you. For watching Apollo."

Thayden closes his eyes briefly, and I can see the exertion it takes to control his emotions. When he opens his eyes again, those beautiful grass-green eyes, I want to cry at the expression in them.

"What did I sign?" I ask quietly, knowing somehow that whatever it is, I don't want to know.

And I'm right.

"You agreed to marry me next month."

CHAPTER NINE

Thayden

TO SAY that the walk back to the parking lot is awkward would be an insult to awkwardness. We are silent, and Delilah keeps at least two feet between us at all times. Meanwhile, I'm fuming, furious at my mother and hoping Delilah doesn't think it's directed toward her.

But who doesn't read contracts?

Okay, fine. I don't read them all. I've scrolled through the Netflix terms of service and clicked the box. I joined my gym without so much as a second glance. Scroll, scan, and sign on the dotted line.

But THIS?

It was probably because she trusted my mom. And why wouldn't she? Who would suspect a mother of tricking someone into a marriage contract?

The wheels are turning in her head. I can practically hear them. But in what direction? That, I do not know.

My own thoughts are all over the place, like someone has dropped a handful of bouncy rubber balls in a concrete room.

With anyone else, I would be relieved by the lack of yelling and anger. But Delilah's quiet stillness feels like the proverbial calm before what I suspect will be a fierce Southern storm with gale force winds.

"Dare I ask what's going on in that pretty head of yours?"

We're halfway up the hill to the parking lot when I finally get up the nerve to speak. Delilah is silent for a moment, then answers without looking up from her sneakers.

"Why would your mama do that?"

Her voice is even, but her accent is thicker than usual. I can't get a read on her. I consider how to answer, and I decide on the ugly and embarrassing truth. No point in trying to sugarcoat it.

"I told you my father liked control. When he died, he put a stipulation in the legal documents regarding the family firm. Specifically, that I need to get married in order to take over the company."

"I see."

Does she, though? Can she possibly understand my situation? I know nothing about her family, but it's hard to imagine one as messed up as mine. My dad bound me in one contract; my mom bound me *and* Delilah in another. All with "best intentions."

The Joneses, we are not, folks. The Walkers are a whole different breed of family. We're wolves.

My mother's behavior is reprehensible. She's codependent on my father, *still*. On the other hand, she's lost the love of her life. She wants the best for me, I do believe that, even if I don't believe the same thing about my father.

Mom loved Delilah when she met her this morning. She got attached, thinking marriage was already the plan in the works.

And honestly? Though I was—and am—angry with my mom, a tiny and selfish sliver of my heart *wants* Delilah to be trapped in this contract with me. For the first time I can ever remember, I can't get enough of a woman. *This* woman.

I felt that way before the kiss, and after having a taste of her lips in a too-short embrace, I only want more. Not just physically, and that's new for me. I want something deeper, something real.

Having Delilah around ... I could get used to that. Way too easily. This contract would force her to stay with me.

In marriage. Which you DO NOT WANT.

Right. It's a little odd that I have to remind myself of that fact. It must be the aftershocks of that kiss, messing with my brain. I take a moment to reorient myself.

Fact: I don't want to get married.

Fact: I don't want my father to get his way.

Fact: I don't want Delilah to be a pawn in these games.

Fact: This may have ruined any chance I have of dating her.

Fact: This completely sucks.

Delilah glances briefly at me, then away. "So, your mother drew up the contract? Or did you?"

"I had nothing to do with it. Delilah, I swear, I didn't know she was planning this."

"But you *had* planned to arrange—or *fake?*—a marriage in order to keep your firm."

"No. I'm working to find a way out of the contract. A loophole."

"And if you couldn't find one, would you have married someone?"

I haven't let myself think about that. Now, I look that possibility straight in the face. "I don't know."

We've reached her scooter, and in the faded hush of twilight, this moment feels more serious somehow. Nothing like the light, easy conversation over dinner or the charged electricity in the air as we kissed. My eyes drop briefly to her lips, then away. I don't deserve to think about that now.

Even if it was categorically the best kiss of my life.

Delilah wraps her arms around herself. "Why not just meet a woman and settle down?"

The words are an echo straight from my father's lips, something he said to me over and over again through the years. Even though I know Delilah can't know that, I still bristle.

"I'm thirty-three and haven't met anyone who made me want to consider settling down. I doubt I could do it in three months."

She flinches a little, and I realize that my words may be insulting. Honestly, if anyone could make me rethink my stance, it's Delilah. But what am I supposed to do—admit that on our very first non-date?

"But your mom's contract shortened it to one month?"

I shift, dragging my shoe through the gravel. "I guess you could say my mother is … overeager. You should know that this means she likes you."

"I liked her too. Before this. Now, I don't know how to feel."

"I'm sorry."

"It's not your fault."

But it definitely *feels* like my fault.

Delilah chews her lip for a moment, the motion drawing my attention back to her full mouth. I'd give anything to hit rewind, to not answer my phone, to kiss her again right now.

I force my feet to stay where they are. There's no way she would let me kiss her again. Based on prior experience, I suspect Delilah has a mean right hook.

"Did you know your mama was going to try and trick me into marrying you?"

I hold up both hands. "*No*. We discussed you earlier and I said ..."

I trail off, realizing that in the context, telling Delilah about the whole conversation I had with my mother sounds bad. Really bad.

But it's too late for that.

"You said *what*?"

Delilah still has that stiffness to her limbs, such a contrast to the vivacious, fiery woman I've gotten to know.

It's not like I can make this situation much worse. Unless I lie. So, again, maybe stupidly, I opt for the whole truth and nothing but the truth.

"After she met you this morning, Mom assumed I had asked you to, uh, help fulfill my father's stipulations. When I explained that I'd hired you to take care of Apollo, she suggested I ask you to marry me. For the contract. I told her that I didn't want to marry you. Or anyone," I say hurriedly.

But again, my words make her flinch. "To clarify, you want to take me on a date. You're fine with kissing me. But you don't want to marry me ... or anyone."

Her eyes could burn a hole straight through me. In fact, I think they are doing just that.

"Right." It feels like the word has been yanked out of me, and that one syllable *hurts*.

"What was your endgame with me? Out of curiosity. You don't want to marry me. You just want to ... what? Make out? Make love? Make me yours but not for keeps?"

Wow. Okay, so we've turned from hypothetical marriage-contract stuff, to the most epic DTR talk ever. Straight from a first non-date date to future intentions and marriage talk. I mean, she's right to ask.

And though I haven't ever wanted to get married, I also haven't ever met a woman who made me feel what I feel for Delilah. And I haven't known her long enough or really even dated her to consider what might come next for us.

It feels like both of my parents managed to somehow drop a bomb into my life, decimating any chance I might have with this woman.

I stare down at the ground. "I don't know. But we'll get you out of the contract. My mom wouldn't really force you to marry me."

I don't *think*, anyway. Guess I have another contract to study for loopholes.

I brace myself for something. A slap, a shout, maybe her grabbing me by my shirt collar and shaking me. I do not expect the quiet answer she gives.

"Okay."

Delilah begins putting on her helmet and turns the key in the ignition of the scooter before I can say anything else. Not that I have anything to say. Her key turns, but the engine only sputters. Frowning, she tries again.

"Come on, baby," she mutters.

Her voice is entrancing, so much softer and sweeter than the one she was just using with me. She glides a hand over the seat, a caress, a gentle touch. I find myself tracking the motion.

"You got this, sugar."

Is it bad to be jealous of a scooter? Because I am.

"Want me to try?" I ask.

Her head snaps up. "What—because you're a big, strong man, you think you can turn the key and the engine will obey you? Be my guest." She steps back, spreading her arms.

Delilah has been snippy with me before, but it never carried this thread of genuine anger that blasts me with a shock of real heat.

"No, I just …"

"Go on. You seem to have a way with the ladies. Maybe my scooter just needs you to work that *charm*."

Ouch. The flaming arrows she's shooting are hitting the mark, each one going a little deeper, burning a little more. Too embarrassed to stand there with my hands in my pockets, I try the engine a few times, knowing already it's no use.

"Are you out of gas?"

"No," she snaps.

"I'll call a rideshare to get us back and have a tow truck pick her up."

Delilah waves her phone at me. "You can get a rideshare for *you*. I just messaged Zoey and Gavin while you were trying to use your testosterone to start my dead vehicle. They're fixing to pick me up. Gavin can put her in the back of the truck. I'll be just fine."

I hadn't even thought of Gavin, whose house is less than ten minutes away. It's clear Delilah is trying to get rid of me. But I'm not so easy to dislodge, even when my pride has been burned down to ash and coal.

Delilah slumps on the seat of her scooter, twisting her hands over the handlebars before hanging her helmet over one side. My impulse is to reach out, to comfort her in the only way I know how, which, I realize with startling clarity, is only physical. I am no better than a one-trick pony when it comes to women, and Delilah needs so much more.

I want to be the one to give her what she needs. And, for the first time in my life, I want to change. *Really* change. I want to be a new man. The kind of man deserving of love, who can give as well—no, *better*—than he takes.

Maybe the kind of man who would want to get married and spend his life with only one woman.

The thought is radical, but it doesn't feel that foreign. Not when that woman is Delilah.

But I would need to be a different man. A man not motivated by a complicated relationship with his father. A man sure of what he wants. One worthy to love her and consider a lifelong commitment.

Could I be that man? For her? Honestly, I'm not sure. But it is the very first time I have entertained the idea.

Gavin's truck pulls into the lot, the headlights washing over this miserable little conversation.

Sighing, I say, "Look—I can get you out of the contract. I'm sure there was money involved, and I'll pay it."

"You don't know how much it is."

"It doesn't matter. I'll pay it."

Delilah blinks at me. She looks so young, so vulnerable, so beautiful. I hate that this great night ended so horribly.

"Are we okay?" I ask quietly.

She stiffens. "There is no *we*. But yes. I'm fine. Why wouldn't I be?"

I expect this. I deserve it. And yet her words shatter me.

"Do you still need me for Apollo?"

"Yes. If you're willing."

"Just so long as you're not there."

Delilah turns away from me, walking toward Gavin and Zoey as they hop out of the truck.

"Hey, y'all!" she says, her voice betraying none of the emotion I feel. "Thanks for coming to get us out of this pickle. Where's Ella-bell?"

"Nancy was over for dinner and agreed to watch her 'til we get back," I hear Zoey say.

Gavin makes his way to where I'm standing by the scooter, trying to pick up the pieces of shrapnel from our conversation and put something back together from it.

"Hey," Gavin says, studying me. "Want to help me get this in the bed?"

"Sure."

I know he can tell something is wrong and appreciate the fact that he doesn't ask. We wheel the scooter toward the back of his truck. Delilah and Zoey are having a hushed conversation a few feet away, and Zoey's laser eyes let me know exactly what they're discussing. Me. And it isn't good.

The scooter is surprisingly light as we hoist it up into the back of his truck. Gav jumps up and begins to secure it with some nylon straps. Always prepared, always the responsible one.

Which gives me an idea. "Can I drop by later? I need some advice."

Gavin drops the helmet with a clatter. When he looks up, he's grinning. "I'm sorry. I must not have heard correctly. You want advice? Well, now. I don't know that I can give it. But sure."

Zoey sticks her head over the side of the truck bed. "Are we ready to go?"

"Yep. Let's load up," Gavin says. "Are we taking you home and dropping the scooter at a shop?"

Delilah waves a hand before hopping in back. "Nah. I can't afford to fix her right now anyway. Just take us both home."

It's on the tip of my tongue to offer to have it fixed, to offer her a new one, to offer her one of my cars, when Delilah shoots me a look so hostile that my words dry right up in my throat. Any fixing I do will have to be on the sly.

"You coming?" Gavin asks me.

"Thayden has another ride," Zoey says, slamming her door.

Gavin furrows his brow, looking between me and his wife. "You do?"

"I'm fine," I tell him. "I'll be by later."

And then, maybe Gavin can help me figure out what I'm supposed to do about Delilah.

CHAPTER TEN

Thayden

WHEN GAVIN OPENS HIS DOOR, he takes a quick look at my face and grins, slapping me on the shoulder. "You've joined the club. Welcome."

"Which club is this?"

"The one that starts with that look"—he points to my face—"and becomes official with a walk down the aisle."

I slap his hand away and push past him into the house, chuckling. Gavin is way closer to the truth than he even realizes. At least, according to the contract Delilah signed.

Zoey and Ella are nowhere to be seen, which doesn't surprise me. By now, Ella is probably asleep and I doubt Zoey wants to talk to me any more than Delilah does.

"You look like you need to relax," Gavin says. "Hot tub and beer?"

"Hot tub and water? Assuming you have a suit I can borrow."

A few minutes later, Gavin and I sink into the hot tub. I hadn't realized how tense I was until the warmth of the jets starts soothing the ache.

I tip my head back to look at the few stars I can see. Gavin's house feels like it's in the middle of nowhere, nestled into the hills, but there's still too much light pollution to see much.

"So, did Delilah tell you and Zoey everything during the car ride?" I ask.

"No. She and Zoey mostly talked about Ella and our honeymoon."

"Right—your honeymoon. Sorry." I rub a hand down my face, feeling like a jerk. My best friend just got married, and I had basically forgotten. "Congrats again."

"Thanks. No need to apologize." He pauses. "I'm sorry about your dad. Are you doing okay? I wish I could have been here."

I don't, but I'm not about to tell him that. Gavin may be the closest friend I have, the only one who knows all about my lifelong battle with my dad, but I didn't mind his absence. It was easier to comfort my mom and take care of various arrangements. I avoided thinking too much about the man I don't really miss.

"Are you doing okay?" Gavin asks. "Does tonight have anything to do with your father?"

I drop my head, splashing water over my face before meeting Gavin's eyes. "Yes and no. I need to catch you up on a few things."

I give Gavin a brief rundown of the major plot points, which sound a lot like a B-movie pitch: the clause about the family firm, me hiring Delilah, and Mom tricking her into signing a marriage contract.

Gavin's shocked face says it all. "Your mom tricked Delilah into signing a contract to marry you? In order to fulfill the requirements of your dad's estate?"

"That's the big and small of it."

"I know you're the lawyer, but is that legal? Any of it?"

"Courts hate that kind of clause. Judges often throw them out. I'm going to do my best to contest it, though Duke will fight me on everything."

"That small-minded idiot you work with?"

"That's the one. He'd love nothing more than to take the company or lawyer me to death. As for what Delilah signed, we can get her out of it. Mom clearly withheld information, making it sound like my dog-watching contract. I don't think she would actually try to make Delilah stick to it, as much as she would love to."

Gavin shakes his head. "Mothers. Am I right?"

I laugh. "Quite. Though I never saw your mom try anything like this."

"No, but she did try to set me up with any single woman she met for *years*. Chasing women to their cars at the grocery store, introducing herself to single women at church, flashing my photo on her phone. Never took it this far."

"Consider yourself lucky."

"It sounds like you have three options," Gavin says. "Give up the company."

"Boo!"

"Go to bat with Duke and win."

"Yes!" I raise my water bottle to that one.

"Or get married."

And ... I take a long drink.

I have no response to that. Because totally unrecognizable

thoughts have started to churn in my head tonight. Ones that involve Delilah and a future.

"Awful quiet over there," Gavin says. "You aren't really considering option three, are you?"

I assumed Gavin would encourage that line of thinking, especially based on his greeting at the door. I mean … I'm not considering it. Am I? After the great date with Delilah, that kiss, and the disaster that followed, I honestly don't know what to think.

When I don't answer, Gavin sets his water down and leans forward.

"Marriage in this situation would be ridiculous. Do you *want* to marry Delilah?"

"I want to *date* her." The question fires off so rapidly that my response is just as quick.

"Do you even want to get married?"

"I want to be happy."

"Thayden, do you want to get married?"

"Maybe?"

The intense look on his face relaxes and he leans back again. "You're not ready. Fight Duke. Find a loophole. Or leave the firm—you seem pretty miserable there anyway."

He can't be serious. "It's the Walker Firm. I'm not going to just walk away and let Duke have it. That's my legacy."

"So? Start a new Walker Firm. Build a new legacy that's not tainted with all of your father's control. Clean break, fresh start, no baggage. Date Delilah. Then come back and talk to me about marriage when you're ready."

He makes it sound so easy; his tone is so dismissive. I'm immediately defensive. "Who says I'm not ready now?"

"You're not."

Like most people, I hate being told what to do, or whether I am or am not ready to do something.

"I'm not as opposed to the idea of getting married as I once was."

Gavin throws his head back and laughs, which only makes me angrier. And he wonders why I don't ask for advice. I send a wave of water his way. He sputters, but his eyes are still dancing with amusement.

"You think that because, sometime between yesterday and today, you are less opposed to marriage that you should consider marrying Delilah to save your company?"

"That's not exactly—"

"Look, Thayden. You're one of my closest friends. If you wanted to get married, you'd be a great husband. A great father, even, *if* that's something you wanted. But do not let your father's manipulations factor into that kind of decision. Walk away, man. Walk. Away. I can tell that you really like Delilah, that this is different for you. That's awesome. Don't make it complicated."

"I'm afraid it already is."

Gavin shakes his head, a knowing smile on his face. "You kissed her, didn't you?"

"I did. Before ... all this."

"And how was it?"

I give him a look. A long one with narrowed eyes. Gavin only laughs. Again. Apparently, my plight is quite amusing to him.

"Something funny?" Zoey asks.

Because of course, she chooses this moment to walk outside. I cringe a little but try to keep my expression neutral.

"Hello, wife," Gavin says, grinning, clearly not sensing the undercurrent of danger that I do. Of course, she's angry with *me*, not him. Actually, from her expression, she's mad at him too, probably for conspiring with the enemy.

"Hey, husband. And hello, *Thayden*."

I realize she's holding my clothes in her arms the moment before she tosses them in the pool. I watch them floating in the moonlight for a moment.

"I didn't want you to forget your things when you go," Zoey says sweetly. Then she gives Gavin a look that says they'll be talking later.

She starts to walk away, pauses, and throws both our towels and Gavin's shoes in the pool. "And this is because you're entertaining an unwelcome guest. I'm Team Delilah, for the record."

I'm glad my shoes are by the front door. Though they might be on the lawn by now.

"Zo, hang on a sec!" Gavin calls, but she's already slammed the door. I'm shocked the glass didn't shatter from the force.

Guess that's my cue to head home.

Gavin sighs, then dives into the pool, fishing out the drenched clothes, towels, and his shoes.

"I'm sorry," he says, climbing out of the pool. "She's usually not that vindictive."

"It's fine. Tonight surprised and hurt Delilah, and this is totally what I'd expect from her friends. They've got each other's backs, and I respect that."

Even if it's going to be a cold ride home.

Gavin hangs my dripping clothes along the back of a lounge chair, spreading the towels out on the terrace. We both stand there for a moment, shivering in the air that's cooled considerably.

He sighs. "Look, if you want to win Delilah over, you have to be willing to give up the family firm, if it comes to that. No contracts, no money, no strings. Get your father out of your head and out of your relationship."

The funny thing is, while my father is still in my head, there is someone else who has moved in and is taking up much more valuable real estate. Too bad I think she'd rather list the property than live there.

"What do I owe you for hot tub therapy?" I ask.

Gavin smirks. "How about you stop doing things to make my wife upset?"

At that, I shove him in the pool. He comes up sputtering as I gather my wet clothes. Maybe Zoey's onto something because that was quite satisfying.

CHAPTER ELEVEN

Delilah

JUST STAY QUIET. Make yourself small, and JUST STAY QUIET.

If it works for animals in the wild, why can't it work for me having lunch with my friends? I've been giving myself this pep talk all morning, but as the rideshare drops me off in front of the restaurant to meet my friends, I'm not convinced.

"Hello, ladies!" I call out in a voice that hopefully hides my panic. Everyone but Abby is already seated at the back of the Mexican restaurant.

I love when we choose Mexican, and not just because Tex-Mex is life. I can fill up on chips (free!) and most places have a side menu or soups, so I can look like I'm still eating, yet spend less than $10. You want budget tips? I'm your girl.

I give Zoey a hug first, trying to signal her with what are probably crazy eyes that she can't tell anyone about the stuff with Thayden. Specifically, the whole contract thing. And about the part where I confessed that I'm actually considering the idea of going along with it.

I know. I KNOW. Ridiculous.

I've sent Zoey no less than ten texts this morning, but she did not reply. I can't read her expression, which only makes me more nervous.

"Sleep okay?" she asks, one eyebrow raised.

"You know I didn't," I hiss through clenched teeth. "Read your texts!" Louder, I say, "Marriage agrees with you, darlin'."

She looks amazing though, all tanned and content after her honeymoon. I'm not jealous. I'm *not*. But okay, yeah—I've never been on a fancy vacation. Summers were spent doing pageants when I was younger, and in college, they were for working. Not once have I sat on a beach without a care in the world, sipping some drink out of a pineapple.

Will I ever?

If I marry Thayden like the contract says, I could have a honeymoon in a month. Fake marriages still get honeymoons, right? I snort at the idea.

"Did you just snort?" Sam asks.

"Of course not." I give her a hug before patting Harper and sitting down.

The server is already taking our orders when Abby rushes in, practically throwing herself into Zoey's lap. "I've missed you!"

Zoey laughs. "You saw me the night I got back. And the other day for coffee."

"It's not enough," Abby says dramatically, kissing Zoey noisily on the cheek before flopping in the last empty chair and ordering queso. "The house is empty without you."

"Which is the perfect segue into talking about our living situation," Sam says. We all groan. "The lease is up next month. We'd originally planned to renew, but with certain changes, it's a good idea to discuss options."

"I'm sorry," Zoey says, looking guilty.

"Please do not apologize for getting married," Abby says. "Sheesh. We all knew this would happen."

Just not so soon. Those are the words she doesn't say, but we all feel them around the table. Things are shifting for us, and the last year we thought we'd have living together is quickly becoming something else.

"We're all happy for you!" Sam assures Zoey.

And it's true, even if it does put us in an awkward position. Our house is in a perfect location and is the ideal setup … for five. But without Zoey, we can't afford to split the rent four ways. Add in my uncertain situation, which I do NOT want to discuss, and things get harder. I'm hoping they can figure this out without me weighing in. I honestly don't know my next steps.

Between the kiss and the contract, I'm a *mess*.

"As I see it, we've got three options," Sam says, tossing back her dark hair. "Find a new place." We all groan. "Increase the amount of rent we're all paying." Louder groans. "Or get a new roommate."

"I vote option one," Harper says.

"That's because you're never home," Abby argues. "I don't want to live in some apartment that looks like every other apartment. Gross."

Sam sighs. "Guys, if we all just paid a little more—"

"Not all of us got big advances on book deals," Harper says.

I nibble chips, getting to the end of the basket while they debate. I hate conflict. And if I open my mouth, all my secrets will spill out, so I just keep stuffing in the chips.

The server drops off our plates, hurrying away. My tiny cup of soup looks like a meal for Lilliputians.

"We all knew this was coming," Harper says. "Sam and Abby are practically engaged already. Who knows if either of them will even be living with us still in a year?"

The table goes silent. This is it. The end of an era. We'll stay friends, but it won't be the same.

I stare down into my soup, willing my tears to get themselves back to where they came from. I refuse to cry. But I feel like I'm walking a tightrope stretched out over a canyon. There's no ground beneath me, and balance isn't my strong suit.

"Maybe we could find a new roommate?" Sam suggests quietly.

"No," Abby and Harper say at the same time.

"Abby doesn't want to move out. Harper doesn't want to pay more. Neither of you want a new roommate." Sam makes a frustrated noise. "Delilah?"

Everyone looks at me, and I swallow. "I, um ..."

"Thayden asked Delilah to marry him for money," Zoey blurts.

No. She. Did. Not.

The table erupts into questions and shouts while I shoot murderous looks at Zoey. Thankfully, a mariachi band starts doing a birthday serenade at the table behind us, temporarily shutting us all up.

I take a long swallow of water, not meeting anyone's eyes as I prepare my defense. As soon as the trumpets stop trumpeting, Sam says, "Explain."

"Thayden did not offer to pay me to marry him. His mother tricked me into signing a contract to marry him for money."

"That's ... wow." Abby shakes her head. "No words."

"Clearly, that's preposterous," Harper says. "You can't be forced to marry him. Which means it has no bearing on the discussion about our living situation. I vote apartment."

"Delilah," Zoey says, a note of warning in her tone.

Note to self: do not trust Zoey with secrets.

Abby laughs. "You're not really thinking about marrying him."

It is laughable, isn't it?

And yet, around four in the morning, something hit me. I need the money in that contract. Like, *need* it. It would be life-changing. I know Thayden said he would pay it without the contract, but I can't let him. I *could* let him if there was something in it for him.

If we stick to the contract I signed, I would get out of debt. He would get the family firm. Win, win.

Thayden and I could get married, and it would mean nothing. I could just consider it like a job.

A job that forces me into close proximity with a man who seems to be my Kryptonite.

My friends will not get this. Not without me telling them the *whole* truth.

"I haven't been forthcoming with y'all about the state of my finances. And it's pretty dire. I got fired."

Abby blinks rapidly. "You got fired and got tricked into a marriage contract all in one week?"

"And she went on a date with Thayden," Harper adds.

"And she kissed him," Zoey says, shrugging when I throw my napkin at her.

"Is nothing sacred?" I demand.

"Clearly not marriage," Abby says, laughing. "High five!"

No one high-fives her.

"I thought you had scholarships from the pageants," Harper says.

She looks like she smells rotting garbage when she says the word *pageants*. Out of everyone, she's been the most vocal about my former life and the dozen or so titles I own. Long ago, I stopped trying to convince her they're scholarship competitions. Any time you have girls dressing in swimwear, it's a pageant. Even if there are, in actuality, scholarships.

It's funny. The pageants aren't half as bad as the other things I've done, the ones I never talk about. I wonder what Harper would say about what else I grew up doing for my mama.

The thought chills me, and I take those memories and shove them back in the box where I keep them, tying it with chains and dropping it in a lake.

"My scholarship winnings didn't cover everything. Not nearly enough. I'm looking at almost a hundred thousand in student debt and climbing. If I don't fight to get out of the contract, I could be free, y'all. You have no idea what that means to me."

No, tears. No. You do NOT get to come out. They aren't listening to me, which isn't surprising.

Sam touches my arm. "Why didn't you say something? We would have helped."

Around the table, all my friends nod, which has the tears going full force.

"You can't help with something like that." I sniff. "I love that y'all would want to. This is a gift. I have to take the opportunity."

For a moment, no one says anything. The mood has shifted to sadness, and I'm tempted to tell the server it's Abby's birthday so we can get our own happy serenade.

Sometime around Mama's third live-in boyfriend, I made a promise on a star. Some kids made wishes; I made myself promises. I didn't believe in the power of wishes, but had all the faith I could muster in my own self-determination.

I promised I would never be like Mama, with a bedroom door that revolved, letting in men and spitting them right out at a breakneck pace. I would hold out for something real and lasting—if such a thing existed, and I'm as unsure now as I was then. If I got married, it would be forever.

My nine-year-old self would be ashamed of me now. But my twenty-three-year-old self has a little more living under her belt, a bit less faith in herself, and a heck of a lot more debt.

Sam's brow furrows. "Hang on. You went on a date with him last night. You *kissed* him. Is this marriage real or fake?"

"Fake." I have zero hesitation.

Abby coughs *liar* under her breath.

I shake my head. "Definitely fake."

Harper raises her brows. "I saw you two last night. Attraction off the charts."

"Thayden doesn't want to get married," I say. "Trust me. This would be on paper only."

"No," Sam says. "Kissing makes it messy and real. You're lying to yourself if you think otherwise."

"I'm not going to kiss him again."

That elicits laughter from them all, and my neck is starting to get hot. I'm irritated, and mostly it's because I know they're right. I had those same arguments with myself in the darkness last night while I wasn't sleeping. And I kept coming back to one thing.

"Maybe it's a terrible idea and will be messy and complicated, but ... one hundred thousand dollars. Tell me another way I can earn that now."

They all share uncomfortable glances around the table because they know I'm right. I can't get some big corporate job like Zoey. I don't train elite athletes like Harper. I don't have a book deal like Sam. And I don't have mad tech skills like Abby.

Harper clears her throat. "You could sell your priceless collection of Beanie Babies."

I don't even know what to do with that answer. Especially because I don't have Beanie Babies. But Harper has a sly smile on her face.

Oh my goodness—Harpy made a joke!

"Definitely an option," I say, smiling.

"You could make art from trash," Abby says. "Ironic art. Like ... ashtrays made out of cigarette butts."

I giggle. "Plus, that would serve to clean up litter."

Sam grins. "You could knit sweaters. Like, specialty organic sweaters from lemur fur."

"Do you knit?" Zoey asks.

"Nope."

"Can you even get ... thread or wool or whatever from lemurs?" Abby asks.

Harper holds up her phone. "The internet says no."

"Boo!" we all say.

Just like that, I feel better. Well. Slightly better. There's still the whole matter of convincing Thayden to go along with the contract and marry me when he doesn't want to get married. And the other matter, which is the fact that I really like him. Like Sam said, it is too complicated and messy. One way or another, I'm going to get hurt. Heck, I was hurt last night just hearing Thayden say he wanted to kiss me, but wouldn't consider more.

But *one hundred thousand dollars*. I can manage messy for that.

"I guess that means we're getting an apartment," Abby sighs, and everyone groans.

For now, I ignore my worries in favor of finishing up my dollhouse-sized cup of soup.

———

Apollo greets me after lunch with exuberant licks that get just a little too close to my mouth. There's something so simple about the love of a dog. No complications. No meddling moms and binding legal agreements.

Just a waggly butt and slightly smelly kisses.

Speaking of kisses, I'm still trying to shove away memories of the legendary kiss from my date—correction, *dinner*—last night. If I close my eyes, I can still feel the scrape of Thayden's facial hair against my skin.

And dang it, now I'll probably never feel that again. If I agree to the contract for money, there will be no kissing. Too complicated. Too close to selling myself.

The afternoon drags on, allowing me too much time to think and get nervous before Thayden comes home. When Apollo runs to the front door with his whole backside wagging, I know that it's go-time.

"Hey, boy," he says, tossing his keys in a bowl by the front door and letting Apollo kiss him.

His smile and that rich baritone have me needing to reprimand my body, which has lit up like a human torch. My lips are going rogue, all Pavlovian, tingling in response to the sight of him.

Thayden's eyes land on me, and he grins. I need to look into some kind of anti-attraction pill or maybe a vaccine. I mentally add that to my list of things to google later.

"I didn't expect to see you here," he says. "I thought you wanted to avoid me for a few days."

"I did. But we need to talk."

I stand from the couch and stretch, feigning a casualness I don't feel. Because everything in me wants to react just like Apollo, who ran straight to the door to get kisses.

No kisses. No thoughts of kisses. If this is going to work, kisses are banished to the outside realm of possibility.

And in my memory.

Thayden manages to extricate himself from Apollo's greeting and joins me in the living room. I sink back down on the couch, where I've been trying to read. My eyes keep scanning over the same words again and again as I've thought about what I'm going to say to this man. Now that he's here, all thoughts have fled.

Thayden sits in a worn leather chair facing me, leaning forward, elbows on his knees. I sink back down on the couch, putting a receipt in my book to mark my place because I'm not a savage who turns down the corners of pages.

"Shakespeare, huh?" Thayden sounds surprised. "Are you taking classes or is this what you read for fun?"

"This is one of my favorites. Don't let my accent fool you. I'm no dummy."

If I'm a little prickly about this, it's because every time I answered a question in class, there were snickers. You'd think in Texas, a Southern accent wouldn't be synonymous with stupid, but I guess my Alabama drawl is more pronounced than the typical Texas one. It's something I'll have to get over if I really want to get into academia.

"I never thought you were," Thayden says. "Not with that whip-smart mouth of yours."

His gaze drops to my lips and I remind myself that kissing doesn't exist in this realm. Kissing died out with the dinosaurs. And the stupid marriage contract and the fact that Thayden only wants to kiss, not marry, me.

Apollo nestles his body against the couch so his head is in

my lap. When I start to rub his ears, he groans. I giggle at the almost human sound.

"You're stealing my dog's heart," Thayden says, and my own heart quivers a little, because his eyes are pinned on me, seeming to communicate something else.

"I am so sorry about all of this," he says suddenly. "About my mother taking advantage of you. About hurting your feelings last night. I had a really great time with you last night. Before ... everything else."

He gives me a sheepish grin, and I fight the urge to smile back. I don't know where this conversation is going, and I need to work up the nerve to say what I want to say.

"Delilah, I don't want you to think I just want—"

"I'll do it. I'll marry you like the contract says."

The words tumble out and hang in the room like a stiff fog.

I know my friends were right to be worried. I'm going to hate myself when this is done. And I'm going to struggle every moment I spend with Thayden *not* falling for him.

He looks like I've knocked the wind out of him. "You—what?"

"I think that it's in both our interests to stick to the contract I signed. Get married, in name only. You get your company, and I'll be able to better my financial position."

Now, if that doesn't sound a whole lot fancier than *dig myself out of student debt*, I don't know what does.

Thayden sinks back in the chair. He swallows, and I watch the knot of his Adam's apple bob. Such a nice neck.

"You don't have to do this. If your finances are an issue, I'm more than happy to help. Like I said last night, I would pay you the money."

"I'm not a charity case, Thayden."

"It's not charity. You're working for me."

I scoff. "You can't pay me one hundred thousand dollars to walk Apollo."

"Is that what Mom promised?"

I nod. His expression doesn't change.

"She lowballed you."

"Thayden, that number is ridiculous!"

He sighs, running a hand through his thick hair. "I disagree. But I need to look at the contract."

"We would need to add some stipulations. Addendums, or whatever." I try to say those words casually, like I didn't scour the internet for the correct legal terms last night. "But I want to do it. That is … as long as you do. I know you said you didn't want to get married, but this lets you keep the firm. We both win."

And I lose. But I swallow those words down.

Thayden simply stares, and I internally begin to panic. What if he says no?

Thayden is silent for a long time, staring down at his hands, which are clenched in his lap. It feels like I've thrown my chips on the table and am waiting for him to call or fold.

As always with this man, I'm torn about which one I want him to do. Really, what I'd like, if I'm being completely honest, is for him to sweep the chips off the metaphorical table and throw me down onto it, declaring his feelings for me and then continuing that kiss from last night.

I tell myself that resisting him will be easier when the novelty of the man wears off. Though I suspect Thayden might be like a fine wine, getting better over time.

"Are you sure about this? I was planning to come in and call the whole thing off. Then we could start over, without something like that hanging over our heads."

"Start over, how? With what? We're not dating, Thayden. Remember? Last night was dinner, not a date."

We both know I'm full of it, but for this to work, I have to push the platonic angle.

"And the kiss?" he demands.

It's hard to lie when he's so laser-focused on me.

"That was a—"

"Don't you dare say *mistake*."

Yeah, I was gonna choke on that lie as it came out. But no other word comes to mind. That's also a lie. Lots of words come to mind—toe-tingling, synapse-shorting, future-altering—but none I'll admit out loud.

Instead, I change directions. "The contract will keep us both protected. We'll be very clear about where the lines are drawn. No confusion."

Other than my feelings, which are as muddy as a creek bed after a spring rain.

Thayden looks pained. My desperation, now that I've seen the light at the end of my financial tunnel, means that I can't be too proud here. It feels a little like I'm begging, and I hate that. I'm about to take the whole thing back and tell him to tear up the contract when he speaks.

"When would you want to meet with the lawyers? My offer to pay for your representation still stands."

The man sounds exhausted. Not like he's just solved a massive problem in his life. And I'm not sure how I feel about his answer. A kaleidoscope of emotions flows through me, none of which are good.

"Anytime. I'm all yours."

A day ago, Thayden would have grinned and made some flirtatious remark about me being all his, I would have rebuked him, and we would have sparred with our words. I ache for that back-and-forth.

Instead, Thayden nods, standing in a swift motion. "I'll be

in touch," he says. "Oh, and your scooter is fixed and out front, waiting for you."

"I told you not to fix her!" I'm less irritated and more overwhelmed.

"Well, we don't always get what we want, do we?" He gives me a sad smile before leaving the room, leaving me alone.

From: MamasBoysGirl@DrLove.advice
To: DrLove@DrLove.advice

Dear Dr. Love,

My boyfriend has a really sweet relationship with his mom. That was one of the big things that attracted me to him. I've always heard the way a guy treats his mom shows how he'll treat his spouse.

Except ... I'm pretty sure his mom trumps everyone. Even me.

Anytime she calls him, he stops what he's doing to talk to her. If she needs help, he cancels our plans.

She always seems to call for some favor when we're on dates. I thought it was a weird coincidence until he told me that they share their calendar with each other. They also have location sharing enabled, and I swear, every time he comes over, there's some kind of emergency.

I should also point out that his mom is very capable. She does yoga five times a week, walks 10k races several times a year, and heads up a charity. But if we have a date, suddenly she can't find her keys or her car needs an oil change or she's afraid there's an intruder at the house.

While I want them to stay close, I'm tired of feeling like the third wheel in *their* relationship. Any advice?

Yours,

Mama's Boy's Girl

———

From: DrLove@DrLove.advice
To: MamasBoysGirl@DrLove.advice

Dear Mama's Boy's Girl,

My advice is RUN. I'm not even kidding.

While it's great when a guy cares for his mom, there is a difference between caring for and being codependent with. It sounds like this mama has her claws in deep and isn't willing to share.

Just like you don't want to get between two dogs in a fight, you don't want to get between a boy and his jealous mama. Back away slowly and find a man who is sweet, but not stuck to his mom.

Sincerely,

Dr. Love

CHAPTER TWELVE

Delilah

HOW MANY LAWYERS does it take to change a lightbulb?

Five, and a thousand dollars in billable hours.

What did the lawyer say to the frog?

If you kiss me, I might turn into a decent human being.

Okay, so maybe my lawyer jokes suck. But after almost an hour trapped in this conference room with Thayden hashing out a revised contract with Scott, my representation, I've made up about two dozen of them. It's the only thing keeping me in my seat, because let me tell you—negotiating with lawyers is my own personal purgatory.

Three lawyers walk into a bar and lose their licenses. Because they're supposed to *take* the bar, not run into it!

Ba-dum ching!

I'll be here all night, folks.

Actually, hopefully we'll be done soon. I zoned out a

while ago, to be honest. I should be paying attention. Signing the first contract with his mama should have taught me that lesson. But legal documents are a snoozefest.

"Are those terms sufficient, Delilah?" Scott asks, fidgeting with his glasses.

I shake my head. "I'm sorry. Is what sufficient?"

Thayden groans. "Delilah!"

I whip my head to look at him. "Don't you start with me!" I turn back to Scott. "Can you write something in there about him being insufferable?"

Thayden laughs and puts his head down on the table, but Scott just looks confused.

"Put something in like ... what?"

I cross my arms, glaring at Thayden. "Damages. I want extra damages if he's difficult."

"Define difficult."

Thayden's eyes blaze, but there's a tiny curl to his lips. I've missed this.

The past few days, Thayden looked ... muted. There was no flirtation, no dimple in sight. I thought maybe signing this contract meant signing away that privilege, but today, he's back, and I love it.

Except when I remember that this isn't about love.

Scott sighs. "Can you two—"

"What?" Thayden and I both shout at the same time, and Scott jumps.

"Never mind," he mutters. "I'd just like to get through this. I think the final thing is the adjustments to the compensation portion."

My stomach takes a deep dive. Did Thayden rethink the hundred thousand? I suddenly feel the weight of my debts again clawing at me. I don't want to be selfish. That amount still seems like too much, but I'd gotten used to the idea. I swallow.

"How much less—"

"Not less." Thayden smiles. "I told you my mom lowballed you."

Scott pushes a paper toward me. The numbers make my heart race. Thayden is out of his mind. A quarter of a million dollars for a year of marriage.

"That's—no. Too much. I can't possibly agree to this in good conscience."

Scott turns, looking at me like he's about to mansplain something. The dark look I give him shuts him right up.

Thayden is undeterred. "I disagree. It's asking a lot of you. One year of your time. Keeping this a secret. Putting up with me."

"That's worth at least another hundred thousand," Scott jokes.

Thayden raises one eyebrow, and I can't help but giggle. Scott coughs and checks the time on his phone.

I stare down at the paper. Two hundred fifty thousand dollars. To fake marry Thayden. Actually, the marriage would have to be real, at least on paper. To fulfill his father's stipulation, we have to legally wed.

Thayden has already told me that his mother is chomping at the bit to start planning. Apparently, she doesn't care if this is real or because of a contract. The thought of planning a wedding with Thayden's mama makes my throat feel tight. I know I should probably be angry at her for tricking me, and I am. A little. But having met her, what I saw was how much she loves her son. My own mama tricked me plenty, but love had nothing to do with it. This was more ... matchmaking on steroids.

I fan my face with an empty folder. "Is it hot in here?

Just me?"

"It's just you," Thayden says with a grin.

I point the folder at him. "No flirting! Put that in the contract, Scotty."

I swear, Scott is about to quit his job and walk out. "I can't—"

The conference room door swings open, and a man I hate almost immediately on sight strides in. It's his smile, which is smarmy as all get-out, and his eyes, which stare at my chest first, then my face.

"How's the prenup going?" He chuckles, walking over to Thayden and slapping him on the back. Thayden looks like he wants to drop-kick this guy off the side of the building.

Ah. This must be the famous Duke. Thayden has mentioned him a few times, none of it good. I notice that Scott discretely puts the contract in the folder.

"Please tell me I'm invited to the wedding," Duke says.

"It's going to be small," Thayden says through gritted teeth.

Does he think he has to be nice to this man? Because I certainly do not.

"You're not invited," I say. "I'm Delilah, by the way. You must be Duke."

He only grins wider. "I see my reputation has preceded me."

"And what a reputation it is," I say.

The smile disappears from his face, and he looks back to Thayden. "Don't think I don't know what you're doing. You can't fake a marriage and think that will work."

"We're not faking anything," I say. "We are getting married."

"Maybe that's true," Duke says. "But I'm going to be watching for any sign that you're in breach of your father's wishes. This should be fun. I could feel the tension in this room the moment I walked in. How long will it take you to crack?"

I joked about Thayden being insufferable, but this man truly deserves to have his photograph in the dictionary next to the word. Maybe it's the years of being on a stage that make me get to my feet. Maybe it's the tightness in Thayden's jaw. Maybe it's just because I want to, that I slowly get to my feet and walk around the table, stopping next to Thayden's chair.

Duke's eyes are narrowed, Scott looks petrified, and Thayden looks ... like he knows exactly what's coming.

"You feel tension in the room?" I ask Duke, trailing my fingers down Thayden's neck.

"Uh, Delilah?" Scott says. "I should advise you—"

"Shut up, Scott," Thayden and I say at the same time. Poor guy. I'll buy him a gift basket later. Once I have money in my bank account, that is.

"I think you were confused about what kind of tension you were feeling," I say, my voice almost a purr.

Duke takes a step back, and Thayden's mouth tips up in a grin.

"I'd love to hear more about this tension," Thayden says.

"Oh, you'll more than hear about it," I assure him, leaning down to kiss him.

I swear, this is the last time. I haven't signed the contract yet, so this one is still free.

And I plan to enjoy it. Despite our audience.

Our lips meet in a soft kiss. It's a little awkward since Thayden is seated and I'm standing. It's not like I'm going to climb in his lap. I have some standards. Not very high, obviously, but they *exist*.

One kiss turns to another, then another. I'm vaguely

aware of the door slamming as Duke leaves. Thayden's hands find my waist, and the man clearly has no standards, because he pulls me down until I'm seated sideways on his lap. Our lips never break apart, and there is a desperation to this kiss, like somehow he knows what I already do—this is it. A goodbye kiss in a way. Once we sign, everything changes.

"I, uh, think you made your point," Scott says.

Thayden groans, but Scott is right. I stand, straightening my skirt and walking away from Thayden. Yanking the pen from Scott's hand, I sign and initial on every line. When I'm finished, I shove the contract toward Thayden and reach out my hand.

Looking dazed, he shakes my hand. "What is—"

"I look forward to doing business with you," I tell him.

Then, after giving Scott a friendly pat on the shoulder, I walk out of the conference room before I'm tempted to do something stupid like kiss Thayden again.

He catches me when I'm almost to the bank of elevators. "Let me walk you out," he says.

His hand settles on my lower back. I swear it's going to leave a brand, telling everyone that I'm his.

At least for the three hundred sixty-five days following our wedding.

Thayden leans close, much too close, and his lips brush my ear. "You know what I'm going to enjoy?"

"What's that?"

My breath catches as his lips lightly brush my ear. I know I should step away, but I can't. Especially because other people in the office are watching. I'm sure he's using that to his full advantage too.

Just before the elevator doors slide open, he says, "Finding every single loophole."

My, my. I hope he does.

CHAPTER THIRTEEN

Delilah

I'M IN A WEDDING DRESS. Sure, it's a complete monstrosity of lace and tulle and beading that looks like what might happen if you threw ten wedding gowns in a wood chipper. But still.

I'm in a wedding dress.

"Come on out. Even if it's dreadful. The ugly ones will just help highlight the *right* dress," Thayden's mama calls in a singsongy voice.

Because, in a strange turn of events, I am wedding dress shopping with my future temporary mother-in-law, who tricked me into a legally binding agreement. The greeting card aisle doesn't cover that one yet.

"This one is definitely in the dreadful category."

I pull aside the heavy dressing room curtain and step out, cocking a hip with one hand and tossing my hair with another. If there's one thing I can do, it's smile and walk in a dress. Even one that should be taken out by guys in Hazmat suits and burned.

Thayden's mother is seated on the plush pink sofa, sipping champagne. She almost spits it out when she sees me.

"Oh my," she says with a giggle. Rising to her feet, she follows me over to the small pedestal in front of several floor-to-ceiling mirrors edged in gold.

"I think the correct response is bless its heart," I say, turning to see the back, which I haven't fully zipped. "This poor dress. It's really trying."

"A bit too hard, I'd say. Let's zip you up, just for the full effect."

Elizabeth's hands are warm on the bare skin of my back as she zips, and I'm immediately transported back in time. Not to one specific memory, but a whole warehouse of them when my own mama zipped and pinned and sometimes stuffed me into pageant dresses. I shiver.

"Sorry! Are my fingers cold?"

"You're just fine," I say.

"Well. Let this be the standard from which we rise," Elizabeth says, clucking her tongue.

I take a moment to fully appreciate the awfulness of this dress. It has a sort of Elizabethan collar going up my neck with a deep cutout in front that reveals way too much boobage.

The waist should cinch tight, though this is the sample size and would need to be taken in. The bottom half looks like a colonial hoop skirt tried to have a baby with a mermaid style. There's even a strange row of ruffles over my bottom.

"Will you take a picture with my phone?" I ask. "This memory needs to be preserved."

Elizabeth takes a few photos, laughing as she does so.

If you're wondering how I've gone from being tricked by this woman to laughing as I try on wedding dresses, it involved a tearful apology from Elizabeth earlier and my mommy issues. I'm usually quick to forgive on a normal day, but I didn't stand a chance with Elizabeth.

Not when she hugged me tight and told me that she had always wanted a daughter, and despite what she did, hoped that I could see her as a mother. It's like she had a cheat sheet with all my pain points and knew just where to press.

She held my cheeks and stared into my eyes. "Forget the contract. Forgive me, please, and let me love you like the daughter I never had."

Yep. She said that. I know because I immediately committed it to memory. Those words will go with me to the grave. It's a little sad how desperate I am, to be honest.

And so, here we are.

The sales associate, a squat, gray-haired woman named Hilda, appears from a doorway. "Oh! This is fabulous but much too large for your petite frame."

I'm not sure where Hilda is from, but her accent makes her sound like Arnold Schwarzenegger's grandmother.

Before I can stop her, she starts pulling the dress together in the back, using giant clips to hold it in place. They remind me of the chip clips we have at the house, and now I'm feeling like a bag of Doritos.

"That's really okay," I tell Hilda. "This is *not* the dress."

"Oh," she purrs, "but now that it's more fitted, just look at your shape!"

They don't have a name for this shape. Unless *what not to wear* is a shape.

"It's just not what I envisioned for my big day," I say. The words flow so easily from my tongue. Like this is a normal wedding and I'm a typical bride. Not a wife for hire. I've decided that's what I'll call our arrangement.

"Well, you do have plenty more to choose from. If you need a specific style, just let me know." She unclips me and slides the zipper down enough that I can escape once I'm behind the dressing room curtain. "Such a shame. It's couture."

I glance at Elizabeth, who seems very interested in her nails. Couture, hm? When Elizabeth insisted that I let her pay for the wedding in exchange for getting to help plan, I agreed with the caveat that I wanted simple and small. Not expensive. Definitely not couture.

I cough pointedly, and Elizabeth blinks up at me, sipping champagne like the glass will hide her guilty expression. It does not.

I knew when the bridal salon—not store, but *salon*—unlocked its doors just for us that it was probably way too exclusive and expensive. Then there's the fact that none of these dresses have price tags. I'm also pretty sure the champagne the associate poured us was Dom Perignon.

But it's hard to say no to Elizabeth. She picked me up this morning in a car with a driver and has already helped me choose a date, invitations, and the venue, the rooftop garden of a hotel. It's not even noon and we've done almost all the big things.

It's like a crash course of wedding planning in one morning. I'm sure without her money and influence, we wouldn't have been able to do this. Even a small wedding with about fifty guests—it shouldn't be so simple.

And my emotions about it are as volatile as social media during a political election. I'm not sure how I'm holding it together. The wedding now seems REAL. Despite the fact that it's fake.

And Thayden's mama is treating me like a real daughter-in-law. No, like a *daughter*. At least, what I think would be a normal mom-daughter relationship. She's been pouring kindness and graciousness over me all morning. I'm just soaking up her sweetness.

"Don't fret, dear," Elizabeth says. "We've got plenty more dresses. And I have lunch plans. You deserve it after all this hard work."

"You don't need to do anything more for me," I protest, wiping my eyes.

"Nonsense. Now, let's be rid of that monstrosity and find your perfect dress."

The next few I try are not as horrible, but definitely not The One. I hadn't ever allowed myself to dream of wedding dresses. It seemed so out of reach. But if I'd even so much as created a Pinterest board, it sure would help about now. I have about everything else covered on Pinterest, but weddings ... nope. It felt like I'd be jinxing the idea to pin dresses or flowers or anything else that would be helpful.

When I step into the fourth dress and slide it over my hips, I *know* before I even see it. I don't have a lick of superstition in me, but I swear the hair stands up on my arms.

This one fits perfectly, and I'm even able to zip up the side. Not trusting myself to look in the mirror yet, I hold my breath and walk out.

Elizabeth gasps and drops her glass, which thankfully is empty and bounces harmlessly on the rug. She's in front of me in an instant, holding her hands up to both cheeks with tears welling in her eyes.

"Oh, darling, this ... is exquisite! You're a vision." She sniffs, and I bite my lip.

"You like it?"

Elizabeth meets my eyes, and the emotion there has my heart tilting sideways. "Ignore *me*. What do *you* think?"

"I didn't look yet," I confess.

"Well, let's take care of that." Elizabeth gently lifts the back of the dress, which has a short train, shaking it out so I can walk more easily.

I keep my eyes cast down while I walk to the mirrors, as if looking will break the spell I feel. I'm reminded of the glamours in some of the fae fantasies I've read this past year. Like the moment I slipped into the dress, its magic shimmered over my skin.

When I finally look up, the effect definitely is magical. The dress is deceptively simple, yards of white satin which fit perfectly over my waist and the swell of my hips, cascading gently to the floor. The sweetheart neckline and wide straps are classic, reminding me of something Audrey Hepburn would have worn—simple, elegant, classic beauty.

The waist is accentuated with the smallest line of demure beading. It's perfect. Exactly the kind of dress I can see myself getting married in.

Which means, of course, I can't choose it now. It would be cruel, a lie. This isn't the kind of dress you wear to a fake wedding. It's the kind you wear when you're going to marry the love of your life. Tears blur my vision.

"Well?" Elizabeth asks.

The hope in her voice makes my breath hitch. "I'm not sure. It's a little ... plain."

"Plain?" Elizabeth shakes her head. "No, it's the simple lines that make this dress so beautiful. Many dresses hide behind accoutrements, but this one stands on its own. Like you, dear. Your beauty needs so little to shine. That's why this dress is so perfect."

The tears are flowing now, almost to an embarrassing

degree. "I don't want to ruin the fabric," I say, trying to wipe the tears before they can land on the satin. Elizabeth sniffs, handing me a tissue.

"It's your choice. But I can't imagine a more beautiful dress or a more beautiful bride. I wish your mother could be here."

I don't.

The thought of Mama being here, slimy and thick as a slug, makes pinpricks dance in front of my eyes for a moment. I focus on staying upright, making sure I'm not locking my knees, until my vision clears.

"That's okay," I tell her, not willing to explain the truth. My mama would die if she were here. But not for the reasons Elizabeth might think. Mama would be seeing dollar signs everywhere she looked and finding ways to exploit them. If possible, using me to do so.

"This is just that moment every mother dreams about."

Not every mother. Not the way Elizabeth is. And I feel badly, because even though Thayden's mother knows the truth, she seems to be pinning her hopes on this wedding like it's not a lie.

I turn away from the mirrors, meeting Elizabeth's green eyes. "You know that it's not … real. I mean, Thayden told me what he said to you. That he didn't want to get married. It's just for practical reasons."

Elizabeth's eyes flash. "Nonsense. My son doesn't know what's best for him. He'll come around."

He'll come around.

I hoped, some part of me did, that she would deny it. Maybe tell me I misunderstood what Thayden meant. But no, she only confirms it, even if she doesn't say the words.

I would rather hear almost anything, even hearing that he hates me than he'll come around. If there were trophies for *meh*, that statement would be taking it home.

My stomach twists uncomfortably. Hilda chooses that moment to appear with a veil.

"Oh, we must try the complete look with this one."

And before I can protest, she has pinned it into my hair, moving it over my face. I stare at the stranger in the mirrors, wearing a dress that likely costs more than the sum of all the clothes I've ever owned. This woman in the mirror looks like a bride, beautiful and wanted, like she belongs to someone who will wait at the end of the aisle for her, teary-eyed.

Beneath the veil, I am not that woman. I am a glorified dog walker who signed a legal contract to wear a white dress and say I do.

"Thayden!"

I turn, hearing his mother call his name, and there he is, standing in the doorway of this little salon. In his hands are bags of what looks to be takeout food, and in his eyes, there is only something like shock.

I want to twist my hands together, but Hilda shoves a fake bouquet into them, humming the bridal march. I am frozen as Thayden sets down the takeout bags and crosses the room to me, a terrifyingly determined look on his face.

His mother and Hilda fade away. There is only Thayden. When he reaches me, we're almost nose to nose because of the platform I'm standing on.

For a moment, all time hangs between us, weighty and heady. In a move so swift I can only draw in a shallow breath, Thayden lifts the veil away from my face. With that tiny barrier gone, the moment is even more intense, the very air alive and electric. It's what I felt between us the night of our kiss, but *more*.

His eyes, so green. His expression, so earnest and so full

of longing. I want to sweep my hands over the full stubble on his cheeks, the light beard that almost hides the dimple.

"You're breathtaking." His voice has a low rasp to it that makes me shiver.

"You like the dress?" I ask.

"What dress?" he says, and I can't help it—I grin. And then I laugh, even as a tear escapes.

"Shut up."

"That's not hard. You've got me speechless."

"Thayden," I say, "stop."

"I have something for you," he says, and I realize he has a ring in his hand.

Not just a regular diamond ring. It's a pink stone—large, but not overwhelming—set in a rose gold band. Simple, yet unique. *Beautiful.*

I can't get out a word. Thayden lifts my hand, slipping the ring into place.

"No children were harmed in the making of this ring," he says, a smile on his lips.

I can only laugh, even as tears gather. Earlier this week, Thayden asked about rings. I gave him very little to go on, other than to tell him I didn't want a diamond or any other stone that involved children mining or being harmed in production.

"I don't know what to say."

"You like it?"

"It's perfect. Truly. Too much."

He squeezes my hand. "Nothing is too much for you."

Suddenly, it's all too real. The dress, the veil, the ring—the man looking so earnest in front of me.

The man who doesn't want to get married.

Out of nowhere, his mother steps in, hooking her arm through his. "Thank you for bringing lunch, dear. Though

147

you were supposed to message me so I could come out. It's bad luck to see your bride in her dress," she chides gently.

Thayden kisses her cheek. "I thought that was just the wedding day," he says, eyes flicking back to me. The look in them makes my whole chest flush.

"This isn't the dress," I manage to say.

Three heads whip to me, because Hilda is still standing here, way too close. I can almost feel her breath on my arm, that's how close.

Personal space, Hilda. It's a thing. Learn it.

"It isn't?" Elizabeth tries to hide her disappointment, but I guess she's only good at being sneaky when she tricks people into marrying her son.

Thayden's eyes scan over the dress, and I thought he was being funny when he said *what dress*, but he really seems to be seeing it for the first time.

"No. It's too ... um ..."

White is the only word that comes to mind. Because Thayden's presence, his eyes, his everything, has stolen a good portion of my brain cells. "It's too simple. Don't you think?"

Hilda tsks, like I'm the village idiot, which is how I feel. "Simple means expensive. A dress like this is more than one with all the extras on it. Because it has to stand on its own, the lines, the fit."

"Then it's too expensive," I say. This is not a lie, and it's a relief to say something that isn't.

"Don't you worry about the expense," Elizabeth says. She elbows Thayden, who still hasn't said a thing. Dresses don't seem to be in the man's wheelhouse.

"I would marry you in anything you wore," he says. The words drop from his lips like a vow, and they cause something to shift inside of a deep, locked and heavily guarded vault of my heart.

He doesn't want to marry you, remember? He told you this.
He'll come around, his mama said.

That reminder helps me find the strength to step down off the little dais. I'm breathing heavily when I get to the dressing room. Without looking at myself again, I remove the dress, stepping out carefully, feeling that fairy glamour slip away as well as I sigh.

It's just a dress. For a wedding that is in no way real. Even if that's becoming harder and harder to remember between Elizabeth's kindness and the look on Thayden's face.

I hear the two of them talking in low murmurs and then quiet. Did Thayden leave? Relief and disappointment make for a bitter cocktail.

I remove the veil—because that made things a little too real—and pull on a dress that is just pretty. It's strapless and lace with a bit of a mermaid style without being ridiculously dramatic. This one must be off the rack, because it's a smaller size and I struggle to get it zipped. When I finally do, it's no small triumph. I'm sweating a little and fan myself with my purse.

There is no magic in this dress. It's a white sausage casing. When I walk out, Elizabeth and Hilda don't have much to say.

"You are lovely," Elizabeth says. "But I'm not sure ..."

I stare at myself in the mirrors, angling to see the back, then bouncing a little on my toes to make sure my chest doesn't come flying out of the top. I learned the hard way you need to move in a dress to see what happens when you do. Especially a strapless one.

"Well?" Elizabeth says. "What do we think?"

We. It should feel pushy. If it were my own mama, it would. I would bristle and tell her there's no we, only me.

But it's wholly different with Thayden's mama. I want there to be a *we*, to feel like she's on my team. Like she's family.

Oh, boy. I think I might be falling not just for Thayden, but his mother.

"I haven't found the one," I say, thinking of the last dress and how perfect it was.

It's my dream dress. And this is not my dream. I should pick something I hate, like the first monstrosity.

"Let's get some food in you," Elizabeth says, patting my arm. "Thayden dropped it off and I have a little picnic planned. This is our first stop anyway. And we can always come back if you change your mind."

I know she means about The Dress, and I don't want my face to give away anything. I used to be so good at the fake smile, at giving answers people wanted to hear. Somehow, it's a lot harder to slip into that persona after a few years off.

Maybe because despite all the warning signals, I want to be me. I want to be real, for *this* to be real.

I shuffle away to the fitting room, thinking how mermaid dresses would be the worst for being a runaway bride. The thing doesn't allow me to move my legs above the knee.

I am very ready to get out of the dress, out of this shop.

Only, getting out is not so simple.

The side zipper only moves halfway down, catching on a bit of the dress's thin lining. I work it up, then try to move it back down, but it catches more of the fabric. Which means now it's even higher and tighter.

No, sir. This zipper isn't the boss of me.

With slow care, I try gently to separate the lining from the zipper, twisting in front of the mirror like a contortionist.

"That's it, sugar. Nice and slow."

Honestly, I'm not sure whether I'm talking to myself or the zipper, but either way, my pep talk doesn't work. In messing with it, I've only managed to raise the zipper almost all the way up, and now I really am a sausage stuffed in a casing.

I am *cooked*.

Fanning my face, I try to relax my breathing and weigh my options. As I see it, they are severely limited. Maybe I can roll it right on down and peel myself out. I don't for a moment think the cinched waist is going over my hips, but I am starting to feel the smack of pure, desperate terror.

This attempt fails. I can't even get the top rolled down over my breasts. Which is a testament to the staying power of the bodice. Too bad I need less staying power right now, not more.

Next, I try lifting the skirt up over my head, and this works better, at least until I get to the fitted waist. I tug and pull, hoping to avoid ripping anything, but it feels like my ribs are expanding. Is that a thing? There's fight, there's flight, and then there's the kind of panic no one talks about when you blow up like that blueberry girl in *Willy Wonka and the Chocolate Factory*.

You'd think that the slick of sweat on my skin might help provide lubrication. You'd be wrong.

"Delilah?" Elizabeth's voice is much too close, but before I can warn her that I'm not decent, she pokes her head behind the curtain.

"Hi," I say, smiling brightly and trying to strike a model-like pose. Given the sweat and the flush in my cheeks, I look a bit more like a crazed clown.

"I, um, can't get it off."

Elizabeth steps into the dressing room, pulling the curtain closed. "You change your mind, then? This is the one?"

I laugh, lightly at first, then quickly veering off into the area of hiccuping and even one undignified snort. "You misunderstand," I gasp. "I literally *can't* take it off."

Understanding spreads over her face, and she laughs a little. "Here. I'll help."

"The zipper is stuck."

"I'll get it. Don't you worry."

I am worried though. Even more so when Elizabeth's gentle tugs become more firm, and she mutters some colorful words under her breath before apologizing.

That's when the dress rips. The sound is horrible, because to me, it's the chinging of a cash register, counting up what I imagine to be thousands of dollars.

Elizabeth's wide eyes meet mine. "Oh, dear."

Oh dear is right.

"I'm so sorry," I say. "It didn't feel so tight when I put it on."

"It's not you. It's this hellish dress."

She yanks a little harder, and more of the fabric rips. I brace my arm on the wall for support. I can finally breathe but the relief is short because of the guilt. There is no coming back from this.

"Is everything okay in there?" Hilda calls.

We freeze, our eyes meeting in the mirror.

"We're fine," Elizabeth manages in a melodic voice. "Be out in a minute. Just taking a last look."

We don't move until Hilda's footsteps fade away, and then Elizabeth uses renewed force and vigor, practically ripping the dress open at the side seam.

A giggle chokes out of my mouth. "Does the 'you break it, you buy it' adage apply here? Because—"

"Hush." Elizabeth yanks the top of the dress, which to my utter relief moves down over my hips and pools on the floor. "Get dressed. I'll grab the food. Then we make a run for it."

And then she's gone, pushing through the curtain with a determined look on her face.

Is this my life? Trying on wedding dresses with my almost mother-in-law for a wedding I've agreed to for money, ripping up a dress that probably costs more than my last car?

I don't have time to let the guilt and worry sink in because Elizabeth bursts back through the curtain, looking almost gleeful. She grabs my arm, the one I've managed to get through my shirt sleeve.

"Let's go. I distracted Hilda, and we have a clear shot to the front door."

Still giggling and trying to get my clothes in order, I grab my purse and let myself be swept up in Elizabeth's grand getaway plan, feeling with every step that my own escape from this family is less sure.

CHAPTER FOURTEEN

Thayden

I'M thankful that Gavin mostly works from home now because it means I can burst in on him in the middle of the day.

"I'm ruining everything and I need your help." I slam the door behind me and stride right into the sunken living room, where Gavin is seated with his laptop.

"Uh, Thayden, could you—"

"No. I can't wait or calm down."

I take off my jacket and fling it on the couch, my tie following right after, then my button-down (which may have lost a few buttons in my haste), until I'm stripped down to my undershirt.

I'm burning up. Not with fever, and I'm aware of the cool air blowing through the vents. It's like my heart is on fire, a raging inferno, and I'm cooking from the inside out. Gavin tries to speak again, but I talk right over him.

"I'm doing this all wrong. You said I should pursue her without the contract or strings or whatever, but she wanted to sign. So I did. That was mistake number one."

Gavin starts to stand up. "Listen, man—"

"Please just let me get this out! I'm going to explode otherwise. So, we're getting married. And get this: I *want* to marry her. I know I'm not exactly experienced in serious relationships. Or relationships at all. But when you know, you know, right? Or is that just a phrase people say?"

I'm going to pace a hole through the floor, so I kick off my shoes, one landing on the kitchen counter and the other disappearing behind a chair. My socks are too hot, so I tear them off and toss them toward the fireplace. Gavin opens his mouth again and I point a finger towards him.

"Just cool your jets and let me finish, old man."

He sighs, deeply, his eyes darting between the laptop and me.

"Thank you. So, today, I saw her in her wedding dress. Or *a* wedding dress. And my heart"—I thump my chest two, then three times with my fist—"it's like the thing woke up for the first time. I would have recited my vows right there in the dressing room. Which is ... insane. Am I insane? Look at me?"

I'm still burning up, so I rip my T-shirt over my head to illustrate my point.

"See?"

"Please keep your pants on," Gavin mutters, dropping his head in his hands.

"The point is, I never wanted to get married. Enter Delilah. I thought it was just that she was exciting. She fought me, and I loved that. But it's more. I still barely know

156

her. I don't know her favorite color. Her childhood dreams or future plans. Yet I'm marrying her in a few weeks and I actually want to. For real. What do I do, Gav? Fix me!"

Gavin puts his hands behind his head, leaning back into the couch, the faintest smirk on his lips. "Is this where you finally allow me to speak?"

"Yes. Please tell me you have something to say."

"Can I say something?"

I startle at a tinny, female voice. My eyes dart around the room, finally landing on the laptop. Where there's a gray-haired woman in a suit, clearly on a video call with Gavin.

"Thanks for the heads-up," I mutter, glaring at my former best friend.

He shrugs. "I tried to tell you. You wouldn't let me talk."

I come a little closer to the screen, managing to locate and put on my undershirt. "Sure, uh, go ahead."

The woman smiles. "Don't feel the need to get dressed on my account. I quite enjoy the view."

Gavin snorts, and I cross my arms over my now-covered chest.

The woman continues. "It sounds like you need to do two things. The order is up to you. You need to woo her, and you need to be honest with her."

"Like that's so simple," I grumble.

"Most relationship problems start with communication, or the lack thereof," the woman continues. Gavin just keeps smirking at me like this is the best entertainment he's had in weeks. "But considering what little I heard about your situation, you might need to show her how you feel, so that when you tell her, there's evidence. I don't know the details, but if there's some kind of contract, that muddies the waters."

"Told you so," Gavin says.

"Thanks, buddy. Super helpful right now."

"And," the woman continues with a smile, "if things don't work out, feel free to give me a call."

Well, then. No words. Just … none.

Her eyes flick to Gavin. "If that's all, how about we reschedule this call. My assistant will be in touch."

Gavin leans forward. "Oh, no. Really, if you don't mind—"

"I do, actually. Best of luck, gentlemen."

Gavin punches me in the shoulder as the video call ends. "Thanks for costing me that account. It took a month to get on her schedule."

"Sorry. She had good advice though."

Gavin laughs, shaking his head. "She would know. I think she's on her seventh husband."

"Oh." I'm torn on whether that makes her advice more or less legit. She is at least experienced in marriage.

"I do agree though," Gavin continues. "I might flip the order and say to talk first, then act, but then again, I'm guessing you've been acting like an idiot, so you may need to make up some ground there."

I run my hands over my face. I have been an idiot. It's like the feelings I have for Delilah, mixed with the overwhelming confusion of our situation, has me totally off my game, in every aspect of my life.

I start pacing again, a different path this time, looking out over the back patio and the hot tub there.

"What do I do? I feel totally out of my league here. How do I win her over? How do I show her how I feel?"

Gavin joins me by the window and grabs my shoulders in his hands, steering me toward the couch. "Do you have to go back into the office today?"

"Not really."

"Then sit down. I've got just the thing. Let me grab you a

beer. You'll need it. Promise me this—you won't leave before the end?"

"The end of what?"

Gavin only grins. "Promise."

"Fine. But this better work."

From the kitchen, I hear the clinking of beer bottles as Gavin laughs. "Oh, it will. Maybe not in the way you think. But it will."

———

Two hours later, Zoey and Ella get home and find us still sitting on the couch, a few empty bottles on the table, and the credits rolling for *Pride and Prejudice*.

Gavin seems to be watching me for some sign that I got whatever he thought this would teach me. The biggest life lesson I've come away with is that I'm thankful for technology and indoor plumbing.

I'm also glad I don't have a lot of sisters.

"What's this?" Zoey asks, looking at us warily. I can tell from her expression that she's just as mad at me as when she threw my clothes in the pool.

"Are you guys playing hooky?" Ella asks.

"Not quite. I'm teaching Thayden how to make a grand gesture," Gavin says, giving me a wink.

That's what I was supposed to learn. Okay. Noted. Grand gesture.

"Among other things," Gavin says.

Maybe I'll be watching this movie again in the near future because honestly, I'm not sure what *other things* he means. Period pieces are not my jam.

Zoey leans over the couch and gives Gavin a kiss.

"Ew," Ella says. "I'm out of here." And with that, she's off to her room.

Just when I'm about to excuse myself, Zoey gives Gavin one last peck and stands. She sniffs, glancing at me with glittering eyes, then nods.

"I forgive you," she says.

"Okayyyy." I'm afraid to say more because it might break whatever spell has come over Zoey. A Jane Austen spell? Is that a thing?

"And I'll do anything you need to help with Delilah. If you swear you're serious about this."

She points a finger at me, her eyes suddenly turning hard and terrifying. I want to glance at Gavin, maybe just for reassurance that his wife won't murder me if I screw this up, but I suspect breaking eye contact with Zoey might be a mistake.

"I'm serious," I say, feeling the truth of the words, like they're a rare treasure that's been mined—ethically and not by children—from my very soul.

I *am* serious. And apparently, I need to get my Jane Austen on if I want to figure out the magic that's going to help me win over my fiancée.

CHAPTER FIFTEEN

Delilah

MOVING day comes far too quickly. When we told our land-lord that we weren't renewing, she asked if we could move out more quickly. Harper, Abby, and Sam found an apartment that lined up, so here we are.

Thayden pulls up in a rented truck Saturday morning, looking wholly strange in athletic shorts and a T-shirt. I would have sworn that man slept in suits. Chase pulls up behind them, and I watch from between the blinds as the guys high-five.

"Chase is here," I say, giving Harper a look. "Since when are those two friends?"

Harpy holds up both hands. "Don't ask me. Maybe he got his number the night you had your first date."

"Dinner. Not a date."

"You're about to say I do—are we seriously going to argue

about that?"

"Yes," I growl.

Harper shakes her head, going to the door, while I disappear into the kitchen for a moment. I suddenly feel a pressing need to stick my head in the freezer.

Yep, I'm in full-on panic mode.

You'd think that I should be excited to move into Thayden's perfect house. I've spent enough time there lately. When I'm not with his mother picking out the menu or linens or flowers or a hundred other things I don't think I need for a wedding that's only real on paper, I'm reading on the couch with Apollo for company.

Thayden has been scarce because of some big case on the docket, but he still manages to take up far too much space in my brain. Which I suspect is his exact goal.

First of all, the man has insisted on stocking his kitchen for me. From my favorite snacks (Wheat Thins and Bugles) to those fizzy seltzers in my favorite flavor (pink grapefruit) to the takeout that mysteriously gets delivered at lunch daily, already paid for, including tip.

I'm not sure where he's getting his inside information from, but one of my besties definitely squealed. I can't even be mad about it because I haven't eaten like this in … well, EVER. One of these days he's going to come home to find me passed out on his couch in a food coma and pregnant with a food baby.

Then there are other things. More personal touches that give me heart palpitations. Some are little things. Matching pillows appeared on his couch one day, one with the word *Y'all* stitched across the center, and the other saying *Bless Your Heart*. Both are Texas sayings as much as Alabama ones, but I know Thayden didn't buy them for himself.

Another day, it was a gorgeous leather-bound edition of

Shakespearean sonnets and a coffee mug that reads, *Talk Literary to Me*. I mean, I'm not saying that the way to this girl's heart is through literature, but I'm not denying it either.

Did I mention the fresh flowers that are delivered daily? No note, always different flowers, probably because none of my friends know my favorite flower, which is already hanging on his front porch.

And then there are the daily notes he sticks to the fridge with a magnet shaped like the letter D. His one and only magnet, one that didn't appear until a few days after he gave me the ring.

Sometimes they're simple or sweet, wishing me a good day or telling a joke. Today's note was a line from John Donne: "Come live with me, and be my love, and we will some new pleasures prove of golden sands, and crystal brooks, with silken lines, and silver hooks."

He wasn't kidding about finding those loopholes. The man knows his way around a loophole. Guess I shouldn't be surprised given that he is a lawyer and all.

"D?"

Abby's voice startles me, and I yank the freezer door shut. She's staring at me like I've got a shrunken head.

"Just looking for ice cream."

"Breakfast of champions," she says. "But I think we're out. Are you ready for your big day? Any second thoughts? Cold feet?"

My roommates have all handled this decision differently. While Harper has been dead set against this whole thing, Sam is dying for details, Zoey is oddly silent, and Abby seems to think it's all a colossal joke. If it is, I'm the punchline.

"I'm fine," I say, just as Thayden appears in the doorway, sucking up all the oxygen in the room. With his big case coming up, I haven't seen him in days. Five days, to be precise. I don't resent his work at all, or think about calling his assistant like I'm some kind of jealous wife, wondering if her husband will be home for dinner.

I drink him in, with his beard shaved down to little more than stubble, maybe for the sake of his court appearances. I want to run my hand over his cheek and feel the burn of that five o'clock shadow in my palm. I want to kiss him again and measure the level of burn.

It's five o'clock somewhere, right?

"Hey." Smiling at me with the threat of an apex predator, he lifts an arm to each side of the doorway. He's got on a shirt with the sleeves ripped off, exposing not only his arms, which flex as he moves, but the whole side of his torso. I didn't even know you could have muscles there! But he does. Lots of them.

"Good luck with that," Abby mutters, ducking out the other door to the kitchen.

I cross my arms, doing my best to glare and keep any drool inside my mouth. "Don't break any of my stuff."

"I'll be very careful. Your *stuff* is important to me."

How can the man make innocent words sound like a flirtatious promise? I need him to go so I can stick my head back in the freezer.

Harper saves the day, ducking underneath Thayden's arm, patting his bicep as she walks into the kitchen.

"Looking good," she says. "Can you see the difference yet?"

Thayden drops his arms, glancing down at them as he flexes. Gracious! I didn't sign up for a gun show.

"I don't see it yet, but I can feel it after your workouts."

"Wait—he's working out with *you*?"

I point at Thayden, then Harper. She has the good sense

to look the slightest bit guilty. Not nearly enough, if you ask me.

"Oh, did I not mention it?" she asks.

"You most certainly did not."

Why am I so angry about this? And why am I not better at hiding it?

Maybe because jealousy is like Hydra. Cut off one head and another one grows right in its place. I'm wild with jealousy and then furious that I'm jealous.

"You said Harper was the best," Thayden says. "I wanted to make sure my body was in tip-top shape for my wedding day."

Oh, this man!

And Harper! She's biting her lip to hold back a grin, at least until I turn my crazy eyes on her, and then she clears her throat. I thought she was against this. Now she's training Thayden?!

"Guess we should get started."

"Guess we should," I snap.

And Thayden, still looking like some kind of mythical muscled creature, just grins and grins.

"Are you just going to stand there, or are you going to come boss me around?"

What kind of response can I even make to that? None. That's what.

So, with my chin in the air, I brush past him, leading the way toward my room. And if I happened to take a quick sniff of that spicy, masculine scent when I did, well, so be it.

———

Arriving at Thayden's, I'm faced with another surprise from him. And because he's standing right there to watch my reaction to this one, it's a million times harder to hide my reaction.

"I hope you like it," he says. "This seems like your style. And if it isn't—"

"It's fine."

Fine is totally underselling the makeover he's managed in the guest bedroom. MY new bedroom. Before, it had just been a basic room. A bed, dresser, and small bookcase with a nondescript rug and blinds on the windows.

Now? It's like one of my Pinterest boards sprouted legs and hopped into this bedroom.

I turn my gaze toward him, eyes narrowed. "How did you—"

"I have my ways." He shrugs, looking adorably chagrined.

Again, I smell my friends. All of whom were suddenly busy, their excuses as transparent as tissue paper, leaving me and Thayden to unpack and move my things—meager though they are—into his house.

I am beginning to suspect that my friends are less against this whole arrangement and are now trying some classic matchmaking shenanigans. I'll have words with them later.

Right now, I have none. Because the room has left me breathless.

I should tell Thayden it's beautiful. Or thank him. I should hug him. Or at least look him in the eye.

But I can't say or do any of those things. Because if I face him, he might notice the tears gathering in my eyes. I clench my jaw as tight as I can, hoping that will be enough.

"Are you sure?"

"Yep."

Thayden hovers in the doorway for a moment, giving me ample opportunity to say more. Which I still can't do without releasing the floodgates. I feel like a terrible, ungrateful brat.

Probably because that's exactly how I'm acting.

"Well," Thayden says finally, stuffing his hands deep in the pockets of his shorts, "I'll leave you to unpack. Unless you need help?"

I jam my eyes closed. The man has redecorated his guest room for me, helped me move, and now wants to help me unpack. He *wants* to.

"That's all right," I say.

"Let me know if you need anything. And make yourself at home. This is your place too."

He's wrong though. It's not my place. Not more than temporarily.

"I'll have some dinner ready around six." Without giving me a chance to decline, Thayden closes the door quietly, leaving me alone with the few dozen boxes that hold the entirety of my life and the room that has been exquisitely decorated for me. Exactly three tears track down my face before I give my cheek a little slap.

"Pull yourself together, girl."

I need to unpack, but before I do, I allow myself the indulgence of walking around the room, examining all the little touches that make this unexpected gift so darn sweet.

The bedspread is a fluffy white duvet with a quilt in varying shades of blue folded at the end. The headboard is almost hidden by scrumptious piles of pillows in more blues with a few pops of yellow.

I trail my hand along the gauzy white curtains and then the thicker, deep gray drapes that I would bet are light-blocking. Perfect for this east-facing room. I can't help but take my shoes off to walk through the plush white rug that replaced whatever was here before.

The only piece of furniture he added is a beautiful white wooden bookshelf, filled almost to the brim. He left me two shelves, which is about what I have in my collection. Even though I've technically lived in Austin five years now, I've always traveled light. Maybe that comes from having so little room in the trailer growing up. The truck Thayden rented could have fit our whole house's stuff in it, while my two dozen boxes and one single upholstered chair—the one piece of furniture I wanted to keep—took up only a tiny corner.

I trail my hand along the spines of the books, which have been arranged according to author. Not bad, though I might change it to group them by color. I know it's a topic of hot debate among book nerds, but I just love the way it looks. Thayden has chosen a mix of classics and contemporary books, some looking brand new and others worn. The thoughtfulness of this gesture alone would be enough to undo me.

How is this the same man I slapped the day I met him? Is this the act or was that?

I know the answer. I've come to know him. But in many ways, it's easier to think of him as simply that rich playboy with the silver tongue. What he's done in this room proves he's far from that.

The dresser has a new crystal vase filled with white roses. I can smell them even from a few steps away, but I still bury my nose in the soft petals. That's when I notice the single photograph Thayden has tucked into the mirror. It's a picture of Thayden squatting next to Apollo, who looks like he's just leaving puppyhood. Still massive, but somehow gangly, like he hasn't quite grown into his legs yet. Thayden is grinning around a much thicker beard than what he sports today, and with the way Apollo's tongue lolls out, it looks like he's smiling too.

I catch sight of myself in the mirror, and my smile matches theirs.

CHAPTER SIXTEEN

Delilah

A FEW HOURS LATER, I'm fully moved into my new room. I'm also starving and stinky. Thayden has been narrating what he has done all day, shouting up the stairs every few minutes.

"I'm starting the wash," he'd said a few hours ago.

"I'm going to mow the yard!"

"I'm getting a drink of water!"

I'm not sure if he just feels the need to check in or wants me to feel included. The last thing he said was that he's taking Apollo for a walk. With the house to myself, I decide to take a bath in the massive bathtub.

There may be only one small, full bathroom, but Thayden added a deep soaker tub with two of those fancy rain shower-heads. As a result, there's hardly any room to move between the tub and the pedestal sink next to the toilet. Clearly, the man has priorities. And, like much of the house, they align really well with my own. It's tiny, but adorable.

The bathtub in the house I shared with the girls had basically been designed for toddlers. The one time I tried to take a bath, most of my body had been above the water. I could almost swim laps in this one.

While the tub fills with water and bubbles, I unpack some of my toiletries. Thayden has cleared off half the space in his bathroom cabinet for me, and I notice a few plush blue towels next to his charcoal-gray ones. Is there anything he didn't think of? He's so irritatingly thoughtful that I want to be mad about it.

I'm not sure how I'm going to share a house, much less a bathroom, with him. Not without my heart getting broken.

When I turn off the tap, I listen for a moment, hoping the house is still empty. Not a sound. I've been alone in Thayden's house almost every day for the last few weeks, but this feels wholly different. It's that same squirmy feeling I used to get in my gut whenever I got in trouble as a kid, like me making myself at home is doing something wrong.

I better get over that feeling quick, or this will be a *really* long year.

There's a lock on the door, but it doesn't feel like enough. The idea of even taking off my clothes is making my eye twitch. Maybe I should take a quick shower rather than a long soak, just in case. Or stick a chair under the door leading to his bedroom. Maybe install a deadbolt.

You know. Just *minor* precautions.

While I'm debating, the clock is ticking. Any minute, Thayden might return with Apollo.

This is your house too, I try to tell myself. *You're going to have to get used to showering and changing your clothes here.*

I put my hands on my hips in a power pose, and glance in

the mirror. It's foggy, so I wipe a spot clear with my palm and then resume the position, giving myself the fiercest look I can. I'm no Harper, or even Zoey, but I can look scary if I want to.

"'Make yourself at home,' the man said. And that's what you're going to do. Starting with a bubble bath. Now, get to it."

I let my ponytail down, but before getting in, I flick on the exhaust fan to dispel the billowing steam, then return to my room to locate my phone. It only takes a minute to hook it up to my Bluetooth speaker and blast my '80s Ladies playlist. A girl can't beat Pat Benatar, Joan Jett, or Chrissy Hynde when she needs to feel empowered.

A few shimmies later and I'm feeling more confident about claiming my right to a luxurious bubble bath. I'm also feeling more sure of how much I need a serious scrub. I smell like my middle school locker room after we ran the mile in gym class.

The opening notes to "Walk Like an Egyptian" have just started playing, and I'm walking into the bathroom with my hands pulling up the hem of my T-shirt, when the door on Thayden's side flies open. So much for the lock. I freeze, mouth open, and hands fisted in the fabric. My eyes narrow at the sweaty, shirtless man before me.

Do not look at his bare chest. Do not!

And I don't. Because The Bangles have got my back. I don't need to admire a sexy man-chest.

Okay. Even The Bangles would condone a *tiny* peek. Which turns into a longer perusal, because—good night! There are too many muscles for just one quick scan. I mean, how is it possible to have so many abs?

I jerk my eyes back up to his face, but I don't need to worry because he doesn't seem to notice my blatant ogling.

Thayden's cheeks are flushed, and his eyes ping from the bubbles almost spilling out of the tub, to my hands, which I immediately drop from the hem of my shirt. Our gazes finally connect, his green eyes wide.

I cross my arms protectively over my chest, even though he's the one without a shirt on. "Hey! I locked that! Ever heard of knocking?"

Thayden looks dazed. "I'm sorry. The lock doesn't—it's broken." He swallows, and almost has to shout over the music. "I didn't know you were taking a bath. The music playing in your room—I thought—"

He's interrupted by a deep woof and the sound of Apollo bounding up the stairs. Thayden's eyes widen even further, and he tries to close the door.

Before he can, Apollo's big, gray body barrels through the doorway, knocking Thayden into me. I have time to think one rational thought, which is: *I was wrong. This bathroom is definitely too small.* And then Apollo has leaped into the tub, knocking me and Thayden in with him.

I don't even have time to scream before my head is submerged. Air leaves my nose in a shock expulsion of bubbles. Thayden shouts at Apollo as strong hands pull me up.

I gasp for air, tasting my cupcake bath gel, which unfortunately is nothing like dessert. Thayden pulls me away from Apollo, which means I'm now wet and gasping and plastered to his chest. But at least I smell like cupcakes?

Though the wet dog smell is almost enough to overpower it.

"Out! Apollo, out!"

Thayden's voice is directly in my ear, and I wince, trying and failing to pull away. Our legs are tangled, and his arms are cemented around me, like we're two trees that have grown together, trunks tangling upward, linked forever.

"Sorry."

He winces, shifting slightly so his mouth isn't right next to my ear. His rough cheek scrapes mine, and it's as tantalizing as I remember.

Apollo leaps out of the tub only to leap back in. Water sloshes up into my eyes, and I make a very unladylike screech as his toenails drag over my arm.

"Out!" Thayden roars, tugging me closer so that he's yelling over my head rather than piercing my eardrum. My cheek slicks against his smooth pectorals, and to tell the truth, I'm not so mad about the whole situation after all. I'll have to sneak Apollo a doggy treat later on.

"Out! Now."

With a whine and a lick to the side of Thayden's face, Apollo leaps out again and shakes off, sending water, bubbles, and a fine mist of dog hair over everything. He trots away, thumping down the stairs.

And still, Thayden cradles me to his chest. "Eternal Flame" starts to play, because OF COURSE it does.

With a sigh, Thayden tilts his head until our eyes meet. "Hi," he says.

"Hi."

"Come here often?"

I smack his firm bicep, all I can reach right now since my arms are mostly pinned between us. Thayden grins, and maybe it's that daggum dimple or the fact that his heart is thumping against my cheek, but I smile back. And then I laugh, because there is dog hair on his forehead.

"You've got a little something right ... there."

I lift my head and wiggle my arm free to brush his forehead. My fingertips leave a trail of bubbles in its wake.

Maneuvering both hands, I cover his actual beard with one made of bubbles.

"That's better."

"Is it?" he asks.

"Definitely."

"Well," he says, twisting so that I'm dipped lower in the water but still cradled to him, "you've got a little something yourself."

With the arm that's not holding me, Thayden gives me my own bubble beard. Scooping up a handful, he places a mountain of bubbles on top of my head. "Now you're ready for the ball, Cinderella."

"Does that make you the handsome prince?"

"Nope. I'm one of the mice helping you magically get ready."

I study his face and the bubble beard, which is quickly dissipating. "A mouse, huh? I think I'd peg you as more of a … big bad wolf."

Thayden's smile stretches into something altogether feral in its wickedness, illustrating my point. "Wrong fairy tale, princess."

We're so close. Tension is thick in the air again between us. His lips are within reach. I ache with the memory of kissing him.

But now, we have a contract between us. We're living under the same roof. Crossing these lines is even more dangerous. How would I know what's real? What's fake? How will I protect myself? Maybe we need a different kind of contract. One to prevent moments like *this*, to Thayden-proof my heart.

I pull back. "I should probably—"

"I'll let you—"

We both laugh, and then Thayden and I both begin to

move. Water sloshes over the side of the tub. I fall further in, while Thayden manages to get out. I watch as he grabs a towel, rubbing it over that sculpted chest.

I was just *right there*, and I didn't even write my initials on it! In my mind, I see *Delilah was here*, written in looping cursive. Yep. I was there.

"Do you usually bathe fully clothed?" Thayden asks, grinning down at me. I'm sure he saw me staring hard at his chest, though he probably wasn't imagining me staking my claim.

"Maybe I do," I say, angling my body back until my head is resting comfortably. "Wouldn't you like to know."

His eyes take on a gleam, and though he doesn't say it, I know he's thinking that he very much would like to know.

"Sorry, I forgot to tell you that Apollo loves"—he cups his hands around his mouth, whispering dramatically—"*baths.*"

"Yeah, thanks for a heads-up on that. Side note: I'd like to put in a request for a working lock, please. To keep out *all* the dogs."

Thayden laughs. "And what about the mice?"

"Them too."

"And the wolves?"

That smile is just like a lasso, perfectly thrown, tightening around my poor heart and bringing me down to my knees.

"Definitely no wolves."

Thayden wraps the towel around his waist, then gives me a last look that only further tightens that lasso. "Why don't you let me know when you're done?"

"Don't wait up. I may stay in here all night."

He laughs. "I'm making mushroom risotto for dinner."

"I'll be down at six."

CHAPTER SEVENTEEN

Thayden

IF THE WAY to a man's heart is through his stomach, the way to a woman's heart is through her Pinterest boards. Something I had never heard of before a few days ago. Now, thanks to Zoey, I'm intimately familiar with the site, which is like a pretty way of collecting links and ideas from the internet onto different "boards." I need to thank Zoey again for that tip. Once I got her blessing, D's other friends fell like dominos, supplying me with all kinds of juicy intel, the kind needed to bring Delilah down.

One grand (or small) gesture at a time.

Delilah's Pinterest boards are like a series of satellites, picking up on all her frequencies. I now know her favorite foods, what style of decor she likes, the books she has read and the ones she wants to read, and even the kinds of actors she finds attractive, thanks to a board she titled Man

Candy. I'd probably be more irritated if most of them didn't have dark hair and facial hair. I'm not saying they're my not-as-hot clones, but ... okay, sure. That's what I'm saying.

Whoever invented Pinterest is a genius.

Anyway, I'm not sure what Delilah will think when she learns that I'm cooking my way through her Pinterest boards. It doesn't make me a sneaky person. It makes me *resourceful*. Based on Delilah's expressions, the noises she's made throughout dinner, and how many times she's asked for just a pinch more, I think she would agree.

"This is ..."

Delilah doesn't finish her sentence. Her eyelids flutter closed, and I sip my wine, enjoying the look on her face much more than the chenin blanc. It pairs nicely with the risotto, and also with Delilah, who is a little sweet, and a whole lot spicy, even when I'm plying her with home-cooked food.

"... incredible."

Yes. This *is* incredible. And I don't mean the food.

Her eyes pop open, meeting mine, catching me staring. No point pretending that I wasn't. So, I don't. Hers is a face I could catalogue for days. In sunlight, on cloudy days. I want to know what her eyes look like under different kinds of light. I have a sudden urge to order every kind of light bulb on Amazon just to see the blue of her eyes in them. Then I could make a spreadsheet to name each shade of blue, correlating them with the various wattage and brand. Not that I'm obsessive or anything. I happen to like spreadsheets. And Delilah's eyes.

Those eyes narrow for a moment, which kicks my heart up a notch. That look means she's about to get after me about something. I *love* that look. I'm just like the problem kid in class, who doesn't care if it's positive or negative attention, so long as she's paying attention to me.

"That reminds me." Delilah sets her fork down and rummages through her big leather purse, which has been sitting at her feet.

She pulls out a notebook with a sunflower on the front and uncaps a pen. "After this afternoon's bathroom issue, we need to discuss our house rules."

I groan, then take a long swallow of wine. "Boo! Rules."

She glares. "Why is it no surprise that you don't like rules?"

"Actually, I do like them."

"You mean, you like them so you can break them."

This is not a question, and so I don't answer. I just lift one shoulder and grin at her over my wineglass. I watch her slender hand as it grips the pen with force, writing ROOM-MATE CONTRACT across the top of the page.

Really? Neither of those words inspire confidence that I'm any closer to winning my fake fiancée's heart. Roommate— could there be a more platonic word? It's synonymous with friend. Maybe worse. Because you can be roommates without being friends.

"Haven't we had enough contracts?" I ask lightly, pouring us both more wine.

Delilah takes a small sip, then chases it with water.

"It's practical," she says. "Especially if we want to keep from killing each other. We should draw clear lines. Like, for example, don't come in the bathroom when the door is shut."

I grin. "Okay."

It was an honest mistake earlier, what with the music blasting from her room, but I do not for one second regret the outcome. I even gave Apollo a piece of leftover steak as a reward. Now, he's lying all full-bellied and smelling like a mix of cupcake bath gel and wet dog.

"That was easy."

Picking up her pen, she writes that down on the first line. Her penmanship is classic cheerleader handwriting, each letter happy and bright. She could crank out pep rally posters like nobody's business. I didn't know handwriting could have a mood, but hers does, and it's effervescently chipper.

"Too easy. I thought you might fight me on that one," she says, a little tentatively.

Does she still see me as she did when we first met— some kind of charming playboy, just after one thing? The thought is like the first dab of peroxide on a skinned knee. But it only makes me more determined to do better, to show her the man I'm trying to become. For myself, but also, for her.

I run my finger along the top of my glass until a clear note sounds, garnering her attention. "I want to respect your privacy. The same way I respect you, Delilah."

She studies me for a moment, then nods, her features relaxing just a bit. *Good.* She trusts me, even if just an inch. Still, I'm the boy who can't resist pulling on her braids.

Keeping my expression deadly serious, I add, "If we have to leave the bathroom doors open when it's not in use, that means I have a clear view of your bed when I'm lying in mine."

Her jaw drops, and I slide off my stool in time to miss her jab at my stomach.

"Thayden Walker, you incorrigible knave!"

Laughing, I collect our plates and begin washing up at the sink. "Tell me more. You know I love when you talk literary to me."

"Do I do that a lot?" she asks, taking another sip of wine.

"Around me, in particular. I seem to draw it out of you. Especially the insults."

She sighs. "That you do."

"It's refreshing, actually. I'm being insulted on a higher level."

She snorts. "Get back over here, you scallywag. I'll do the dishes later."

Drying my hands, I lean on the kitchen island. Closer to her, but not quite close enough for her to smack me.

"Now, see—that's more pirate than high literature. And I don't think you can pull off pirate speak."

Delilah looks like she's going to argue for a moment, then says, "Arrrrrr," and bites her lip. The giggle she is trying to hold back escapes, and the sound travels down deep in me. It's like she's skipped right down into my soul's wine cellar and uncorked a rare bottle of merlot. She doesn't seem to even realize the power she has over me.

I gesture to her paper. "What else? I was serious about wanting to respect your boundaries. I've never lived with anyone before. You might have to train me."

Her eyes go wide. "Not even in college?"

I shake my head, tasting the bitterness before I even say the words. "Daddy paid for a loft, since I went to his university of choice."

Her expression softens, and though I want her to look at me that way, I don't want her to look at me that way because of my father. Not because of pity or even compassion.

"I'm very much looking forward to living with my first woman," I say, waggling my brows. I know this will steer us back into the safe space where she throws me glares she doesn't really mean.

She also throws pens, apparently. This one bounces off my chest and hits the floor. I pick it up and hand it back, making sure our fingers brush. A pink flush tints her cheeks, and I'll take that as a tiny win.

"I've got an idea," I say. "Why don't you get comfortable in the living room and start working on the list, since you're the expert. I'll make you a coffee."

"I'll be up all night," she says, wrinkling her nose, making me want to leap over the counter and kiss the tip of it. My self-restraint is becoming legendary.

"And I already didn't sleep last night."

My eyes snap up to her face. I can tell she didn't mean to say that by the way she dips her chin, avoiding my gaze.

Honestly, I'm glad to know I wasn't the only one. Last night, all I could think about was having this woman here in my house, sleeping a bedroom away, with only layers of wood and drywall between us. I swallow hard, just thinking of it.

Ducking to catch her eye again, I say, "What about a decaf peppermint mocha?"

Her eyes brighten, then narrow again suspiciously. "How do you know everything I like? Are you a stalker? Did you hire a private investigator?"

I feign seriousness. "No. Should I? Might be a good idea, considering."

It's only a flash, but true panic skates across her features. I don't like whatever put that expression there. No matter how I've tried asking, she's managed to put off any talk about her past.

I know four facts: she's from rural Alabama; she doesn't know her father; she isn't close with her mother; and she competed in a few local pageants as a child. I want to know more, to know it all. I especially want to know why the idea of me digging makes her panic. But I don't want to go about it like I've learned her favorite things. I want her to tell me because she trusts me enough to say the words.

She swallows the concern quickly, feigning that sauciness I know and love. "Only if I can do the same. Though I'm not sure I want whatever skeletons might pop out of your closet."

No, she definitely would not. Though I've been forthcoming about my past, not even I want to revisit past-Thayden. We need to bail out of this conversation, for both our sakes. Though I do want to circle back later. I hate the idea that her past is painful. I'd like to make the future something far better. If she'll let me. And right now, while she's writing up a roommate contract, that's a big *IF*.

"Whipped cream or no whipped cream?" I ask, before turning to my espresso maker. I already know the answer. And I already have homemade whipped cream in the fridge.

"Whipped cream, please," she says.

"Got it. Now go get to work on our … *list*." Sounds marginally better than contract, doesn't it?

I normally don't use the espresso maker, or even find myself in the kitchen this much, but Delilah is giving me excuses to do a lot of things I haven't done in a long time. Or ever.

I've definitely never pampered or pursued a woman like this before. Especially not one who seems to wear Thayden-repellent in a fine mist over her skin. I'm doing all the things I can, small gestures and a few larger ones I have planned, but her polar ice cap doesn't seem to be melting. If anything, it's like a winter storm is constantly hovering around her heart.

Gavin says to just keep going, slow and steady. I'm not planning to give up anytime soon, but I'd love to see a sign that she's cracking. Even a little bit.

Though she didn't say much, I saw the wonder in her eyes when she saw her newly decorated room. I would have loved a hug, don't get me wrong, but seeing that look was enough. I'm like a starving dog, hanging out under her table for the smallest scrap. It's a little embarrassing, honestly. But I'm still down here, head on my paws, waiting with those same doleful eyes Apollo gives me when I've grilled a T-bone.

As the espresso machine screams, heating the milk, I wonder, not for the first time, what I'm doing. I wanted to pursue Delilah. Now, I want more. The contract keeps her here, keeps her close, but it also keeps her at a distance.

The Walker Firm has been a matter of pride for me. Until lately. It's not just Delilah either, but the case of my father's I was forced to pick up, the one that's kept me working eighteen-hour days, six days a week. Stuck with Duke, a man I dislike even more now than I did before. I'll be working tomorrow at the crack of dawn since I took off today to help Delilah move.

The hours aren't what bother me or being in the courtroom. It's the man I'm defending. He's facing a whole laundry list of things, and I honestly think he's guilty of at least eighty percent. White-collar things, but still. And I'm standing up there, defending the man, trying to help him get away with tax evasion, fraud, and some light laundering.

Duke isn't bothered in the slightest, but I hate myself a little more every day that I show up to the courthouse and see our client's smug face, sure he'll get off because the Walker Firm is known for this. Pay us enough, and you won't need a get-out-of-jail-free card. We ARE that card.

But as soon as I take over, I can change that. I can shift the firm to less of that work and more pro bono cases. I can say no to clients that were an automatic yes from my father and his boys' club. I can hold out hope that Duke will leave, or I can fire him, along with anyone else who shares that same, skeevy dirty-lawyer vibe.

I have to wonder if this really is how my father envisioned the firm. As much as I despised how he treated me, I always thought he was honorable. Now, I'm just not sure of much. Other than the fact that the only thing making me happy right now is the woman who wouldn't be here except for that stupid contract.

I deliver her peppermint mocha, sitting in a chair across from her with my latte. She's filled up a whole page with that cheerful handwriting and moved on to the next. She presses so hard that I might be able to read the words by running my fingertips across the paper.

"Let's get after it," I say. "Roommate contract. How does this work?"

Delilah takes a sip of her drink, her eyes rolling back in her head just a little. "Were you a barista before you were a big law-man?"

"I think law-man usually refers to a sheriff in a western movie, and no, I was not a barista. I just happen to like coffee. And I don't want to pay Starbucks for it."

"Hm," she says, looking suspiciously at me.

That's right. Suspect away. I DID figure out all your favorite things so I could win you over. Yep.

Delilah sets down the mug, then tucks her feet up underneath her. She changed into pajamas while I made our drinks. They are far more wholesome than what I might pick out, given the chance, but it's probably for the best. The long pants are a gray cotton that looks soft, and the matching gray V-neck top hangs loose over her shoulders. It's still feminine and pretty, though. I want to drag her into my arms and kiss her just as much as I would have if she were wearing something lacy or that revealed more skin.

Delilah takes another sip, her tongue darting out to lick the whipped cream from the corner of her mouth. I track the movement, warmth burning in my chest.

When she sets down her mug, it's like a gavel calling the court to order, and I shake my head a little, trying to focus on the task at hand.

Right. Another set of rules governing our relationship.

"Let's do this," she says, tapping the notebook. "Roommate contact."

"Can I ask where you got this idea? Is this something y'all did at your other house?"

"Yes, but it started before that. My freshman year, I didn't know anyone, so I got a roommate by the lottery system. Hateful girl."

She shudders, and I have an intense longing to know that story, like I want to know all her stories. She glosses over it, just as she does most of her past.

"The only way I survived the semester was because of the roommate contract."

"Did you get a new roommate after the first semester?"

"Yep. Sam." She smiles. "But that's getting off-track. Our RA made us sit down and discuss our preferences. Everything from whether or not it's okay to blow-dry your hair while your roommate is sleeping (it's not) to whether it's okay to have a boyfriend sleep over."

A jealous alpha beast starts clawing its way out of my basement, and it's all I can do to slam the doors on its gnarly, clawed fingers.

Delilah having sleepovers? Nope. That is not anywhere my mind needs to go, now or ever. All I need is a list of names and I will be tearing off people's limbs.

"I see." Maybe I sound a bit stiff, but at least I do not sound jealous. Not at all. Law-man is ice cold over here.

186

"I can see the wheels turning, mister. And we voted no sleepovers in the room, so take a deep breath."

"I'm fine." Mostly. Sweat is beading on my hairline and I'm holding my mug so tightly it's a wonder the thing hasn't shattered.

She huffs, rolling her eyes a bit, then continues. "The contract helped. There are so many things you don't consider until you live with someone. Even if you don't fully see eye-to-eye, laying out the expectations and getting into specifics can head off conflict before it starts." She takes a sip of her mocha.

"Would you have lived with someone before marriage?"

She almost drops her mug, and I understand her startled expression. I have no idea where that thought came from. Or how it escaped. Maybe because my whole focus is not letting the jealous monster out of the basement, I got a little loose with everything else.

"I ..." She blinks rapidly, eyes skating around the room, touching on everything but me.

"I'm sorry." I wave a hand, shifting in my seat. I'm so hot now that I wish I'd made iced coffee instead so I could pour it over the top of my head. "I didn't mean to put you on the spot. You just seem old-fashioned in some ways." She seems to take offense at that, and of course, the words just keep coming out. "Classic. Classy?"

"Keep on digging that hole with your mouth, charmer. See where it gets you."

When she's fired up, that accent slides into place, turning her *gets* into *gits*. A slight difference, but I'm tracking all her syllables. Another spreadsheet. Soon, my laptop is going to need new memory because it will be filled with all things Delilah.

I chuckle. "Sorry. Forget I asked. Go on. Back to the *contract*." I make a face.

"Fine. A few softballs to get us started. Like a lightning round. I'll name something, and you say whether it's your job or mine. Then I'll share my answer."

This feels like the worst kind of trap. There will be no right answers, only booby traps and snake pits.

"Who will do most of the cooking?" she asks, pen hovering over the page.

"Me."

"Dishes?"

"Me."

She narrows her eyes. "Cleaning?"

"The housekeeper."

"I mean, like day-to-day stuff. Putting away mail, making sure shoes aren't all over the house. Basic stuff."

I look around the room, where the only thing out of place is Delilah. Though to me, she looks like what was missing in my little house.

"Both of us?"

"Who puts the trash cans out by the curb? Also, what day do the trash cans go out by the curb?"

"Me. And Monday."

Delilah drops her pen on the notebook. "You can't do everything."

"I said we'd both clean up after ourselves. That's you. Do you really want to cook? Or roll the trash cans to the curb?"

"Maybe." Her chin juts out a little, that adorable nose lifting. Wow. Not once have I ever thought of a woman's nose or anything else as adorable.

"Okay. Maybe you should just tell me what you want."

"I want to be useful. I don't want to feel like I'm a hotel guest and you're the concierge or somethin'."

I spread my palms out, a sign of surrender or frustration. I'm honestly not sure which. "I'm not trying to be that way. I guess I'm just used to doing everything myself."

"Well, times are a'changing."

"I couldn't be happier about that."

"Then let me do some things around the house. Think you can do that, tough guy?"

I can't decide if the nickname is a good or bad one. "Fine."

I take a sip of my latte. This woman is like one of those complicated knots I never learned to untie because I wasn't a Boy Scout. Just when I think I've got it, the thing is even tighter than before.

"Let's keep going," she grumbles.

We go back and forth for almost an hour, bickering and claiming household things like who's going to lock up at night (me) and who's going to mow the lawn (her). I am willing to bet she has not once ever operated a lawnmower. But I didn't fight her when she shot me a murderous look about it. I cannot wait to watch her try to mow. I'll need to buy a new porch swing and a six-pack of beer.

"Let's move on to physical touch."

And like THAT, I am focused on the conversation. "Physical touch—I'm for it."

Delilah makes a little growl of frustration. She is so cute when she's irritated with me.

"Considering this isn't a real relationship—"

"Ouch."

"Well, it's not, is it?" Her raised eyebrows challenge me.

Not yet. "Go on."

"I think we should avoid physical touch as much as possible, unless it's needed. Like in public, since we are supposed to be in a relationship."

She is killing me, carving me up like I'm a Thanksgiving turkey, slice by slice.

"So, what kind of public touching are we talking about here?" When her eyes turn to slits, I hold up both hands. "Hey—you were the one who said we should be specific."

"How would you like to touch me in public?" She must see the heat I feel traveling through my body, because she quickly waves her hand. "Scratch that. Let's stick to hand-holding when necessary, kisses on the cheek, and side hugs."

"Side hugs? Are you serious right now?"

"As a hurricane."

I run a hand over my jaw. "I'll see your side hugs and raise you a kiss on the lips."

Her cheeks color, and her eyes flash. "Closed mouth."

"Fine."

"Fine."

I feel like I've won a tiny battle. Because you better believe the next time I'm in public, I'm kissing my fiancée on those luscious lips. Even better, the fact that she didn't shoot me down tells me she doesn't hate the idea.

"So, other than a few, brief and occasional touches in public, we keep our hands to ourselves."

"Does that include your violence?" I ask.

"What violence?"

And like that, she's all wide, blinking eyes. Gorgeous and so, so guilty.

"How about this." I lean forward, putting on my court-room voice. "For every act of violence against me, I get my choice. A hug. Hand-holding. Maybe a k—"

"Don't finish that sentence." She's already scribbling on the page. "Fine. If I smack or elbow you—"

"Or kick, bite, hit—"

"I get the point. For each offense, you may hold my hand. Or hug me."

"What about cuddling in—" I backtrack away from the word bed, seeing flames about to shoot from her mouth. "I mean, cuddling on the couch."

"Fine. With a time limit of five minutes."

I have traveled back in time to junior high, where there were so many rules. You liked a girl, asked her out, then got to hold hands for a week or two in the halls, maybe—*just maybe*—hug. And if you convinced your parents drop you at the movies, you might make out in the darkened theater.

I feel ridiculously old thinking this. Because I'm pretty sure being a teenager looks a lot different now, what with all the TikToks and Snapchats.

And I, a fully grown man, have a five-minute cuddle limit, which I get only if my fake fiancée smacks me.

Swell.

As she writes, my gaze is drawn to her fingers, long and delicate. The pink nail polish is chipped on her index finger. I bet she'll touch it up by tomorrow. As I watch, that same hand drops to rub Apollo's belly, and he stops mid-snore to groan in pleasure, rolling over to give her better access. She whispers something to him in a honey-sweet tone, but I'm not even sure she knows what she's saying, because her eyes are on the contract.

I've never hated contracts so much, not in all my years of lawyering.

I want to yank the page out of that notebook and crumple it up before I tug the ponytail holder out of her hair. I want to make a whole different set of rules just to break them.

But I simply watch her, becoming the best student of this woman I can, because I have big plans to ace this class and go on to get my doctorate in all things Delilah.

"Let's go a bit deeper," Delilah says, "why don't we start with sleepovers. What's our rule on that? Is there some kind of sock-on-the-doorknob rule or what?"

I swear my heart has filled up with cement, all four chambers. I can hear the beats slowing as it thickens.

"Like, you and me ... sleeping over in each other's rooms?"

Please say that's what you mean. I know it isn't. But I want it to be. I cannot handle the alternative thought I have.

Delilah laughs. *Laughs.*

"Nice try. No, I mean if you have other women sleep over." She tries to keep that same amused look on her face, but it's all wrong. Her eyes aren't blinking, and her mouth is pinched. She is legitimately concerned about this possibility.

My cement heart hardens, then cracks wide open.

I'm across the room in a flash, all up in her space, defying her no-touching rules. I've tossed the stupid notebook and its ridiculous list over the back of the couch.

Cupping Delilah's face in my palms, I am practically vibrating with the need to set this beautiful, confused woman straight.

"No other women have crossed this threshold, save my mom and housekeeper. And now you. I have no plans, now or ever, of having any kind of sleepover with any woman other than you."

Too much? Probably. I have basically committed my life or a life of celibacy to her. At least as long as I live here. I guess if I can't win her over, I'll have to move.

Her eyes in the dim light are deep pools of inky blue, like someone's left a pen open on a white tablecloth and it's bled through the fabric. She almost looks scared, making me want to back off before she flies off like a startled sparrow, but when I shift, she covers my hands, still on her cheeks, with her own. Her eyes, though, they kill me. So vulnerable and sweet.

"No sleepovers?" Her voice is soft as a wind chime in a spring breeze.

"No." In contrast, my voice is a husky growl. The air between us is alive and moving, shifting and sparking with tension. It's a replay of the moment before our previous kisses, when the attraction rolled in like a storm.

I think of our first kiss, outside Mozart's. It seems like such a simpler time. She was still pushing me away but starting to melt. I was hoping for … I don't know what. My plans for sure didn't include marriage—yet. We didn't know about my mother and the contract. We didn't have RSVP cards stacking up on the dining room table. Now, the tension is here, the desire, but it's like we're feeling it across a chain-link fence.

"I wouldn't have lived with someone before getting married," she says suddenly.

I knew it. Swallowing, I don't even nod or blink because she's a scared rabbit who has spotted the fox.

"You're right. I am old-fashioned. Or … something."

It's on the tip of my tongue to apologize, for making her compromise on something she wouldn't have chosen for herself if I were a *real* fiancé. But her hands grip mine even tighter, keeping my palms against her soft cheeks as she keeps talking. It's a different sensation to feel the movement as she speaks, and I barely keep myself from rubbing my thumb over her lower lip.

"I want something real. Honor and faithfulness and 'til death do us part."

I'd like to think that she means with me, that this is like a coded message, telling me that she wants what's between us to be more than a contract, more than a promise jotted down on a piece of notebook paper.

My mouth opens and closes, seeking the right answer, wishing I had a Pinterest board to tell me the right thing to say. But I don't. I've never made these kinds of promises or commitments. I've never tried to convince a woman to stay. My vocabulary is wanting, while my tongue seems stuck with the same cement that filled up my heart.

Apollo shoves his big head between us, burrowing his nose in Delilah's lap. And like that, I've missed an opportunity, letting it wink out like a dying star.

Delilah pats my hands once, twice, then lets go in favor of scratching Apollo's ears. If I could, I'd take back the steak I gave him earlier.

"Would you mind grabbing my notebook that you so carelessly tossed over the couch? I remembered one more thing I want to make sure gets into our contract. I also need to see how many times I get to hit you for that five minutes of cuddling."

Just like that, we're back to light banter and talking about contracts.

I stand, my joints aching not with the movement but with resignation at the thought of moving away from her. As I pick up the notebook, Delilah catches my eye.

"We need to cover where Apollo will sleep at night."

One look at my dog, with his boxy gray head in her lap, and I know just who will be sleeping alone for the foreseeable future.

From: CantHardlyWait@DrLove.advice
To: DrLove@DrLove.advice

Dear Dr. Love,
 There's this guy I like, and I'm pretty sure he likes me. He's really shy, and I'm not, so I was thinking about making the first move. But my parents always taught me to let the guy be the initiator. If he doesn't make a move, he's not interested.
 I'm tired of waiting! Do you think women should wait for a guy to make the first move? I'm tired of waiting.
 Sincerely,
 Can't Hardly Wait

From: DrLove@DrLove.advice
To: CantHardlyWait@DrLove.advice

Dear Can't Hardly Wait,
 While I love it when guys make the first move, that's my personality. It doesn't have a thing to do with what I'm packing in my panties.
 It sounds like you are feeling the sparks, but you have a shy guy. He might really appreciate you taking the pressure off. I say go for it!
 -Dr. Love

CHAPTER EIGHTEEN

Delilah

THIS ISN'T GOING to work. I turn on my side again. Maybe with a pillow between my knees? There certainly are enough pillows in this room. Nope. Still not comfortable. I try my back again, staring up at the unfamiliar ceiling.

Last night, I conked right out after the Roommate Contract with Thayden. This morning, he was already gone for work when I woke up. I might have slept all day if Apollo hadn't stuck his cold, wet doggy nose in my face. Clearly, the bed is amazing. The bed is not an issue. It's the proximity to the man one room over that has me flopping around like a trout on a riverbank.

We're feeling much too ... domestic. Even after a day or two. Thayden might have been gone all day, but he brought home Vietnamese takeout—somehow, he seems to know that baking cookies is the extent of my kitchen prowess—and we ate at the dining room table with a bottle of wine.

Together, we did the dishes, complete with a very small water fight and a lot of laughs. We took Apollo for a walk. I found myself continually cursing that stupid roommate contract I insisted on, because Thayden kept his distance when all I wanted was to hold his hand while we walked. Technically, I guess I could have claimed the *in-public* clause and just grabbed his hand, but the man would have seen right through me.

Basically, tonight was like a really fantastic date where at the end of the night, instead of kissing, you both go upstairs to your separate rooms without so much as a handshake.

And then, of course, we went to brush our teeth at the same time.

"You first," he'd said, as we each awkwardly hesitated in our respective doorways.

"No, it's your bathroom."

"I insist."

I finally dragged him into the small bathroom by his shirt collar. "We're adults. We can brush at the same time."

Or so I *thought*.

If anything could kill attraction, it would be a benign act like toothbrushing. Ew, right? The foaming mouths, the spitting. But Thayden brushing his teeth, catching my eye in the mirror and grinning while toothpaste dripped from his lips— was somehow just as alluring as he is in a suit. Or pajamas. The man could probably crawl out of a dumpster and still make my stupid heart pitter-patter.

Living with him is the worst idea I've ever had.

"Stop sighing in there," Lucifer himself calls from the other room. "You're too loud."

Per the agreement, both doors to the bathroom are

cracked open. Not enough to see each other (because he was right about the straight view from his bed to mine) but open enough he can be distracted by my sighs.

"Don't you have a noise machine?"

"No. I've never needed one."

At that moment, Apollo lets out a snore that sounds like a bear. I can practically feel my bed vibrating all the way from Thayden's room. I can't hold back my giggles. Thayden muffles his own laughter.

"You sure about that? Apollo," I call. "Wanna snuggle, you quiet boy?"

"Hey! No fair!" Thayden says as I hear the *thump-thump* of Apollo's front and then back paws hitting the floor. Apollo's nails tick along the hardwoods, and he noses his way through the bathroom. Leaving, of course, both doors wide open as he jumps in my bed. Thayden gives me a little wave.

Hello, temptation. Thy name is Thayden.

I should have planned for this. Because now I've got a massive dog all up in my space. And I can clearly see Thayden in his. He shifts, putting his hands behind his head and leaning against the headboard, watching me with that trademark smirk. At least it's dark enough that I can't make out the dimple. With my inhibitions lowered as they tend to be when sleepy, that dimple might be my undoing.

"Well, hello," he says.

"Don't start."

"What, specifically, should I not start? I'm not the one who made Apollo open the doors. You called him in there. Was this your plan or just a benefit?"

"Neither."

I sigh, scratching the big dog's neck. He's got his head on my stomach, and if I couldn't fall asleep before, there's no way I can now. He's already snoring. And Thayden is still staring.

"Quit it! Why don't you be a gentleman and close the doors?"

"I'm comfortable right where I am, thank you."

I let out a frustrated groan and Apollo sighs heavily, shifting so his body is alongside mine, his head claiming the pillow next to me. He still smells faintly of my cupcake body wash.

"I can't sleep with you looking at me," I call to Thayden.

"And I can't sleep with you in my view. But neither of us was having much luck anyway. Is the bed okay?"

"Better than what I had. Thank you."

"You don't need to thank me. Say the word and I'll replace it."

I roll my eyes. "No. I've got enough money now to replace it myself."

One of the agreements we made in the negotiations with Scott is for me to receive payment in the form of a few lump sums. I got the first yesterday, and immediately paid off a big chunk of my loans, leaving me a comfy cushion. I already feel the burden lifting.

Thayden scoffs. "I won't let you."

"You can't stop me."

"I'd like to try."

"I'll bet you would."

We're like expert tennis players, volleying back and forth, the ball never hitting the net, never going out of bounds. Instead of exhausting me, it's invigorating. The man might drive me a little batty, but he wakes me up. Being around him, I feel more content yet also more alive than I've ever felt.

"Do you usually struggle to sleep?" I ask.

He shakes his head. "Nope."

I bite my lip, trying not to smile. Okay, fine. So, I love the idea that he can't sleep because of me. I like disrupting his life. It's only fair, since he's torn mine all to pieces.

Yeah, and put it back together. Now you've got money to pay off the loans and the best mattress you've ever slept on. The best nighttime view too.

"I've had trouble since my dad died," Thayden says.

Oh. I'm instantly deflated. I feel guilty and small thinking that it was me keeping him up. His grief is way more important. And it only makes my heart go out to him more.

"But now ... I've got other things keeping me up." He winks, and I feel my whole body shudder.

And just like that, I'm buoyed back up, my pulse skittering through my veins and my cheeks heating. Thayden grins, his teeth so white in the dark. Maybe I need to switch to whatever toothpaste he's using.

"How about your family?" he asks.

A perfectly normal question that I perfectly don't want to answer. Ugh. I've made it through years with my friends not asking, not pushing for answers. Thayden's like a dog and my past is a big, juicy bone.

What he doesn't know is that if he yanks at this particular one too hard, it's attached to a whole skeleton. I can't imagine what Thayden would do if he found out about my mama, about my past and what I've done. He would probably toss me out and ask for the money back. Considering I've already used a big chunk to pay off most of my debt, I'd end up being his indentured servant or something.

"My mom mentioned that you didn't think your mom could come to the wedding," he says, continuing to needle at me.

"She can't." Mama would take one look at this crowd and

come up with a plan to rob them blind. Or be some kind of leech, blackmailing me for cash. Lord knows she's got a pile of dirt on me that I'd love to stay in the ground.

"That's a shame."

It really isn't.

"No other family?"

"Nuh-uh."

"I'm sorry." His tone is either pitying or just compassionate. I can't tell which.

"I'm not. I don't know any different."

"Now, I'm really sorry," he says.

I give him a little nod, rubbing Apollo's ears and looking away.

Thayden thinks about this for a moment, and when I look back at him, his face is a thing of beauty draped in shadows. I haven't found a light yet that doesn't love this man's features.

"New topic. Any ex-boyfriends I need to be jealous of?"

"No. Not many. Most couldn't get past my defenses."

He chuckles. "You do have a pretty deep moat. And a sturdy castle wall. The flaming arrows are also a nice deterrent."

"They sting, don't they?"

"They do." He grins, looking like he doesn't mind a bit.

"Hasn't stopped you."

That grin widens into something so gorgeous that I have to grab Apollo's collar to keep me in my bed.

"I like a challenge," he says. "Well. When the prize is worth the fight."

My heart speeds up. My neck feels hot. My toes curl. I need an exit from this dangerous path, and I need it now.

"Are exes really the topic you want to bring up?" I ask.

"I'm not sure we have time to get through your past in just one night."

Thayden groans, covering his face with a pillow. He then tosses it. The pillow makes it through the bathroom and slides across my floor with a whoosh. Apollo looks up at the sound, then lets his head flop back down, as though he can't be bothered by our shenanigans.

I grin. "Great arm, tiger. Did you play baseball?"

Thayden shakes his head, chuckling. "Will you ever stop giving me a hard time?"

"Doubtful."

"Good. Now, don't freak out. I'm going to help you fall asleep."

He swings his legs over the side of the bed and begins crossing to my room. I point a finger at him.

"Don't you cross this threshold."

He pauses in the bathroom, just outside my door. "Why not?"

"I've poured a protective layer of salt around my room to keep your kind out."

Thayden laughs as he confidently steps high over an imaginary line, and my pulse is now performing a complicated drum solo. Pausing just over the threshold, Thayden looks around dramatically, as though waiting to be turned into dust.

"Guess I'm not the monster you think I am," he says.

"That remains to be seen. Don't come any closer! I've also got holy water and I'm wearing a garlic necklace."

Thayden stands next to my side of the bed, so close I can smell that masculine spicy scent I've gotten addicted to. I try not to take big, deep sniffs. Even if I want to. Not breaking eye contact, he picks up my water glass and drains it in a few deep swallows.

Now, why is that so sexy?

Oh, right. Because everything the man does is.

"I'd like to see that garlic necklace," he murmurs, and before I can react, he's dragging a fingertip over my neck in an invisible circle. I grab his hand, because my skin cannot handle any more of his light touch. I swear I'm about to start glowing like a nuclear reactor. They glow, right? Or maybe that's nuclear waste in superhero movies. Either way, the man needs to get his paws off me.

"Unaffected by salt, holy water, and garlic," Thayden says. "Maybe I'm just a mere mortal after all."

"Maybe I should try a silver bullet," I say, still clutching his hand.

"Turn over, Delilah," he says, and the low timbre of his voice makes me drop his hand and comply.

The bed creaks and dips as he sits down near my hips. I'm now framed in by a massive beast on one side and a man on the other. The pulse in my neck throbs as Thayden's palms stroke their way up my back. I groan as his fingertips thread their way through my hair.

"Relax," he says. "I'll take care of you."

I don't have the strength to tell him that's what I'm afraid of. Nor the energy to fight the magical touch of his fingertips as they gently massage my scalp.

"My mom used to do this for me when I couldn't sleep."

"Mmm," is all I can manage. I'm drooling onto my pillow. But I'm sure Apollo is doing the same next to me. I wonder what that was like, having a mother who would help you sleep? As opposed to one who was always sleeping with the kind of men that made me wish I had a double lock on my door.

"So, you're a fan of the show *Supernatural?*" Thayden asks. I'm thankful for the change in subjects.

When I mumble an agreement, I can almost hear his smile. "Sam or Dean?" he asks.

If I tell him the truth, that bad-boy Dean Winchester is my favorite, I'll never hear the end of it. He's far too much like Thayden, at least in the way he behaves. Maybe I do have a type.

"Castiel," I say.

"I should've known you'd pick the angel," Thayden grumbles. His fingers reach my temples, and nothing has ever felt so good. I try to hold back a groan, needing to keep some semblance of composure. The man is turning me to mush.

"Story or song?" Thayden asks.

"Song," I mumble into the pillow.

I don't want to admit that no one ever sang me a lullaby. It's too deep a truth, too much of an admission to how starved for love I really am.

But maybe I should have thought this through. I'm already melting for Thayden. Having a private serenade will make it worse. His speaking voice is bad enough, deep and rich. He's going to slay me with a song.

Thayden clears his throat, opens his mouth, and then does the absolute worst rendition of an Ed Sheeran song I've ever heard.

Probably the worst rendition of any song that *anyone's* ever heard. It's really, really terrible. Cats howling and fingernails on chalkboards have nothing on Thayden's singing voice, which is somehow *nothing* like his speaking voice. Next to me, Apollo's groan pushes me over the edge from giggles to outright laughter. Thayden's fingers freeze in my hair.

"Story!" I gasp. "I choose story!"

Thayden's hands grip my shoulders and he gently rolls me over. I cover my face with my hands, but it does nothing to stifle my laughter.

"What?" he asks. "Not good? Don't like Ed Sheeran? How about Sam Smith?"

Thayden starts in on a song with a falsetto that sounds like an ostrich dying. Apollo grunts, then jumps off the bed and pads back to Thayden's room.

"Please!" I gasp through my laughter. "No more!"

Thayden crosses his arms, staring down at me in confusion. "What is it? You don't like singing?"

My laughter dies off and I sit up. I'm staring. I can't help it. The man who seems flawless and charming in so many ways is a terrible singer and has *no* idea.

"Are you serious? Thayden, you can't sing. And if you really don't know that, you're tone-deaf."

A muscle in his jaw tics. "No one's ever complained before."

"How many people have you sung for?"

"A few."

I bite my lip. "Were these … women that you dated?"

He clenches his jaw. "Maybe."

I can't contain my laughter. "No wonder things never got serious! You probably scared them all away!"

Thayden puts a hand to his chest. "Delilah Hart, you wound me."

"'Tis but a scratch," I say, the line from *Romeo and Juliet* somehow popping into my head.

Thayden's eyes light up. "'Ask for me tomorrow, and you shall find me a grave man.'"

I stare at him, all rational thought ripped from my body. Quoting Shakespeare is *way* too much. If I have an Achilles heel, that might be it. Thayden looks smug, as well he should.

"I played Mercutio my senior year. And did an excellent job, I'll have you know."

My lips twitch. "Probably because there's no singing in the play."

Thayden drops his head. "I can't win with you."

"I'm sorry," I say, touching his arm and offering a smile. "But friends don't let friends sing tone-deaf."

He narrows his eyes. "Fine. But no more laughing. Roll over and I'll tell you a story. Quick before I change my mind."

I roll over because there is no way I'm turning down more of a head rub. I can only hope Thayden is a better storyteller than he is a singer.

He must be, because within minutes, I'm drifting into sleep. In the morning, I have a fuzzy memory of lips brushing my cheek and Thayden whispering, "Sweet dreams, my Southern belle. This could be real, anytime you want it to be. Just say the word."

But it was probably more dream than memory because those are the words I really long to hear from the man who never wants to get married.

CHAPTER NINETEEN

Delilah

IF I HAVE my own patron saint of homemaking, it's Bridget Jones. Because I am a flaming train wreck when it comes to anything at home. Quite literally in some ways, I think, watching the firemen move around the yard from my spot with Apollo on the sidewalk.

Before this, there was the lawn-mowing incident. When I insisted on taking that job, I had no idea how difficult it would be. I've seen people mowing lawns my whole life. Never did it look hard. Hot, maybe, in the summer. Not back-breakingly exhausting.

Thayden watched me from the shade of the porch, grinning, while I sweated, battled, and wondered if I needed to start training with Harper. I wanted to smack him, and that was before he leaned on the porch railing and told me the dang thing was self-propelled.

"Just push that lever," he said, tipping his beer to me.

When I did and the mower jumped forward on its own, I wanted to throw him off the porch but settled for soaking him with the hose. He finished mowing the lawn shirtless, and I almost had to spray myself down watching him.

Really, there was only that incident and this one, so maybe Bridget Jones is a stretch. I'm not doing *so* bad.

Thayden sighs through the phone. "Are you standing outside with a bunch of hot firemen hitting on you?"

I wouldn't have called him, but the alarm company does it automatically when there's a trigger. Lucky me, the fire alarm also calls the actual fire department.

The rugged sound of Thayden's voice, the spark of jealousy I hear in it, has my stomach tumbling like clothes in a dryer. When one of the hot firemen in question walks by, winking, I feel nothing. Not even a tiny flare of nerves.

What has Thayden done, ruining me for perfectly good firemen?

Apollo growls, as though he heard my thoughts, and I grip his leash tighter. Thayden hadn't been wrong when he said Apollo doesn't like men in uniforms.

"No ..."

"Delilah. Don't make me come home."

"They're not hitting on me," I say.

Even as I say this, one of them rolls his T-shirt sleeves up to his shoulders, revealing his bulging biceps. Still no reaction. I'm more than a little concerned about the depth of my feelings for the man I'm living with and fake engaged to.

"Shouldn't you be more worried about me burning the place down?"

"No. I have insurance. I could be there in ten minutes—"

"Don't even think about it. You've got your big case."

A case he's been moaning and groaning about for days.

He's probably less jealous and more looking for any excuse to get away from Duke. I can't blame him. Meeting that despicable excuse for a man once was enough for me.

"The case doesn't matter. *You* matter."

I matter.

I bite my lip to hide my smile. Another fireman strolls by, grinning at me in a way that's just south of friendly. They should be clearing out by now. Must be a slow day at the fire station.

Why in tarnation are they getting out the hoses? *There aren't even any flames.*

I swear, all I did was blacken some toast. Really, really blacken it. And a cookie sheet. Which is unfortunate, as cookies are about the only thing I can safely bake. I'll have to buy Thayden a new one.

The lesson learned today is: don't use the broiler to make toast, then forget about it. Or ... don't cook.

This wouldn't have been such a difficult lesson, except for the whole thing where Thayden's fire alarms send a signal right to the fire station. You can imagine my surprise when I hopped out of the shower to alarms downstairs, black smoke in the kitchen, and sirens as the truck pulled up out front.

I'm definitely not telling Thayden I was in the shower. I managed to get clothes on before they got to the door, but I have a feeling he'd be on the way here before I got to that part. Especially if he knew my clothes consist of tight workout pants and a tank top with no bra.

"Delilah?"

"What's wrong, darlin'?"

"That. That's what's wrong."

Drat. That *darlin'* just slipped out. I force a laugh. "Sorry, should I have called you a knave? An incorrigible rake?"

"You know I like your literary mouth. It's when you call

me *darlin'* I get worried. Tell me—are they wrapping things up? You said it was just burnt toast."

"And a cookie sheet. Whatever. I'll buy you a new one."

"Don't worry about it. Burnt toast and a cookie sheet. Right. So, they should be packing up?"

"Mm-hm."

Another fireman walks by, balancing an ax on his shoulder. *What does he need* that *for?* His white teeth gleam as he smiles. Two others are dealing with the length of hose that has been unwound in the yard for no purpose I can gather. Apollo lies down on the sidewalk with a another growl.

"*Are* they packing up?" Thayden asks, his voice at a level that I'd call intense.

"Not exactly."

"I'm on my way."

"Thayden!"

He's already hung up. I'm smiling, but I'm also furious. Maybe I'm smiling because I'm furious? It's ridiculous how much I enjoy sparring with that man. With him, anger is never just anger. It's like joy, but hot. Heated joy? I think I'm getting addicted.

Right now, I'm feeling a whole heap of heated joy at the idea of Thayden rescuing me from the evil clutches of flirty firemen.

Speaking of which ...

Apollo growls again as a big, beefy shadow stops in front of me.

"Hello, ma'am." It's the ax-wielding fireman, though now he has both hands on his hips and a wide smile on his face. I'll call him Mr. Ax. This pose is clearly designed to show off his arms. They're nice and muscly, I suppose. Pre-Thayden Delilah might have been impressed.

Before Thayden, I might have smiled back, a real smile.

Not my pageant one. Instead, I find myself running my left hand through my hair, making sure he sees the ring. He does, but that doesn't seem to have any impact. Okay—he's *that* kind of man. Which makes me even happier that Thayden's on his way.

"We have a few questions we'd like to ask," the man says, his tone serious, but his mouth still smiling. "I'm Breck, by the way."

I prefer Mr. Ax. "Breck, hi. I think I've answered all y'all's questions. I left the broiler on. Burned toast. I'm a terrible cook." I force a giggle and give Apollo a little more slack to lean forward, a growl still in his throat. "What can I say? My fiancé isn't marryin' me for my culinary prowess."

A blink of confusion. Oh, was *prowess* too big a word for the little ol' fireman? Darn.

"It happens to the best of us," Breck says.

"Oh! Has it happened to you? Is that how you developed an interest in being a fireman—burning your breakfast?"

"Er—no."

Thayden's car screeches up to the curb in front of the house next door, the closest he can get because of the fire truck. It's hardly parked before he's sprinting toward me, glaring at the mess of firemen on the lawn.

"Darling!" Thayden shouts, and I have to bite back my smile.

So, that's how we're playing it. I don't miss the sneer Thayden throws Mr. Ax as he throws his arms around me, lifting me off the ground. Apollo wags his butt happily, shoving his head between us as best he can.

"Sugarplum!" I laugh. "I'm so glad you—"

Suddenly, Thayden is kissing me and my words are gone.

This is not the kind of kiss we agreed to in the contract, which I should be mad about, but almost immediately, I'm

213

lost in his lips, the scrape of his beard against my cheek, the feel of his arms around me. My mind blanks out and I'm pretty certain the earth halted its rotation around the sun for a moment there.

Too soon, Thayden sets me back on my feet, grinning smugly as I stumble a bit. I always thought shaky legs were an aftereffect of kissing only found in novels. Nope, it's real-life stuff. Thayden wraps an arm around my waist, dragging me to his side. I don't even want to fight him.

I'd like more kissing instead. Which I definitely can't admit. So, I give him just a little bit of fight, pulling away until he clamps me even tighter against him. I feel like I fit here, like I've been made to fit tucked into his side. I'm grateful for Apollo. If I weren't holding his leash, I might be tempted to run my hand over Thayden's chest.

"Hello," Thayden says, smiling at Mr. Ax. "I'm her fiancé. Wow, do I need to roll my shirt sleeves up? My biceps feel left out."

I choke back a laugh. Territorial Thayden is hilarious. Mr. Ax frowns, swiping at his sleeves until they cover his arms again.

"I think I've seen you around the gym," Mr. Ax says.

They're shaking hands now, shaking and shaking, and I swear Mr. Ax winces. I could call Thayden off, tell him to stop being such a jealous caveman, but I'm shamelessly basking in it. I wonder how he'd be with a woman he *really* wanted to marry. That thought sobers me up a little bit.

But only a little bit. Because I'm the one Thayden is holding tight. He's jealous of me talking to other men. I can just pretend that all of this is normal. It's real. We are an engaged couple with no roommate contract. No complications.

"Yes. I work out with Harper Graham," Thayden says. "Heard of her? Trains all the elite athletes."

"I think maybe I have."

He hasn't. It's clear. I almost feel sorry for this guy. The other firemen are rolling the hose back up, putting away their gear and their flirty smiles. They're like wolves smelling the alpha's pheromones in the air, backing down with their bellies low to the ground.

"I guess we'll just be on our way, then."

"Oh? I thought you had questions? My fiancée said things looked serious and you were concerned."

Thayden glances at me, brushing hair off my cheek. I want to lean into his touch, to climb him like my own personal extension ladder. I flutter my eyelashes instead, pleased when he leans in to kiss my lips again. Was I really the one to put limitations on the physical touching? I should rethink that. Or, Thayden and I need to spend more time in public, so he can freely kiss me like this.

The fireman begins backing away. "Oh. No. We were just … checking the equipment."

"The equipment needs checking on my lawn?"

"We'll be getting out of your way," Mr. Ax says.

"Yes, you probably better," Thayden says.

"Thank y'all," I say sweetly, but Mr. Ax ducks his head, slinking away. In moments, the truck rumbles away.

I expect Thayden to let me go, but he spins me, pulling me flush with his chest. The green of his eyes is a stormy sea, and my breath hitches. He pulls one hand away from my waist to tuck a strand of wet hair behind my ear.

"What am I going to do with you?" he murmurs.

"Not let me cook anymore?"

He hugs me close, my cheek pressed to his chest where the

steady thump of his heart matches the melody playing in my own chest. With one hand on my waist and the other cupping the back of my head, he's made me a very willing prisoner.

"I'll make every meal for you if you want. Breakfast, lunch, and dinner. I don't need to go to work. I'll just stay here and be yours."

He says the words with such passion and such sincerity that it takes my breath away. Is that true? Has he changed his mind about what he wants in the future? Have *I* made him change his mind about marriage? The thought is too unbelievable, too much what I *want* to be true.

"Thayden—"

"I know. I know."

Abruptly, he releases me, stepping back a few paces. I hate the distance between us. I watch as he visibly reins in his emotions, finally settling on a familiar teasing smile that's somehow missing the true depth of his happiness.

"I'll let you be and get back to work."

I don't want him to go. I don't know how to tell him. My emotional center feels off-balance, or off-line. Off-*something*, for sure. I just stand there, gaping at Thayden as he walks backwards, away from me, toward his car. The driver's side door is still hanging open.

That roguish grin still in place, dimple in full effect, Thayden points a finger at me. "None of that counts against me."

"What?"

"The touching. We're in public. So, don't think you get free rein to smack me a bunch of times or kick me in the shins later. We're even Stevens."

My stupid roommate contract. Ridiculous rules. I thought they'd keep me protected, give us—give *me*—some safety from this man stealing my heart. But since we made them,

I'm basically thinking about them all the time, thinking about how I can violate them, most especially. Loopholes, indeed.

I'm not protected at all. In fact, each morning I wake up in his house, each time I meet his eyes and see his face, hear the rumble of his voice, whether he's serious or teasing or anything at all, I'm just falling further and faster and harder.

My smile fades as he blows me a kiss, hops in his car, and drives back to his work.

CHAPTER TWENTY

Thayden

APPARENTLY, registering for wedding gifts is a rite of passage. One that Gavin says I'm going to hate, except for the gun. Whatever *that* means. But time with Delilah is time with Delilah, so I refused her suggestion to set it up online. In person, baby. In. Person.

My mother suggested Crate & Barrel, but Delilah has me in a packed Bed, Bath, & Beyond. On a Saturday. Not something I've experienced before, and not something I want to experience again. It's the kind of thing I'd wish on my enemies. Except that I have Delilah at my side. We could be touring a sewage treatment plant and I would be A-okay.

"They have the best return policy," she said earlier with a shrug.

That shouldn't have made my insides recoil, but it did. Maybe I'm just being sensitive, but I can't help but think about the fact that at the end of a year of marriage, she plans to return me.

Not if I can help it. But I really need to get on with telling her that. These gestures only go so far, and my words haven't been doing the job. Are there life coaches who can help you tell someone you love them? Probably at least some solid YouTube channels. I'll get on that later.

Apparently, the computers that let you do this yourself are broken, so we have to deal with a human. And there is a long line to set up the registry, because apparently, every engaged couple is registering today.

And all of them but us look starry-eyed and giddy. Except for the one guy whose fiancée practically dragged him in by his ear. That guy looks like he's about to either throw up or make a break for a rideshare to another city. Maybe another state. I sort of feel like we're cattle in the shute, waiting to be branded.

"And when is the big day," a woman asks wearily when it's finally our turn.

"Two weeks," Delilah says. "November third."

The woman, who looked half asleep suddenly is on high alert. "So soon?"

Not soon enough. After never having a serious relationship, you'd think I would be running away from marriage, not wishing we could move the date up. Every day we don't get hitched is another day Delilah could change her mind.

"Yes. We're very excited," Delilah says. "We just don't want to wait!"

She elbows me in the side. I grin, because that pointy elbow will get me a hug, hand hold, or cuddle on the couch.

"Absolutely. I'd marry her today if she didn't mind just going to the courthouse."

True story.

"He's just so irresistible," Delilah coos, linking her arm through mine.

I stare down at her, wishing that I didn't read humor glinting in her eyes. I love her teasing, but I want those words to be true.

A few minutes later, we've been handed the guns Gavin mentioned, which are essentially the tool employees use to stock shelves and do inventory. It's not until I scan my first bath towel with a satisfying beep that I understand the appeal.

"Sweet," I say, staring at the little screen.

"Do you even want that towel? It's chartreuse."

"It's what?"

"The color." She taps the towel, which is green. Not whatever she just said. Delilah wrinkles her nose. "Ew. And it's not soft. Let me show you how to undo it."

I keep a firm grip on the gun, which means Delilah has to lean close to push a few buttons. I try to smell her hair without being obvious about it. Hopefully, I don't *accidentally* scan more bad towels and need her to do this again.

"Got it?" she asks.

"Yep. Lead the way. Where do we start?"

She eyes the aisles, which are jam-packed with families and blue carts. "Kitchen, then general household, bathroom, and we'll end in the bedroom."

"I like the sound of ending in the bedroom," I say, only because I know it will earn me a smack on the arm.

Instead, she goes for the back of my head.

"That's ten minutes of cuddling," I say, pulling out my phone to make a note. Like I'd forget.

"Five. I think you're misremembering the fine print."

"And I'm thinking you didn't read the addendums. Cheap shots to the head or groin count extra."

Delilah groans. "You're impossible."

"Impossibly charming. You said so yourself."

An elbow to the ribs is another five minutes. Forget bath towels and appliances. I plan to rack up the time today. We've started watching Netflix together at night, and I would love nothing more than to have her in my arms for all forty-seven minutes of that stupid British cooking competition she loves.

An hour later, we've barely made it to the bathroom section. There have been several minor arguments, and one actual scuffle when she tried to forcibly pry my gun from my hands. All I did was try to scan a whole shelf from the As Seen on TV section. Some of those gadgets actually looked useful!

I'm weary, tired of being run into by carts and hearing whining children, but I've earned myself almost a whole British cooking show of cuddle time. Delilah is exhausted, but I've been keeping her alive by passing her gummy bears out of an industrial-sized bag I found on an endcap. She let me feed her the last one with my fingers. So, while I hate this store, I'm in no hurry to leave.

There's nothing I really need, so I follow along, noting what Delilah likes. She tends to start with what she really wants, but then she scans the cheaper version. When she's not looking, I use my gun to remove the cheaper item and replace it with the one that made her bite her lip and stare with dreamy eyes. I feel like she does this with the rest of her life as well. She knows what she really wants, but is afraid to go for it, settling for something that's just ... okay. I'd like to see that change. I want her to dream big and feel deserving of those dreams.

I watch her study a row of bath mats. If I could, I would run this scanner over Delilah, locking every feature into my personal wish list. Her golden hair—scanned with a beep. *Mine.*

The delicate line of her neck. Beep. *Mine.*

I would crouch down and scan her delicate ankle, the one with the half-moon scar close to her heel.

I want to hold the gun over the shell of her ear, which holds my attention for far longer than it should. So many women have pierced ears—why doesn't Delilah? It sparks a rabid curiosity and also makes me want to take the lobe gently between my teeth.

I wonder if I could add that to the roommate contract ...

I would scan things below the surface too. I want to capture the fierceness that seems woven into her very joints. I'd scan her sweetness, something I usually see her bestow on others, almost never on me. I'd let the little red light flash over her memories, one by one by one. I want them all. Mine, mine, *mine.*

I want all of *her.* If I thought I could keep her, I would hoist her over my shoulder, deposit her in one of the wonky blue carts, and sprint out of the store, pushing her toward home. *Our* home.

"Is this ugly?" Delilah moves in front of me, holding up a yellow ceramic elephant.

"It's ... yellow. What's it for?"

She turns it over in her hands. "I think it's a soap dish."

"Must not be a very good one if you can't tell for sure. Do I need a soap dish?"

"You need some color in your house."

"*Our* house."

My emphasis on the word startles her. She blinks hard, twice, then shoves the questionable yellow soap dish on a shelf. Feigning a casual gait, she browses away from me, moving down the aisle.

"It's *our* house, Delilah."

"It's *your* house. I'm just a ... temporary houseguest."

I stalk after her, resisting the urge to smash the yellow elephant as I pass by the shelf. "You should think of it as ours. Because it is."

I take a chance and brush her hair over one shoulder, revealing her neck. I want to press my fingertip to the top of her spine, then move down over the slope of her shoulders. I want to trace and study every line and curve.

"I think of it that way," I murmur, leaning close enough that she has to feel my breath on her skin.

She spins, her fiery eyes meeting mine. "Is that really how you think of it?"

"Yes."

I hold her gaze like a man gripping a rope as he dangles over a canyon. "That's how I want to think of it. And how I'd like you to think of it."

"I didn't pay for it. I'm not paying rent."

"Don't care."

"I hardly do anything to earn my keep."

"You're not little orphan Annie, having to slave away for cold porridge."

"What?"

I shake my head. "Mom's favorite movie," I mutter. "The classic, not the updated version."

"Haven't seen either."

"The three of us will have a movie night and remedy that."

She ignores me and presses on. "My name isn't on the title."

"Do you want it there? Let's go to my office now. We'll write up the paperwork." I'm being serious, and she knows it.

Her eyes go wide, and her head is shaking. "Thayden, no."

"Why not? What would it take to make you feel at home? Like it's your home too?"

What would it take to make you know that you're mine?

"Nothing. I—"

Laughing a little, she swats at my arm. Another five minutes tonight. And she knows it too, seeing my expression shift into something slightly smug. I know I'm not going to convince her about the house, at least not yet, but I can still celebrate the fact that I've earned so many minutes today. Small wins.

Delilah grumbles something darkly that sounds like—and probably is—a Shakespearean insult, maybe mixed with something deeply Southern. *Fie* and *forsooth* were both definitely in there and *tarnation* too.

"What did you say?" I ask.

"Hm? Oh, nothing. I think I'm done in the bathroom area. Almost finished!"

Which means it's time to look at bedroom things, and now I'm thinking about Delilah and bedrooms. I can't be thinking about that, at least ... not yet. There are a few important conversations we need to have before that would ever be on the table.

Like one where I actually tell her how I feel, and that I want this marriage to be real. So far today, she's rejecting anything that looks like real interest from me, anything that would push us past the realm of fake relationship into a real one. I'm trying to give her time, but we don't have an abundance of it.

"What do we need for the bedroom?" I ask.

Pillows are piled high and the shelves filled with sheets go above my head. Delilah stops in the middle of an aisle, then hesitates, scuffing her toe along the ground. Her mood has shifted again, her fire dimming.

"Hey, D. What is it?"

"It's ... nothing."

"You can tell me anything."

"I like my bedroom," she starts, sounding softer and less confident than I've ever heard her. "I love what you did to make me feel welcome."

Knowing it will knock off some of my couch time later, I sling an arm around her shoulders. "I know you do. Now, what else do you want? Just ask and it's yours."

She looks up at me, her eyes still a gorgeous blue under these regrettable store lights. "I don't want to sound ungrateful."

"You won't. You don't."

"You went to so much trouble to make my room perfect. And I don't want to waste money or be a diva."

"D, whatever you want, you can have it."

I'm not sure why this is hard for her. She knows money isn't an issue for me. Everything in this place is on sale, and we're talking about other people buying it for us anyway. She could scan half the building and it wouldn't matter. We could leave and go straight to the furniture store and buy a whole new set. I'd do it.

Delilah doesn't move, frozen with her eyes on the dirty floor and the scanner in her hands. This is much bigger than a wedding registry, than wanting new sheets or a framed art print. I know this, I can *feel* it, but I don't know why. It's another one of those mysteries about her that I want to find out.

Curling my arm tighter around her shoulders, I lead her down an empty aisle until we're nestled out of sight by a hanging display of curtains and a rack of alarm clocks.

"Hey. Delilah, look at me."

There's a firm set to her shoulders and a tightness to her jaw. With hands gentler than I've ever used, I brush fingertips over her cheeks, cupping her jaw, urging but not forcing her to meet my gaze.

When she does, she's fighting to blink back tears. The sight makes me split in two—one half a vengeful warrior wanting to slay what hurt her and the other a tender man I've never been before, one who wants to hug away her sorrows.

"This—what's on this gun—is more than I've ever had." She shakes her head, laughs a little. "I mean, ever. You could add everything up and this is still more. I didn't have a shower caddy when I started college."

I don't know what the heck a shower caddy is—I can only think of golf caddies and I know that's not what she means. It's also not the point. This is guilt. This is shame. This is feeling like she doesn't deserve nice things.

I've been so spoiled. Though I've appreciated the things I've had all my life, I didn't question them. I haven't lacked. In the shadows of Delilah's eyes, I see longing, the echo of want and need. Without details, she has just now told me more than I knew about her childhood situation. Convincing her she's worth a thousand Bed, Bath, & Beyonds is going to require a careful touch.

"People are happy to celebrate with us. You're helping them know what you want, what they could give."

"But this isn't real." Her smile tips up, then collapses on itself. "They're buying gifts for the sake of a lie."

I'm so tired of the way she thinks of this as a lie. I've basically given up my dignity, given up on any hope of defying my father's wishes. I'm not thinking of him at all anymore. Only Delilah. Only, ever her.

Simple attraction has moved firmly into something that is so unfamiliar that it just might be love. And I'm realizing it right here in this stupid store.

I can't help my reaction. I lean in, sweeping my lips over hers. One brush, then two, lingering when she doesn't shove me away.

She exhales a contented sigh, and I let my lips claim hers in a kiss that's probably breaking some kind of store policy.

No, it's *definitely* breaking store policy. Especially when she shoves me. Away, I think at first with disappointment almost crushing me, but no—she's pushing me back into the curtain display, following me in.

There is the sound of metal rings scraping over the display bar and then the curtains close around us. We're in the semi-dark, everything smelling of new fabric, and Delilah attacks me, kissing me like this is a battle she plans to win.

But I've got my own competitive streak. We're kissing like this is a continuation of some earlier argument and both of us need to get in the last word.

Fine by me, because her lips are on mine and her hands are in my hair. She smells like forever, *my* forever, and my palate is ruined by the taste of her lips. Food and drink will always be bland now, because I've had *Delilah*.

At least, until she grabs me by the shoulders and shoves me again. This time, she steps back. Her eyes are wild and startled in the dim light. Like mine, her breathing is ragged and rough.

Way too easily, she composes herself, smoothing her hands down her clothes like she didn't just shove me into a curtain display and kiss me like we were teenagers.

"There went all that cuddle time you were saving up," she says lightly.

Her hand is on the edge of the curtains. I don't want her

to open them. I don't want the harsh lights beating down on this moment, washing it away. I don't want her to dance just out of reach again.

"Delilah," I say. It's *all* I can say.

It's not enough. She shakes her head slightly, and opens the curtains, disappearing into the aisle and leaving me in the dark.

I run my hands through my hair, then smooth it down. This isn't a loss. It was a step forward. A big one.

And then ... ten steps back.

Still, I felt the passion and urgency in that kiss. It matched mine. It's there. That thought makes me step out, blinking at the store, which is no less ugly than it was moments ago.

Delilah hands me back my gun. I guess I dropped it? I don't even remember.

Knowing it's what she needs right now, I give her my best rakish grin. "So, can I upgrade my cuddle time for kissing time now? Okay. Done."

Her finger finds my chest, and she jabs. I'm going to have fingerprint bruises all over my body, and I'm going to be the happiest man around.

"Not a chance. This was a one-time violation."

I grab her hand, pulling her toward me until our chests are touching. "Don't tell me you didn't love it."

She says nothing, but the flush in her cheeks and the widening of her pupils tell me everything.

"A one-time violation. Don't make me add addendums of my own," she says. "You wouldn't like them."

"Maybe I would. Maybe I like everything that comes with you. The whole package." Again, I'm telling her the truth, just as I did that day the fire department came. I'm not sure if she doesn't hear the truth in it or if she doesn't trust me.

Maybe, because of my inexperience with all of this, I'm just doing it wrong. I mean, who declares love in the aisle of this ridiculous store?

Delilah wiggles out of my grasp, which seems to be the theme of my life these days, and gets back to scanning like the conversation and the kiss never happened.

I follow her as she silently studies sheets and pillows, testing things with her fingertips, smelling a set of blankets before aiming the gun at them.

When she excuses herself to use the restroom at the end, I return the guns and get a printout of our registry. After the bathroom, Delilah was going to find new cookie sheets, which she insists on buying me. With a coupon.

"It's a little light," the woman says. "Are you sure that's everything?"

I scan the list. It's not nearly enough. This whole store wouldn't be enough for Delilah.

"For now," I say, then have a realization. "Actually, could you do me a favor?" I pull out my wallet and slap the card on her desk. "Go ahead and buy it all. Put it on this card."

Her eyes widen. "Everything?"

"You said it felt light," I say. "Now it's too much?"

She purses her lips. "Are you sure?"

"She's all that matters," I tell her. "I want her to have it all. But she'll be back any minute, so get my card number and run everything later. I'll sign what I need to."

Nodding, she enters the information into the computer, while I mentally hurry her along before Delilah finds out what I've done.

I'm going to keep pushing her, keep pursuing her, and keep spoiling her until Delilah stops thinking that she doesn't deserve every single thing I want to give her.

CHAPTER TWENTY-ONE

Delilah

WHEN THAYDEN SLAMS into the house a few days later, I drop the book I'm reading, wincing as it lands page down on the floor. Total book crime. Not as bad as dropping it in the bathtub or intentional bending the corner of a page down in lieu of a bookmark, but still. The pages of *Mrs. Dalloway* are creased when I pick it up and set it carefully on the table.

I can hear him cursing and banging around in the kitchen, so I trail after Apollo, watching as Thayden takes out his frustrations inside the fridge.

"Rough day at the office, *honey?*" I lean on the doorframe, doing my best June Cleaver voice. Not that I honestly know what June Cleaver sounds like. Just that she's apparently the epitome of a housewife.

Me? I'm a joke of a housefiancée.

Thayden spins, looking shocked. His features relax when

he sees the tilt of my teasing smile.

"I thought—" He shakes his head. "Never mind. Yes. Today sucked."

I watch as he pours a glass of orange juice and slams it back like he's at a bar. What is it about watching a man's throat as he drinks that's so sexy? I noticed that the night he came into my room for that terrible serenade. I'm beginning to suspect that everything Thayden does has this effect on me.

Now, more than ever. If you don't want to fall in love with a man you're attracted to, you shouldn't live with him. Actually, in some cases, that might be just the ticket. You'd see all the dirty laundry, everything hanging out in the comfort of home and get over it, right quick.

But living with Thayden? The man is a splinter. He used to make me uncomfortable, and I happily would have yanked him out of my life. Now, though, I've seen even more of the man's character, the good, solid stitches in his fabric. I *like* him. More than that, I enjoy being around him. I feel bereft when he leaves for work, and I sit on the couch, pretending I'm not waiting as excitedly as Apollo, who starts pacing around five o'clock, even though it's been much later since Bed, Bath, & Beyond.

I would think the man is avoiding me after that life-altering kiss if he weren't working that big case with Duke. In truth, I avoided him a little after that. It was too much. He's too much.

I'm set up to marry a man I really adore, while knowing he didn't want to get married. Not by contract, not ever. Even if he's attracted to me and likes me, and sometimes says super sweet things that make my heart want to burst.

While I'm still staring (fine—I'm *ogling*), Thayden sheds his suit jacket, tossing it over the island toward a stool. It slips off, puddling on the floor. I step forward, shaking it off and draping it over the stool. And when I look up, Thayden has lost his tie, probably thrown in another corner of the room, and has unbuttoned the top half of his shirt, revealing the planes of his chest and the dip between his collarbones.

The man is like a pie set out in a window to cool, and I want to take a big bite.

Instead, I sit on the stool next to his jacket, watching him scroll through messages on his phone, wondering what went on at work. He almost never talks about his job, but for the past few weeks while he's been in court, his mood has gotten darker and darker. I can almost imagine a tiny storm cloud hovering over his head.

"Wanna talk about it?" I bite back the *darlin'* that's on my tongue. For anyone else, it would be a normal token of affection. With Thayden, I hold back.

"Not really."

"Okay." I start to get up, but he shoves his phone across the sleek white marble. I have to stop it from going over the edge. Already, it's lighting up with texts that look work related. Not that I took more than a peek. But it is comforting that it's not other women.

"I'm sick of it," he says, and I settle more firmly in my seat, waiting.

He drags his big hands through his hair, then grips the counter. For once, the strands don't settle back into place, and I fight the urge to crawl across the counter and smooth it back down.

"I hate my job. Everything about it. I hate what I do, who I represent. I hate the lies, the pageantry."

His eyes flick to me at that last word, like he's insulted me by insulting pageants somehow.

I shake my head. No love lost between me and pageants.

"Go on." I wave a hand. "Let it out."

"Do you ever wonder what you're doing with your life?"

I try not to smile, but it doesn't work. "I'm twenty-three. My *job* is taking care of your dog and marrying you for a year. So, um, yes. I've questioned my life choices a time or two."

His lips twitch, but his eyes look sad. "You've never told me. What do you want to do?"

I swear, he started to say when you grow up, and I definitely would have thrown the man's phone at him. But he stopped himself, and he's being vulnerable. Might as well try it out myself.

"Academia," I say, shifting my weight a little. The stool suddenly feels too small, too hard, too ... something. "I want to be a literature professor."

For a moment, he looks shocked. Then, I can see him thinking, and he finally nods. That little gesture calms the wild staccato of my heart.

This is the first time I've admitted it out loud, other than that one time, to my advisor, who had explained how rigid the world of academics is. How it's not for everyone. Aka— not for little ol' me.

Thayden raps his knuckles on the counter. "I could see that. You would be amazing. All you do is read books that look like they come from school-assigned reading lists."

I grin, trying to hide how much his words mean to me. "I read other stuff too."

Thayden leans on his elbows, bending his whole body toward me. "Like what? Do you have a secret stash of bodice rippers hidden under your bed?"

"What's a bodice ripper?"

"You've never heard that term?" he asks.

I shake my head, and he grins.

Standing up to his full height, Thayden unbuttons his

shirt and pulls it open, flexing. He isn't wearing an under-shirt today, which means there is a lot of tantalizing skin on display. Whatever a bodice ripper is, sign me up!

"You know, those romance novels where the guy is all, like this, and the woman's all"—he pulls his shirt tight around the waist, and with his other hand, opens the V of his shirt feigning cleavage—"like this."

He flutters his lashes, and I laugh so hard I almost fall off my stool. He relaxes the pose, grinning at me and leaning on his elbows again. I don't mind one bit that he hasn't buttoned his shirt back up.

"No judgment if you do read them," he says. "My grandma loved them."

I laugh even harder. "No!"

"Yup. Kept stacks of them under her bed, just behind the dust ruffle. It's a grandma thing. Though they're very educational for young men too."

My laughter chokes to a stop. "You didn't steal and read your granny's romances!"

"Okay. I didn't."

"Thayden!"

"What? You should be glad. I mean, the things I know now—" He grins like he's auditioning for the role of the sexy villain in a movie, wicked and irresistible.

I scream and cover my ears, even though I'm hot under the collar and really, *really* want to hear the end of that sentence. What things *does* he know now?

I drop my hands when he stops talking, still grinning at my reaction. I could confess to my occasional reading of para-normal romance—who can resist a hot fae male? Not this girl —but decide to stop while I'm ahead. I turn things back to him.

"Why don't you quit?" The smile drops from his face, and

Thayden just stares.

"What?"

I shrug. "You hate your job. Quit. Let it go. Find a new thing. Or start your own firm, doing things the way you like."

I know he has to have considered this. Whatever else the man might be, he is logical. But I swear, it's like I've just told him there's a colony on Mars. I've hit a nerve, ending the light banter and sweet back-and-forth.

"I can't."

I say nothing. He has family money. I don't know how much, but I do know it's enough that he could probably not work again and be just fine. I shouldn't be surprised. After all, he agreed to marry me in order to take over the family firm.

Should I even be encouraging this? Because if he quits, he doesn't need to marry me, which means I don't get the money. The rest of the payout, which is set to be delivered after the wedding. Would I have to give back what I already paid down on my loans?

My chest is suddenly burning, and I rub a hand over my breastbone, trying to soothe the ache. No, even if I'd have to pay Thayden back, I'd rather encourage him to do what he wants than to keep him trapped in this arrangement he's never seemed too keen on.

"Why don't *you* go back to school?" he asks, and I neither like the sharpness to his tone nor the accusation beneath it.

Maybe the accusation is my own, and I'm just hearing an echo there, the word *coward* whispered on the wind. The burn behind my ribs shifts toward anger, not worry. I'm suggesting a course of action for him out of goodness, and he's tossing my ambition at me like a barb. If that's how he wants to play things, fine.

I stand, smoothing down my skirt. Apollo appears, or

maybe he was there all along, and leans into me. My hand finds his ear, rubbing in that familiar way that's become like a reflex.

"We've got marriage counseling to get to," I say. Neither one of us is thrilled about this, which is a requirement of the man Elizabeth found to do our ceremony. "And then dinner at Zoey and Gavin's."

Somehow, I'm looking forward to the dinner even less. I don't know if it's Thayden's mood, or the fact that it's hard to pretend in front of my friends I'm not falling in love with this man more every day.

"Right." Thayden straightens and turns away from me, heading for the laundry room.

"Meet me at the car in ten minutes," he calls back over his shoulder, making me feel like an errant child.

"Fine."

"Fine."

———

The only thing more awkward than the car ride on the way to the reverend Billy Blanks's office in a nondescript building is the silence when the good reverand dives right into questions we don't have answers to.

Like the doozy he opens with: "Would you rather start with money or sex?"

He smiles at our shock, probably used to it if he starts all his sessions in such a way. I narrow my eyes, studying his shiny, bald head and his black, pleather vest. He has a baby face, and I don't mean in the regular way. His face is moon-like, puffy and round and as smooth as the shiny, white dome of his head. It's like someone took an infant's head, resized it, and plunked it down on top of this lumpy body.

I'm not sure where Elizabeth found this guy, but I know she was desperate with the short timeframe. She was able to plan so much in so short a time but finding someone to marry us gave her a lot of trouble. The plaque on his desk says Billy Blanks, Reverend at Large. Is that a thing? And doesn't some famous fitness guy share the same name? IS this the famous fitness guy? I wonder if I can do a discrete Google search or send a picture to Harper.

"Why would you ..." Thayden coughs, leans forward in his chair, and does his best to pretend I'm not here. I wouldn't have been surprised if he cupped his hand around his mouth like he's telling a secret. "Why start there?"

The rev, which seems like a suitable name for the man, only smiles. "Those tend to be the biggest points of conflict in a marriage. I don't like wasting time, and the wedding is a little over a week away. No point in beating around the bush. Sex or money? Or, we could always start with family history?"

"Money!" we both say at the same time, practically at a shout.

After exchanging a quick glance, Thayden and I both go back to pretending like we don't see each other. The tension from our conversation in the kitchen still lingers, and I hate it.

I sniff. "We can start with money. Though we're just fine."

Thayden's head whips to me, and the rev smiles even wider. On anyone else, that response might make me storm from the room, but there's something genuine about the man. And I've seen my share of disingenuous church people, so I'm good at sussing out the difference.

"That's an interesting statement. Thayden, do you agree? Should we move on because money isn't an issue for you?"

"No."

Now my head jolts, and my eyes are beady slits before I've even turned them on Thayden. I can't explain the reason for my immediate anger at his response.

"What do you mean, no? No, it's not an issue or no, you don't agree?"

"I mean ..." Thayden pauses, licks his lips, and then speaks carefully, like he's weighing out his words ounce by ounce on a digital kitchen scale. "I mean, things are fine now in both those departments, but I wouldn't say money isn't an issue. I think we could head future conflict off at the pass by addressing it now. In a safe space. With a neutral party to ... referee."

Oh, he's gonna need a referee. I'm fixing to red-card my way right off the field.

"Delilah? Are you amenable to that idea?"

I answer because he used the word *amenable*, a vocab word I remember from ninth grade. "Fine."

The rev turns back to Thayden. "Why don't you start? What makes you want to discuss money? Are there potential problems you could see down the line?"

I cross my arms. *Yeah, buddy. Go ahead and start. Hit me with a list of those potential problems.*

Thayden stares down at his hands, big and awkward in his lap, like he doesn't know what to do with them. I'm doing my best to watch him while studying the Pink Floyd poster above the rev's desk. Now, why does he have a Pink Floyd poster in the office where he's doing marital counseling?

"I guess ... I've often dated women who were interested in my money. And only my money."

My cheeks are two red suns, blazing with jealousy and an anger stemming from I don't know where.

239

"Delilah, that seems to have gotten a reaction from you. Want to share?"

What I want to do is smack that smile off the rev's smooth cheek. This isn't preschool show-and-tell. No, I do not want to share that I feel immediately jealous of those women he's *often* dated, or the shame from knowing I am, quite literally, marrying him for money. This whole conversation is making me sweat. So, yeah, maybe I have some deeper money issues.

For a moment, the room is silent. I stare at a potted plant on the corner of the desk. It's in serious need of water. When I say nothing, Thayden continues.

"Delilah seems opposed to me buying her things, to me treating her like I want to treat her. If I offer to pay for something, she resists, even if she needs help and I'm more than happy to offer it with no strings."

I think of him fixing Annabel Lee. The meals he's ordered for me when I'm at his house alone, the room makeover before I moved in. The man certainly has tried to spoil me. And he's right. As much as I secretly love it, I've resisted.

"Money is, and has always been, an issue for me." I swallow past the thickness in my throat, then meet Thayden's eyes. "But I was never interested in you for your money."

The green in his eyes seems to glow, brightening to the gleam of emerald. He nods, lips twitching like there's a smile he's holding captive.

"I guess I'm just not used to people doting on me. And I'm not used to a lifestyle where money isn't an issue, where you weren't having to count change down to the penny to make sure you could afford to pay rent. It's an adjustment."

"Good, good," the reverend says. I almost forgot he was here. "Thayden has admitted insecurities about being used.

You've shared that your past financial situation impacts you even now. Any fears or insecurities about marriage, Delilah?"

Where should I start the list? With my trust issues or the fact that I saw so many terrible relationships playing out right in front of me? Now, there are added fears, specific to Thayden. That this marriage on paper is really written more on my heart. Which means at some point, probably when the lines between real and fake blur more than they have, this man is going to break me.

"I, um, didn't have an example of a healthy relationship growing up." I can hear my accent slipping, like it's been let out of its cage. I can only hold back so much at a time. "I didn't know my father. And my mama went through men like a box of tissues. I didn't want that for myself, but I ..."

The thick rug under my feet suddenly needs my attention. I can see the lines from where someone has vacuumed recently. They missed a spot, where a dust bunny the size of my fist blows softly in the breeze from the AC vent. I didn't want to talk about this. Why am I talking about this?

But when no one speaks, I flex my fingers and continue.

"I won't be my mama. I only want to do this once. And I want to get it right."

Except ... the very fact that we're here in the office means that I've broken my own promise to myself, the one I made on a star so long ago. Mercutio is dying somewhere, probably calling out a plague on both our houses for this.

Out of nowhere, Thayden reaches over and grabs my hand, lacing our fingers together. I'm instantly anchored.

"I want that too," he says.

Does he though? Does he really? I study him, trying to see the truth through his words.

"Well, good. It sounds like you're on the same page," the rev says.

Same page, maybe, but I can't help but wonder if we're holding very different books.

"Perfect." The rev claps his hands. "Now, let's talk about sex. You know what they say: happy wife, happy life." He pauses dramatically. "In bed."

Thayden's hand freezes in mine. I cannot look at him. I cannot look at the rev. I mean, in a normal context, this is a healthy thing to discuss. For couples to discuss. Privately.

Right here, right now? Nope. Not a chance. Not with this questionable reverend and the man with whom this topic is irrelevant.

The rev links his fingers together and stares cheerfully at us across the desk. It's unsettling. What is he a reverend *of*, exactly?

And why didn't I ask this question earlier? It could have saved us from having this awkward exchange.

I am going to fade out of existence, just like that wilting plant on the desk. Maybe that's how it died, listening to this man awkwardly counsel people.

"I don't think ..." Thayden starts.

"Let me press pause."

The rev opens his desk drawer, and I squeeze Thayden's hand because I do not know what he's going to pull out. A pamphlet on sexuality? A Georgia O'Keefe painting? A gun?

A photocopied page looking like it came from an anatomy textbook is not what I expected. I don't even know if it's worse or better than the other options. He presses it into Thayden's hand. At second glance, it looks like one of those fancy adult coloring pages, not a textbook diagram.

Oh wait—it IS a coloring page. Which brings a whole new meaning to *adult* coloring. The rev pulls out a ten-pack of markers next. Crayola washable markers, just like I used as a kid.

Nope. No. Not even a little bit.

We are NOT color coding the finer points of the female anatomy together with a wacko baby-man who I suspect is not a legitimate reverend of anything.

Thayden and I stand at the same time, hands still joined like we're two superheroes ready to fight injustice, not two very uncomfortable people who do not need to color lady parts on a printed paper.

"I think we're done here," Thayden says. "This is highly inappropriate."

The man taps the markers. "But we haven't even—"

Before I can blink, Thayden calls out a rushed goodbye, and yanks me toward the door. No need to tell me twice. I'm hot on his heels, slamming that door closed forever.

We run, not walk, down the hallway, and Thayden crumples up the coloring page in his hand, lobbing it at the first trash can we see. It goes right in and sinks to the bottom.

I'm giggling, and Thayden tosses me a boyish grin.

"Well, that was enlightening," he says. "Ready to tie the knot?"

"I feel perfectly prepared for marriage now," I say, laughing harder as we reach the door and push through into the sunlight.

Thayden grabs his phone with his free hand. He still hasn't let go of mine, and honestly, I'll take any touch I can get from him right now, so I don't resist. I hated the way it felt earlier when we weren't speaking. Thayden and I give as good as we get, but most of the time, it's in good fun. When it's real conflict, I hate it.

"Mom?" he says, giving me a side eye. "I don't know where you found the esteemed reverend Billy Blanks, but we're going to need a new minister."

CHAPTER TWENTY-TWO

Thayden

AFTER WADING through various exercise videos from the *other* Billy Blanks, I discover that our newly fired marriage counselor is a reverend of the internet variety. I have no idea how Mom found him, though she swears a friend of a friend vouched for him. I actually applied to become a reverend myself through the site listed in his bio, and once I pay the nonrefundable $49.99, I'll also be a reverend.

A lawyer and a reverend—what a catch I'll be! If only the one woman I wanted to catch would let me.

When Zoey lets us into the house she and Gavin now share, the smell of garlic and ginger have my mouth watering. I guess arguments and then awkward counseling sessions can increase your appetite.

"What is that?" Delilah asks, sniffing the air like a puppy. "Did you cook, darlin'?"

Zoey laughs. "Nope. Indian takeout. I've got a bottle of wine open in the kitchen."

"Yum."

Delilah doesn't wait for me, moving toward the open kitchen like she's sleepwalking. Clearly, our disastrous counseling session and the tense conversation beforehand had zero impact on her appetite.

Zoey touches my arm, and I hang back for a moment. Since what I like to call our *Pride and Prejudice* moment, Zoey has been on my side. But I've also seen her fearsome, angry face. I remember her tossing my clothes in the pool. Zoey is like the ocean, and it is a foolish man who doesn't have respect and maybe a little fear of that.

She studies me, and I have to wonder what she sees.

"Gavin's in the shower. He'll be out in a minute. Everything okay?" she asks. "How's it going?"

I rock back on my heels, almost embarrassed enough to lie. "Not … great. I don't think I'm making much progress."

Unless you count occasional cuddle sessions while watching Netflix, random kisses that we pretend never happened, and hand-holding as we're running away from internet reverends. We've made some forward progress, but I feel more like we're going in circles.

Zoey sighs. "Hang in there. Don't give up."

"I'm not planning to, but I don't have a lot of hope. We make good roommates though. Decent friends."

We'd make better than okay friends if Delilah let me in. But it seems that most of the time, when I try to get to know her better or bring up more serious topics, she manages to deflect. She's like the conversation crossing guard, rerouting traffic around a massive pothole that she doesn't want me to see.

She did tell me what her big goal is today, which honestly

shocked me. Both the dream itself and the fact that she told me. It took me a moment to think about Delilah in the front of a classroom, lecturing with a dry-erase marker in one hand and a projector remote in the other. And then, I could really see it. Maybe a little *too* well, because the mental image of Delilah at the front of a classroom is one I like. A lot.

Talking about future employment plans shouldn't be a big deal, but it was like pulling teeth to get her to admit that, and then she didn't offer anything more, like why she isn't pursuing that path now. If I had to guess, it's money, which is a sticky subject between us already, as evidenced in our counseling session.

Despite his inappropriateness, the Reverend Billy Blanks did have a point starting with money. Delilah may not think she has hang-ups about it, but she does. Big ones. I almost feel like my wealth doesn't work in my favor in terms of an actual relationship. Of course, that same wealth got her to agree to marry me, so it's a real catch-22.

"Come on," Zoey says. "Let's see how dinner goes."

Delilah stares at us with eyes like slits as we walk toward the kitchen, but she doesn't say anything. I'm surprised when she hands me a glass of red wine.

"You look like you could use this," she says.

"Thank you." I take a sip, noticing that Delilah seems to be staring at my throat as I drink. When she catches me watching, her cheeks flush.

"We could both use a drink after that horror show," she mutters, but she's smiling.

"What horror show?" Zoey asks while setting out plates.

"Counseling," Delilah says, sipping her wine and tearing off a piece of naan from one of the bags.

Zoey swats her hands away and lines up all the takeout containers on the counter with serving spoons.

"Marriage counseling?" Zoey asks, glancing at me.

"My mom hired someone to do the ceremony," I explain. "He required at least one session with him beforehand. Which we cut a bit short."

"We also fired him." Delilah turns to me. "Do you trust your mama to find a new one? I'm not so sure."

I pull out my phone and show her the screen, still open to the site where you can make yourself a reverend of whatever. "I could marry us myself once I put in my credit card number."

Delilah just stares at the phone. "Shut the front door."

"It's already shut."

Zoey snorts at my lame joke, and Delilah didn't seem to hear. "How did you find this site?"

"Believe it or not, this is where our esteemed counselor got his license. No big surprise, right?"

"What did he do that was so bad?" Zoey asks, pouring herself a glass of wine.

We exchange a look and immediately burst out laughing. We're still laughing a moment later when Ella comes in from the outside patio.

Delilah stage whispers, "It's not fit for small ears. Tell ya later."

Zoey's eyes go wide. "That bad, huh?"

"That bad," I confirm.

"What was bad?" Gavin asks, emerging from their bedroom and kissing Zoey on the cheek. He kisses Ella's cheek as well before grabbing a glass of wine.

"Their counseling session," Zoey says.

"I hate counseling," Ella says with an eye roll. "Daddy makes me go."

Kids in general make me nervous, but I'll be honest, Gavin's kid terrifies me more than most. I know it's not her

248

fault—it's definitely her mother's—but she's way too much of an adult trapped in a child's body. I'd never tell my best friend that, obviously. Maybe I just need to spend more time around her.

"Mine makes me draw pictures of my feelings. She hasn't figured out that all of my drawings are ironic."

Nope. The more time, the more terrifying Ella is. Gavin and Zoey exchange a look over Ella's head.

"How's your music career, sugar?"

Ella brightens, losing that cynical stoniness. "I'm singing for another wedding this month, and I've been asked to play at a festival." Her face darkens slightly. "For children. But I'm the only non-adult performer."

"I'm so proud of you," Delilah says, giving Ella's shoulder a squeeze.

We fill plates, buffet-style, and move to the big dining table. "This is new." I take a seat next to Delilah and across from Gavin. Ella sits at the head of the table, like a tiny queen.

"I didn't really need a big table before." Gavin smiles at Zoey, and I won't roll my eyes. I won't. They're still in the honeymoon phase of things, and besides, I'm truly happy that they found each other.

Suddenly, the thought that *I'm* about to be in my honeymoon phase hits me.

I haven't even told Delilah about the honeymoon yet, mostly because I'm afraid she'll say it's too expensive and she can't possibly go. She's probably got a rolodex of excuses all ready for things I suggest. Especially if they involve me spending money.

So, I wouldn't say that I'm planning a kidnapping exactly, but my plans are maybe a little closer to involuntary than I'd like.

"D, we actually wanted to ask for some advice for Ella. You know, about performing and being on stage as a child. That kind of thing," Zoey says.

Delilah sets down her fork, her lips pinching. She hides the expression behind her napkin. "Oh?"

"They don't want me to turn into a monster," Ella says, scoffing. "Like on all those TV shows with the girls who dance and stuff."

Gavin's expression is serious when he looks at Ella. "We are proud of you, and we want you to ... pursue your dreams."

His tone gets a little funny when he says that, and Zoey gives him a small nod. Clearly, they haven't fully been on the same page about this.

The truth is that Ella can sing. When I heard her at their wedding, I almost fell over. She looks like a child, acts like a half-adult with a teenager's attitude, and sings like she's on stage at the CMAs.

Delilah folds her napkin in her lap and smiles faintly at Ella. "What do you want to know, Ella-bell?"

Ella mulls this over, chewing slowly. "I want to be a star." Her gaze slides to Zoey and Gavin. "One who gets there because of talent and grit. And they won't let me if I get all diva-like. Maybe you could help me with that."

I hear Ella mutter, "I'm not a diva," under her breath.

Delilah hasn't said anything, and I'm frankly wondering why Gavin and Zoey are asking. From my understanding, she competed in a some local pageants as a kid. Hardly the same as heading to Nashville, which Gavin has mentioned is Ella's new dream.

Unless Delilah didn't tell me everything. Suddenly, I feel foolish. Because I bet I'm the only one in the room who doesn't know the truth about her competitions.

"Zoey tells me your college tuition was paid for by pageants," Gavin says, when Delilah is still sitting, staring at her wineglass.

That's definitely more serious than a few small competitions. It feels like a stick has been jammed into my chest, lodging next to my heart. Why wouldn't she just tell me? It's not like it's a bad thing. She should be proud of the accomplishments, not playing them down. And why does Gavin get to know?

"Enough to pay for some of my college," Delilah says. Her eyes flick to me, then land on Ella. "The key is to remember that when you're on stage, when you're performing, it's you, but it's also someone else. A … projection of you and who people think you are. But it still needs to be true to you. It's a part of you and should match up, but you should hold enough back to keep from disappearing under all those lights and the weight of other people's opinions."

There's stunned silence for a moment. Delilah takes a shaky breath, then says, "It's a job, and even if you love it, it's not who you are but what you do. Remember that and you'll be fine."

Ella's eyes are wide, like she didn't expect actual advice. I catch movement, Gavin and Zoey, their hands finding each other on the table, squeezing as a look passes between them. So easy. So natural.

I'd like to hold Delilah's hand, but I'm never sure if she's going to bite mine off at the wrist. Still, I can partially see her vibrating with emotion next to me, like something is rattling a door, trying to force it open.

Casually, I slide my hand toward her lap, trying to find hers without accidentally touching her thigh or stomach. I know she'd snap off my hand then.

But I've barely gotten there when her fingers find mine,

grasping and squeezing hard, with a desperation that makes happy, warm feelings expand in my chest. I feel *needed*.

And though what I really want is all of her, not the tiny scraps she's throwing me, I'll take anything I can get.

The rest of the evening passes quickly, and we head out when Gavin and Zoey tell Ella to go brush her teeth. She surprises everyone by giving Delilah a massive hug, one that I'm jealous of.

"Thanks, Auntie D," Ella says. "Goodnight, Uncle T."

My heart climbs my throat like it's a rock wall, grappling for hand and foot holds while I swallow. When Ella skips down the hall, more childlike than I've ever seen her, Zoey sighs, and I see that her eyes are wet. She hugs Delilah next, then shocks me with my own hug.

"Thank you," Zoey says, then clamps her trembling jaw shut and follows Ella.

Gavin looks thoughtful as he walks us to the door, and Delilah and I don't speak until my car is following the twisty road through the hills.

"So," I say, dropping a brilliant conversation bomb into the middle of the car.

"So."

"Today was ..."

"Yeah," Delilah says. She throws her head back and laughs. Then she laughs some more.

I should be turning out of the neighborhood, but I'm stuck at this stop sign, totally distracted by Delilah. I love the unbound version of her, when she lets loose either in laughter or a verbal tirade.

"That was like a real couple date," she says.

I answer carefully, unsure from her tone what she thinks about that. "And no one died. We could make this as real as you want it to be," I say, my tone light.

"I'll bet," Delilah says, scoffing.

I know that I'm a coward for not telling her I mean it. That none of this is fake to me, though it might have started as an arrangement. One I didn't want in the first place but has now provided me with daily access to this woman. It gave me the excuse to be near her, to have her under my roof, to get to know her better. At the same time, she feels somehow further away because of the contracts and papers and agreements between us.

I want to ask her to be mine, for real, but I'm not sure the protocol for asking a woman to go steady when she's already wearing your engagement ring on her finger.

A car honks, making me slam on the brakes.

"Careful there, Danica Patrick," she says.

"Oh, you're comparing me to female drivers now?"

Delilah turns the full force of her glare on me. "What's wrong with being compared to a woman driver?"

"Not a thing. Danica would do laps around me."

"Yeah, she would."

I manage to pull out of the neighborhood, careful this time. "Are you big into NASCAR?"

I've never understood the draw of racing. Or boxing. I'm a baseball and football fan, the pure American stereotype.

"And if I am?"

"I guess I'll need you to teach me what the big deal is."

She makes an irritated sound. I love that sound. I love her irritation, because it's not true irritation. It's flirty. And more than that, it's real *feeling*. I want her to feel everything with me.

"I'm not. But I also don't like football. American football, that is."

"Oh, no—are you one of those?"

She's laughing again, and I want to drive in circles around

253

the city keeping this moment alive. So, I turn the wrong way, heading up the MoPac Expressway, no destination in mind.

"I suppose next you'll tell me you like soccer."

"Hey! I played soccer." She pokes me in the arm. "I'll have you know I was brutal."

"I have no doubt of that. Did you frame all your red cards?"

Delilah shifts in her seat, turning sideways so she's staring at my profile. I feel the sudden urge to run a hand over my face, just to make sure I don't have masala sauce in my beard or something.

"I'm only brutal to you," she says softly. "What do you think that means?"

I bite back what I hope it means, which is that she likes me. If I'm the boy pulling her pigtails, she's the little girl stomping on my foot.

I need to keep my eyes on the road, though I want so badly to look at her. It's probably better I don't, though. Might scare away this honest mood.

"I'm not sure, but I hope you don't stop anytime soon. I happen to love your fire."

The conversation dries up a bit then, but it isn't uncomfortable. When she cracks her window, I do the same. We're off the highway now, driving hilly, country roads. She has to know we aren't headed home, but she only relaxes on a sigh as night sounds fill the car.

Hoping I don't kill the mood, I grip the wheel a little tighter, and say, "That was some good advice back there. For Ella."

Delilah hums a noncommittal response. I'm surprised when she speaks a moment later. "Why don't you just ask the questions that are on your mind?"

I'm not as subtle as I like to think. This woman steals any

bit of game I have. But if she wants direct, maybe this is the time for it. I can't look at her, not without driving off the road. I can't do more than hold her hand either. She's safe, leaning against the cracked window, face shrouded in the dark.

"I get the feeling you hated the pageants, though it also seems you were more successful than I realized."

"I was never Miss Alabama, much to my mama's shame."

We both carry this, the bitter and painful hang-ups about terrible parental figures. It's the first time I've heard her say as much, and I clamp my mouth shut, letting her have the stage.

"I loved the pageants. At least, at first. All the lights, all the attention. I was a little starved for it."

I can almost imagine Delilah as a little girl, preening up under the lights, longing for someone to care about her for more than the show she puts on.

"It was more than that to my mama. I was her ... meal ticket. Her piggy bank, essentially."

I frown. "I thought these were scholarship programs."

"They are—technically. And they can be expensive as all get-out to compete. But there are some cash prizes to be had, plus other endorsements and deals. Mama found a way to make it her business. To make *me* her business. In more ways than one."

She opens her mouth to say something else, but then sighs, leaning her head against the window. I hazard a glance, and she's staring up into the rising moon, which casts a buttery glow over her cheek.

"Ultimately, they got me what I wanted—escape. I won't go back," she says softly, more to herself than me.

Reaching across the console, I touch what I can reach, the inside of her elbow. She doesn't respond by giving me her hand, but she does relax, letting me pull her arm toward me. I trace the crease of her elbow, skating my fingertips over her skin until she shudders.

I know better than to ask anything else, and she's given me more than she usually does, albeit leaving a bunch of blanks I can only guess at. I once wondered how she could understand the dynamics of my family, the manipulations of my father. I realize now that she and I have more in common than I ever would have thought.

We drive like that for another hour, no direction, no destination, until I finally circle back toward home. Pulling in the driveway, I realize that she's fallen asleep.

Being as careful as I can, I manage to carry Delilah upstairs, tucking her into bed, my peaceful, brutal, beautiful fake fiancée.

As she rolls over in bed, without even opening her eyes, she mumbles, "I would have framed my red cards, but they wouldn't let me keep 'em."

I press a kiss to the side of her face, between her cheek and her temple. "I believe it."

From: StuffyLover@DrLove.advice
To: DrLove@DrLove.advice

Dear Dr. Love,

My fiancée is pretty much perfect ... except for one thing. She still sleeps with stuffed animals.

I'm not talking about keeping one or two stuffed animals as keepsakes. She has thirteen stuffies she's had since she was a little girl. And she sleeps with every. Single. One.

We're planning to move in together when my lease runs out, but I can't share the bed with those things. I swear, they're STARING AT ME. I think they see me as a threat.

I want them to go, but she said she doesn't want to "hurt their feelings." I feel ridiculous breaking up with my ideal woman because of stuffed animals, but I just can't do it. Help?

Scared,

Stuffy Lover

From: DrLove@DrLove.advice
To: StuffyLover@DrLove.advice

Dear Stuffy Lover,

First of all, let's clear up a common misconception: Outside of *The Velveteen Rabbit* (one of my favorite books), stuffed animals are not alive. They are not watching you. They do not see you as a threat.

THEY ARE NOT ALIVE.

Still with me? Great.

That said ... it's a little odd that your fiancée still has so

257

many stuffed animals, much less wants to sleep with them. If she thinks getting rid of them or putting them on a shelf will hurt their feelings, maybe you need to remind her of what I told you: they are not alive.

I've never told someone to break it off because of an inanimate object, but honestly, if she is willing to put their "feelings" ahead of yours, you might need to start a new search for the perfect woman.

Oh, and by the way, there's no such thing. You're welcome.

-Dr. Love

CHAPTER TWENTY-THREE

Delilah

"Now, y'all know I have to object to a kidnapping," I say, not objecting at all as Harper ties a silky blindfold around my eyes. I know it had to have come from someone else, because Harpy would have used a sweat-soaked bandana.

"Ow. A little looser there, unless your intent is to Homer me."

"What?" Harper loosens the knot, but only a little.

"No, *who*. He was a blind Greek—oh, never mind. Where we headed, ladies?"

In truth, I wouldn't care where we end up. I hadn't realized how starved I was for my girlfriends until they showed up on Thayden's front porch earlier tonight. I protested, of course, but that only led to them carrying me out to the car.

"Thayden, save me!" I'd cried, but the man only grinned from the front porch, dimple on full display.

"Be good! Remember curfew is midnight!" He waved before shutting himself back in the house.

I wonder what he's doing now. Things have shifted between us since our dinner with Gavin and Zoey. The clock is winding down, and that might be it, but it feels like something bigger.

He made a crack that night about this being as real as I want. It was cruel, because I've come to realize that I want it all. I want *him*. I don't want to give up this life with him. Not at the end of a year. Not ever.

But maybe he wasn't joking. Maybe I'm not the only one who wants something different than when we started. Something more.

It was on the tip of my tongue to ask him, but instead I got as close as I ever have to revealing the source of my biggest shame, my biggest regret. And that will always stay a secret. Unfortunately, one I share with the one person on the planet I can't trust: my mama.

"Yo, D!" Abby tugs a lock of my hair.

"Ow! Yo, what?"

"Just making sure you're with us, not daydreaming about your intended." She's leaning close and I'm thankful no one else can hear her over the music.

"That obvious?"

Abby hoots a laugh. "Didn't think you'd admit it."

That makes two of us.

When we finally get out of the car and the girls tear off the blindfold, we're standing in front of an unfamiliar house. A very large, expensive-looking house. The moonlight glimmers on the lake behind it, and I can almost see the dollar signs hanging in the air.

A rental for the night? I'd suspected as much when I saw

Thayden hand off a duffel bag to Zoey. But I'd been more distracted by the idea that he'd gone through my drawers than to give thought to our destination.

Before I can ask any of the questions forming, the front door swings open. "Come on in, ladies," Elizabeth calls, waving.

I shoot Abs a dirty look, but she only shrugs. "She offered. And look at this place! You think we'd say no? Come on, Miss Priss."

Zoey hands me my bag, and the rest of them start unloading the trunk of Zoey's brand-new SUV.

"Welcome," Elizabeth says, drawing me in for a warm hug.

It's hard to get used to her warmth, to the way she shows affection seemingly without asking for something in return. Other than a hug.

"I hope you don't mind that I'm tagging along. I don't want to stifle your fun."

"I doubt you could, even if you tried. I just hope we don't scandalize you," I tell her.

She laughs. "Nonsense. I could use a good scandalizing. I'm glad you're here.

"Thank you for hosting. And for taking care of all the planning. You are amazing." I really couldn't have done this wedding without Elizabeth. Not just the payments, but all the details. She kept me mostly in the loop, seeming to sense that I wanted some idea of what was going on, but that I was happy to let her take control. Especially because it brought her so much joy.

"You know I didn't mind! It's been my dream."

She squeezes my hand, and I swallow. There's always that little niggle of guilt knowing Thayden and I aren't having a real marriage in the traditional sense. No matter how much I really wish we were.

"Now, come inside. It's criminal that you haven't been here yet. I hope you won't be a stranger."

She turns, grabbing my hand and leading me into a grand foyer with rich hardwood floors and a straight view to the glass windows at the back, looking out over the lake.

"I've also procured a box of Thayden's things and left them in your room for you." Her eyes sparkle, reminding me of a fairy godmother. "I figured you might want to do a little light snooping."

Childhood photos of my Thayden? "Now you're talking."

———

A few hours later, we've enjoyed the pool and hot tub, eaten a lavishly catered and casually served meal, and have showered, returning to the great room in our pajamas, Elizabeth included. Though the silk pajama set she wears looks like it cost a pretty penny.

Harper leans over the back of the couch where I'm sitting to whisper in my ear. "Hey," she whispers. "Don't let this make you feel … pressured."

I turn my head slightly, and her mouth is set in a serious line. Serious even for her. "What do you mean?"

"It's time!" Sam calls, plopping down next to me so close our thighs brush.

I want to grab Harper by the arm and demand she explain, but I suspect I'm about to find out. Too late to make a run for it? Abby plops down on my other side, grinning like the devil. Yep. Too late.

Zoey walks in from the direction of Elizabeth's bedroom, carrying an armful of gift bags.

"Nope. No, you don't." I try to get up but am veritably wrestled back into place. Abby may not be much bigger than me, but she has at least as much gumption, plus Sam on the other side, digging long nails into my thigh. I told them already, multiple times, in fact, that I wanted no showers. No bridesmaids either, just to save everyone money and make the wedding ceremony as simple as possible. That's maybe the only big thing I fought Elizabeth on, and she let me. Now, I've been hoodwinked into a shower by them all.

"Ow! Fine!"

Zoey smiles, setting the gifts down on the tufted ottoman in front of me, while Elizabeth passes out glasses of champagne.

"Now, the first rule of this secret shower is—"

"No talking about secret showers!" Abby says, eliciting a few chuckles.

Sam continues. "The first rule is NO THANK-YOU CARDS."

My mama may have been pure trash, but she was a Southern woman. Thank-you cards are more than an expectation. They just *are*.

"But—"

"No."

I'm surprised at Elizabeth's firmness. Usually, it's the older generation who staunchly insist on this.

"Fine."

"Lie! You agreed too easily," Abby says.

"We thought this might happen," Zoey says. "And we have a contingency plan. Every thank-you note received has a cost. For me, it's babysitting Ella."

That's not so bad.

"For the weekend."

"Uh ..."

Sam grins at me. "For me, it's dealing with my Dr. Love inbox for a week."

"A *week?*"

"A week. Calendar week, not business week. I get an influx on Sundays."

"Doesn't Taylor handle that?" Sam has a fabulous assistant who's kind of an unofficial extra to our tight-knit group.

"I'll give her a paid week off." Sam's grin is wicked.

I glance at Elizabeth, realizing suddenly that Sam just talked about her secret identity. She follows my gaze, waving a dismissive hand. "Elizabeth knows. It's fine. Now, time to open presents!"

It's only when the first gift bag is in my lap, spilling pink glitter all over me, that my hands begin to shake.

"It won't bite," Abby says, knocking her bony shoulder into mine, and spilling glitter over the couch.

My eyes zoom in on the silvery tissue paper. I squeeze the sides of the bag, hearing it crinkle. I know they all know the truth. This wedding is a sham. An arrangement, as Thayden likes to say. But it's still so far from what Gavin and Zoey had. And from what Abby and Zane will probably soon have. These gifts make me feel, more than ever, like a massive fraud.

"D?" Sam asks.

I can't look at her. I can't look at any of them. Taking a deep breath, I force myself to smile. I can do this.

Just pretend it's your birthday.

Logical Delilah, a little less bitter than she was a month ago, shows up at just the right time. But I can't pretend it's my birthday when I pull a short, silky negligee from the bag. Or the sexy black lace set from the next.

I've been sealed inside a Tupperware container, hearing the laughter and conversation around me as though from a distance. I smile and say thank you as my hands touch these soft, intimate things, meant for a real marriage, a legitimate relationship. It's like I'm glued to a screen where an infomercial plays on a loop, reminding me of that contract meeting, and what I signed away. I've never had anything like these beautiful, sexy nightgowns. I've certainly never worn them for any man, and it's not like I'm going to be wearing them for Thayden. I just don't understand.

It's when I pull out a pink nightgown, full-length but still somehow romantic and sexy, that I find it hard to breathe.

The nightgown falls from my hands. It's so light, I expect it to shift in the air, floating down like a feather. But it just falls, a pink puddle of fabric at my feet.

"I can't," I say, my voice shaking. "I can't."

"You can't what?" Sam asks gently.

I don't even know. Any of it? All of it?

"They're gifts," Zoey says. "We gave them with love. You *can*."

"I can't take them. I can't wear them. I can't pretend anymore."

The room goes still. I'm still staring at the pretty pink fabric, fighting the urge to pick it up off the floor. This pretty nightie doesn't deserve my poor treatment. It's not the nightgown's fault.

There's a creak, a shuffle, and a shift as Sam moves. The sweet scent of roses hits me before Elizabeth's arm goes around my shoulders. I can't help it. My mama issues make me lean into her. She manages to keep me in her arm while picking up the nightgown and smoothing it over my lap.

"Did I ever tell you about Thayden's eleventh birthday?"

I shake my head, sniffing once, and taking a tissue Abby holds in front of my downturned face. "No."

She clucks her tongue. "Well, I'm not surprised you didn't hear it from him either." She laughs softly. "He wanted to go roller-skating. Shocking, considering all his friends were doing laser tag and paintball. Other, more boyish things. But my Thayden wanted a boy-girl roller-skating party."

I smile, because I can see that somehow. A gangly and adorable Thayden insisting on a skating party.

"It became immediately clear, to me at least, why. Her name was Cassandra. Cass, he called her. It wasn't until the end of the night that there was a couples' skate. And my boy practically elbowed people out of the way to get to Cass."

The story is still adorable. But I also have a violent urge to track Cass down and give her hair a good yank.

"It was only one song. She broke his heart a week or so later, by 'going with' some other boy, but it didn't matter."

Oh, it does matter. And I want to yank out two fistfuls of Cass's hair now.

"The point is that my son planned a whole elaborate birthday all around a single goal—to hold Cass's hand during couples' skate."

I wait for a punchline or a life lesson. Hearing none, I shrug. "So, he really liked this Cass girl."

Elizabeth squeezes me closer. "My son really likes *you*, dear. All of the details are just part of the way he protects himself. However this started, it's now all a part of a bigger plan. A real one."

"But he didn't want to marry me. He said he told you that. I was the one who insisted we do the contract."

Elizabeth shakes her head. "My son told me he didn't want to marry you because of his father. He didn't want to trick you or have some arrangement forced on him. He thought you were worth more. But, when given an option to have you any way he could, he took it. You are his Cassandra. And all the plans and papers are just a cover."

While her words are sweet and help soothe the ache, they're coming from his mother. Not from Thayden himself.

But he has told you, love-sick Delilah says. *Remember when he kissed you? When he told you a bedtime story? When he mentioned it being real?*

"If you're pretending," Sam says, using her official Dr. Love voice, "it's pretending that you don't have real feelings for the man. That you don't actually want to marry him."

Sam's right, but that doesn't make me want to smack that self-righteous smirk off her face.

"He's trying to Darcy you," Abby says, and my head snaps up, a jealous snarl on my lips.

Isn't Cass enough? There's a Darcy too?

"Down, girl," Abby says with a laugh. "*Mr.* Darcy."

"What?"

Zoey pipes up. "I came home to find him watching *Pride and Prejudice* with Gavin. Thayden is working on grand gestures."

Harper speaks up. "And small ones."

I look at Harper. There's a challenge in her eyes. Like she's daring me to listen to her, to believe their words.

"We've been helping," Sam says, biting her lip. "Don't be mad."

I'm anything but mad. My brain has broken at these revelations. Like an egg, it's cracked, and I'm leaking yolk on the floor.

Though it's honestly not so surprising my friends have gone Team Thayden. I knew he was getting inside information from them. I just didn't suspect … this. A grand plan to win me over, for real.

"I thought—he said he never wanted to get married."

"That has always been his stance," Elizabeth says. "Until lately. And it has nothing to do with the contract or the firm. It has everything to do with you, my dear."

Elizabeth beams, looking so proud. So … hopeful.

That same feeling, hope, is a small paper boat, bobbing and listing on the water. It's cheerful with its perfectly creased corners, happily moving along.

But the boat is not in a stream. It's in the water running along the gutter, and I see the sewer drain up ahead, ready to suck it down. And are those … yellow eyes??

I never should have let Abby talk me into seeing that Stephen King movie.

I shove away the fear and wrap my arm around Elizabeth, giving her a hug. I want to believe this. I want to believe that underneath it all, this is just a bigger skating rink, another set of plans Thayden has set in place to hold my hand. Maybe I'm not the only one wishing all this were real.

Until he does more than try to *Darcy me* as Abby said, I won't know for sure how he feels, or what this is. I'll still be the boat, on a crash course for the storm drain.

But their words are comforting enough to get me opening gifts again. After taking a few fortifying sips of champagne.

And when I open Abby's gift last, a duct tape negligee she made herself, complete with a little bunny tail, it's just the lightness I need to begin breathing again.

At least, until I remember that I won't get to see the humor and heat in Thayden's eyes as I walk out wearing duct tape lingerie. Because no matter what my friends and Elizabeth tell me, I can't imagine this ever being real, no matter how much I want it to be.

But after opening gifts, we head outside to wind down, and I find myself looking up at the stars, making not a wish, but another promise to myself. Before we say I do, I'm going to confess my feelings, whether he returns them or not. I might make a fool of myself, or ruin the easiness of living together, but I'll never be able to look at myself in the mirror if I don't at least give the truth a chance.

CHAPTER TWENTY-FOUR

Delilah

I HAVE no grand plan when the girls drop me back at home the next evening after a day lying by the pool. Tomorrow is the rehearsal dinner. Our wedding is the day after. Usually, you'd have the kind of talk I want to have when you're dating, not ... NOW.

The whole drive home, I try to come up with words to say to Thayden. I've got nothin'. I figure I'll just go with my strengths and wing it. How hard can it be to burst through the front door and tell Thayden Walker, the handsome, charming, *sweet* millionaire, that I actually want to marry him on our wedding day?

No biggie.

When they pull up to the curb at Thayden's, I break Olympic records sprinting to get my bag out of the back.

"Wow. Are you in a hurry?" Harper asks.

"Something like that."

I've got to see a man about a marriage.

"She must really miss her man," Abby teases. "Go get 'em!"

"Yeah, yeah," I mutter. "Thanks for the bachelorette party, y'all! Even though I told you no gifts!"

"No thank-you notes!" Zoey shouts as I run up the side-walk. Apollo's booming bark sounds from inside and the girls lay on the horn a bunch of times.

Guess there won't be an element of surprise.

I pull out my key, but practically fall inside the house when Thayden opens the door.

"Whoa there," he says, grinning as he catches me by the elbow.

Apollo shoves his way between us, forgetting all polite-ness as he tries to stick his tongue in my mouth. Way to set the mood, buddy.

"Get back," Thayden says, nudging Apollo with his hip. "Let the woman breathe. How are you?"

I'm out of breath, to be honest. Definitely time for some cardio with Harper if running up a sidewalk has me this out of sorts.

"Fine," I say between gasps. This is truly a perfect start to the conversation.

Step one: Prove how out of shape you are.

Step two: Do your best impression of someone going into cardiac arrest.

Step three: Choose one-word answers.

Step four: Confess your undying love?

"Well, come on in. I'll grab your bag. Did you miss me?"

Thayden gently slides the strap from my shoulder. His touch electrifies me, making it even harder to breathe.

I may not have breath, but I do have way too much

courage. Or is it a lack of self-preservation? Either way, I decide to go for it. Because what man can resist a woman who goes for what she wants?

I launch myself at Thayden. "Yes! I missed you!" I say, basically becoming Spanish moss hanging off the tree that is Thayden. He stumbles back a step but manages to drop my bag and wind his arms around me.

"Well, now," he says, the smile thick in his voice and his breath hot on my neck. "I could get used to this kind of welcome home."

"Could you?" I pull back to look at him, and he blinks a little at the expression on my face. "I mean, would you want to?"

A tiny furrow creases his brow. "Yes? I mean, would I want to ... what? What are you asking me, Delilah?"

Now or never, D. Now. Or never.

"Would you want *this*? With me? For real?"

I realize that I'm clutching his shirt in both fists, secure in his hold. I think I've tipped the balance from confident to desperate. Thayden opens and closes his mouth, and I can read the confusion in his eyes.

"I'm doing this all wrong," I say, loosening my fists and smoothing the wrinkles out of his shirt.

"Oh, I don't know," Thayden says, his eyes dropping to my lips. "I like several things that you're doing right now."

Same. But maybe he should put me down if we want to have a civilized conversation. Or, just, you know, a conversation at all. Because now my eyes are on his mouth, the memory of our kisses so fresh in my mind.

Now he's leaning closer ... and closer ...

"WAIT!" I put a finger to his lips, stopping his forward motion. It doesn't make me want to kiss him any less. If anything, I only want him more now that I feel his lips against my fingertip.

"Yes?" he says, lips tickling me as he speaks around my finger.

"Oh, right. Um. I just ..."

I trail off, realizing suddenly that the room is flickering. All the lights are off, and the house is lit only by dozens of candles all around the room. Is this for me? The thought makes me want to grab his shirt again with my fists and drag his mouth to mine.

Wait—was this for someone else? I sniff, like I could possibly smell another woman's perfume in the air.

"Did you just smell me?" he asks.

"No. I mean, I sniffed. But not you. I thought—what's this? What's going on?"

"Nope. You first." He's grinning, and I've never wanted to smack that smile off his face so much.

I glare at him. "Not until you tell me why you bought out a candle store."

He chuckles. "You don't think it's romantic?"

"It could be. Or maybe we should wait and see—I'd love to catch up with my firemen friends."

Now, it's his turn to glare. "Delilah," he warns, and the feeling of his mouth moving on my finger is still doing unwanted things to my insides.

"Just answer this: did you do this for me or for someone else?"

His eyes blaze with a heat that threatens to melt me. "There is only you. No one else."

I take a shallow breath, because I'll chicken out if I take a deep one. "I'd like for us to be more."

"More?" He's exaggerating every move of his mouth on

my finger, like he's placing not so secret kisses on my skin. "More what?"

"More than roommates. More than friends. More than fake—"

"*Arranged.*"

"More than an *arranged* marriage." The enormity of what I'm asking hits me, and I'm suddenly shaky.

Thayden presses a delicate but intentional kiss to my fingertip. "Funny you should bring that up."

Carefully, he walks me over and sets me down on my feet near the couch. I hate not being in his arms, but I'm curious at the papers he has spread out over the coffee table.

"What's this?" I ask, looking down in surprise as Thayden weaves our fingers together.

"This," he says with a flourish, "is me asking you to renegotiate our roommate contract and our other contract into something more … permanent. Less roommatey."

I squeal and Thayden picks me up in his arms, spinning me around while I cover his face in kisses. Apollo wants to get in on the action, leaping and wiggling that big ol' butt all over the place.

In a movie, the camera would have panned out on us kissing, giving us our happy moment. Music would crescendo. The credits would start to roll on our happy-ever-after.

In reality, Apollo knocks over all the candles on the table, setting our contracts on fire, and giving us quite a different ending.

"Hello again," I say weakly, watching the same handful of firemen I met recently march up to the house again. "I promise the fire's out now!"

"We still have to check, ma'am. More toast?"

Thayden practically starts growling when the man gives

me a half smile. His face goes all serious as he turns for the house. I squeeze Thayden's arm.

"Be nice!"

"If they want me to be nice, they should stop being so nice."

I lean my head on his shoulder. "You don't have anything to worry about, darlin'."

Thayden visibly jerks and turns to face me. "I've graduated to pet names?"

I giggle. "Maybe. Though I think I prefer *tiger* for you. What with all the growling."

He leans in, growling all the way to my lips. The hum and vibration make me smile even as I kiss him.

I don't have to worry about being in public, though we are, or about the stupid contract, which I'm pretty sure burned to a crisp inside before Thayden dumped Apollo's water dish all over it. At the back of my mind, I know there is more conversation to be had, more things to work out to make this arrangement real.

But for now, I let Thayden kiss me breathless while Apollo leans against our legs. The stars I made promises on shine overhead, and firemen clean up the mess we made inside the house while we shamelessly make out on the sidewalk. At least until his phone buzzes with a text.

"Don't check it," I whisper against his mouth.

Thayden groans and pulls away. "I have to. It's Duke."

He frowns down at his phone for a moment, then drags a hand through his hair. I can tell by his face what this means.

"Don't wait up?" I guess.

Thayden leans in and kisses me again, slowly. "I have to go. Tomorrow should be our last day in court. Then we get to practice getting married, and then we get to actually get married."

He's grinning, and I'm filled with wonder. This is the same man who said he didn't want to get married. And he wants to marry *me*. In two days.

I stand on my toes and kiss his stubbled cheek. "Take care of your case and I'll see you in the morning."

"I'm sorry," he says. "I don't want to go."

"I know."

"Especially because these guys are here," he grumbles.

I laugh and shove him lightly. "Go on. Don't worry about me. I've got my eyes set on only one man!"

As Thayden jogs off to his car, in the middle of a team of firemen in uniform, I know it's true. He's it for me. And in two days, we're going to have our happily-ever-after.

CHAPTER TWENTY-FIVE

Thayden

MY INFAMOUS TRIAL ends early on the day of my wedding rehearsal. At least that's one thing I don't have to worry about, though the guilt of getting this man off with barely any repercussions sits like a stain on my soul. I need to wash that stain right off and focus on the weekend ahead, which looks even brighter after last night with Delilah.

We didn't exchange *I love yous* yet or anything, but we're on the same page. And we're getting married. All of this totally out of order, but who cares? We don't need to follow some checklist. She wants me. I want her. What started as something that could be summarized in a legal document has grown into something much more.

"You okay?" Scott asks when I stop by the office after lunch.

It's the last time I'll set foot in this place for a few weeks, what with the wedding and extended honeymoon I've secretly planned. Honestly, I can't wait to get out of here, and not just because I'm excited to spend ten days with Delilah on St. John. Maybe we'll just stay there. Buy a little house boat or a cottage, and not return.

"I'm great. Just tying up the last things before tonight." I grin, but Scott doesn't smile back.

"Right. Tonight. The rehearsal."

Scott tugs at his tie, shifting in front of my desk. His nervousness hangs in the air like a cloud of spray deodorant in a junior high boys' locker room. Honestly, I don't want to deal with this right now. I don't need rain on my parade. But I like Scott. Enough that he got shortlisted as a wedding guest.

"Everything okay?" I ask, hoping he'll blow me off and save whatever drama he's got for after my honeymoon.

"I don't want to say."

I pin Scott with a look. "What's wrong? Spit it out."

He chews the side of his lip for so long that I'm about to just walk out, when he finally blurts, "I found a loophole."

That's all? We're way past me needing to push Delilah into loopholes. I chuckle, grabbing my briefcase. "Thank you. But don't worry about it. Delilah signed willingly, the wedding is on, and it's all fine. More than fine."

"No, I mean, I found a loophole in your father's will."

My limbs are dense and cold, like I'm standing neck-deep in a snowdrift. "What?"

"I sent an email with scanned copies, highlighting what I found."

I slip my phone from my pocket, the picture of calm, and open my email, clicking away until I have it right there in front of me. The escape clause. I really don't read too carefully because I don't care.

But Delilah might. My stomach drops. Despite everything she said last night, all of this started with the contract. If that's off the table, what does that change? Does it change? No. It couldn't. It wouldn't.

Would it?

I won't know until I ask her. And that's the very last thing I want to do right now.

"If you read the highlighted part, the language states—"

"I see it."

"Thank you," I tell him. "Good work."

"You don't look happy. Do you need help with anything? Making calls? Canceling reservations? I'm here to help."

"We're not canceling anything."

Are we?

I desperately want to speak to Delilah. I should call her, tell her that she's free if she wants to be. I'll still pay off her loans, of course. The money is hers. She'll fight me, but I'll insist—calling it a sign of good faith since she was willing to do this so I could keep the firm. I should call my mother and tell her.

But I don't do any of that. I stand there, clutching the edge of my desk.

"Take the rest of the afternoon off," I tell Scott. "You've earned it."

Looking unsure, he nods and slips out of my office. I walk to the big windows, my view of the small city. I press my forehead to the glass, watching it fog over as I sigh. The buildings, people, and sky are now hidden behind the haze of my breath.

It's the view that somehow makes realization strike. I

don't need this view. I don't need the contract. I don't need the firm.

I still need to make a grand gesture, and I know exactly what it's going to be.

From: WickingAway@DrLove.advice
To: DrLove@DrLove.advice

Dear Dr. Love,

I'm very athletic and am more at home in athletic wear than anything else. My wedding is coming up, and I commissioned a special wedding dress that's in my style. My best friends think that I'm going to lose my fiancé when he sees my dress—which is custom made from a company that specializes in sportswear.

It's still a wedding dress ... just one that wicks away moisture and that maybe I could run a half-marathon in.

Are my friends right? Do I need to worry about being left at the altar over my dress?

Sincerely,

Wicking Away Wedding

———

From: DrLove@DrLove.advice
To: WickingAway@DrLove.advice

Dear Wicking,

Honestly? I need to see this dress. It sounds epic, and one of my best friends would love it.

I know it's against tradition, but if you're worried, maybe it's time to show your fiancé the dress. Ultimately, if he doesn't want to marry you because you could run a marathon in your gown, that's way too shallow.

In that case, find a guy who shares your passion for fitness and would be happy exchanging vows in track pants.

-Dr. Love

From: WickingAway@DrLove.advice
To: DrLove@DrLove.advice

Dear Sam,

Score! It's Harper. I got one by you. You're slipping. And now you owe me a dinner. Guess what? We're going vegan, baby.

-Harpy

From: DrLove@DrLove.advice
To: WickingAway@DrLove.advice

I hate you. And I hate eating vegan. My intestines don't like it either. Also, is that wedding dress a thing? Now I have to know.

Maybe you and Chase could finally get together and you could make that dress a reality.

-Sam

From: WickingAway@DrLove.advice
To: DrLove@DrLove.advice

Shut up. And prepare your intestines.

-Harpy

CHAPTER TWENTY-SIX

Delilah

"LAST CHANCE TO BACK OUT."

The voice by my ear makes me jump. Abby laughs, then stops abruptly when I don't join her. We're standing on the rooftop terrace of the hotel where I'll be getting married tomorrow. Tomorrow. I'm getting married.

Tomorrow.

Married.

"Whoa." Abby throws an arm around my waist. "Are you nervous? Do you have cold feet?" Bouncing on her toes, she jiggles us both and keeps going before I can even begin to answer. "Don't tell me you're still overthinking this."

"I'm not sure it's possible to overthink it. If anything, I've *under*thought it."

The conversation with Thayden last night seems like a dream. Especially since I haven't seen him in person since. I guess he and Duke took care of whatever client emergency they had last night, and this morning, he was gone when I woke up. It's hard not to question things when our switch from fake to real happened so quickly.

I don't want to be THAT GIRL who worries endlessly and gets all needy. But I've had too many hours by myself to start questioning everything. I'll feel a lot better when I see Thayden tonight. I need the reassurance of his smile and that look he gets in his eyes when he sees me. How did I not see it for what it was earlier? Maybe he hasn't said the L-word yet, but I swear, I already see it in his eyes.

It's almost like Abby somehow picks up on my brainwaves. She jiggles us both again.

"You love Thayden. He *loves* you. Ring, vows, kiss the bride, and we party like it's 1999. Then you ride off happily into the sunset. The end. Simple. No overthinking."

I have to laugh. "Abs, are *you* okay? How many flat whites have you had this afternoon, darlin'?"

"Not nearly enough. I'm fine. I started taking this medication for a rash. Wanna see?"

Abby lets go of me and turns, starting to hike up her blouse. I grab her hands, holding both in mine. "No! I don't need to see your rash. But maybe you should drink some water and sit down. Where's Zane?"

I feel like tonight, Abby might need a babysitter. She's a little unpredictable on a typical day. Whatever medication she's on has made her a bit loopy.

"I'll find him. He owes me a kiss. Congrats, D. Glad you finally figured out that y'all actually both want to tie the knot."

She kisses me on the cheek before darting off, probably to make out with Zane behind one of the large flowering plants. The rooftop is teeming with potted trees, topiaries, and walls with climbing vines. It looks almost like a country garden in the sky. Fairy lights twinkle overhead, and some gauzy white sheets have been hung at what will be the front. Rather than having fabric or ribbon on the backs of the chairs, each chair has its own cascade of bougainvillea. The effect is stunning.

And expensive.

"Do you like it?" Elizabeth appears by my side, linking her arm through mine.

"It's more beautiful than anything I could have imagined. Thank you." I give her a hug that's hard to finish. I feel the need to really hang on. "How did you know my favorite flower?"

I pull back, watching her beam. "I took a page from Thayden's book and spied through your friends. And something called Pinterest. He set up an account for me."

"Pinterest!" I slap a palm on my forehead. "That man! I was wondering how he knew the things he knew."

"Where is he, by the way?" Elizabeth asks. "He's late for his own rehearsal."

"I know he had the big case wrapping up."

"That ended hours ago," Elizabeth says. "He sent me a text."

I know I shouldn't immediately go into crisis mode. But Thayden didn't send *me* a text. Now he's late for our rehearsal.

But he found my Pinterest boards because he wanted to learn my favorite things! I wonder how many times I'll have to talk myself down tonight.

Elizabeth squeezes my arm. "Don't read into it. He'll be here."

"How is everyone reading my thoughts tonight?"

"Because you broadcast them right across your face, dear."

Abby reappears, not with Zane but his father. She's dragging him by the arm, and he has a half smile on his usually serious face. "Elizabeth! I need you to meet my bonus dad," Abby says. "He's walking Delilah down the aisle."

"How wonderful to meet you," Elizabeth says warmly, shaking his hand.

"It's a pleasure to meet you as well." Mr. Abramson smiles again, his eyes crinkling a little. He turns and gives me a pat on the shoulder. "Are you ready for this?"

"'Course I am! Thank you for doing the honors."

"We just need my son," Elizabeth says, glancing at her watch. "Have you heard from him?"

"I'll check," I say.

I turn, discreetly pulling my phone out of my bra. I knew I should have chosen a dress with pockets. I make a show of frowning at my phone screen, even though I know Thayden hasn't texted or called. My whole body attuned for the feel of that vibration next to my heart.

"I'm sure he'll be here soon," I say, anything but sure.

"Can I introduce you to some friends?" Elizabeth glides away with Mr. Abramson on her arm. She looks radiant, probably how I should look right now. Instead, I probably look about how I feel—like roadkill trying to drag itself off the highway before it gets flattened again. Why isn't Thayden here?

I meet the few friends of Elizabeth's I don't know, thankful for my pageant training, helping me float through while worry is practically choking me. Manners make a perfect mask.

There's a ruckus as Thayden steps off the elevator. My heart seems to slide right into place when his eyes seek mine out. He winks, and all is right in the world. I sigh, my shoulders sinking with relief. He hugs his mama, slaps Gavin on the back, and gives Chase a fist bump. Then, he stalks toward me.

His eyes have an intensity that roots me in place. When he reaches me, my heart is beating to some kind of complicated Latin rhythm and my mouth is dry.

"Hey," Thayden says, cupping my cheeks with his hands. His kiss is soft and sweet, but he gives my lip the slightest nibble as he pulls away.

"Thayden!" I hiss. "Everyone's watching!"

His smile is completely rakish and thoroughly unashamed. "They're going to watch tomorrow too. Tonight's the rehearsal, and I take rehearsing quite seriously. Better try that again."

I giggle, pushing him away as he bends to kiss me again. Laughing, he links his fingers with mine. "Sorry for making you wait! I had a little business pop up, but I'm ready to get this show on the road!"

The coordinator pops out from wherever she was hiding and ushers people into place. Within moments, everyone is seated, and I'm at the back of the row with Mr. Abramson. We're at the end of the aisle, and I can't take my eyes off of Thayden.

He's stunning as usual, and I wonder if I'll ever get used to his good looks. I see him as so much more than I did a few months ago. When I'm reading now, I always find pieces of him. He's my Puck. My Prince Charming. My Darcy.

Mr. Abramson gives my arm a gentle tug. "That's our cue."

"Sorry."

"No need to apologize." He hesitates, glancing at Thayden, then back at me. "I said this to Zoey, and I'll say it to you. There's no shame in turning around now if you want to. Better now than later."

It's the most he's ever said to me, and the genuine care has my tear ducts kicking into high gear. I stare down the aisle at Thayden, who is grinning like he simply can't wait for me to reach him.

"Thank you for saying so. But I'm ready." I use my free hand to wipe away the few tears that escape. Little traitors.

We float through the simple ceremony while the minister walks us through the parts. It's surreal to look at Thayden, repeating vows and saying I dos. I giggle through most of it, and he keeps trying to kiss me. I feel like we're a sitcom with all the laughter from the studio audience.

It's over in a blink, and then I'm on Thayden's arm, walking back down the aisle as our friends and his mama clap.

"Part one is done," Thayden says, leading me toward the elevator. Our dinner is downstairs in one of the restaurants' private rooms. "I'm ready for part two. Think we can just move it up a day?"

I shove him. "No."

"That's five minutes cuddle time," he says.

"Nope. That contract burned up in a fire last night."

"Darn," he says.

I clutch his shoulder, finding his ear with my lips. "Since you're my real fiancé now, the cuddle time is free."

He grins, placing a quick kiss on my temple. "And can I upgrade that cuddle time for anything else?" His voice is teasing, but still low and husky.

"Not a chance. Not until tomorrow night, tiger."

"Mm. Even if I have a surprise for you?" he asks. "A grand gesture, if you will."

My interest is piqued, but I love having the upper hand. "We'll see how you behave tonight."

The elevator doors open, and Thayden pulls me inside,

tasting my lips with his as he closes the doors on Abby and Zane. "Hey!" she protests, but I see Zane's smile before the doors zip closed.

"I have no intention of behaving," Thayden whispers against my mouth, kissing me senseless for ten whole floors.

We're still laughing and teasing, flirting shamelessly as we make it to the private room downstairs. No one else is here yet, mostly because we commandeered the elevator. But as everyone arrives, I'm hardly aware of anyone else. Thayden procures me a glass of some kind of wine, but I can hardly taste it. I'm too distracted by the man doting on me.

What was I worried for earlier? It seems silly. Tonight is going to be fine, and tomorrow will be perfect. Thayden's smile and that same look of love in his eyes assures me of it.

That is, until I look up at the doorway as two familiar women enter. One who should be here and another who should be thousands of miles away.

My glass drops out of my hand, shattering on the wood floor. Thayden immediately takes my arm. I hardly feel his fingers on my skin, which has gone cold.

"Delilah? What is it?"

I cannot speak. I cannot even point. My eyes are fixed on Elizabeth, walking through the room with my mama.

CHAPTER TWENTY-SEVEN

Thayden

I FOLLOW Delilah's wide eyes. My mother is walking next to a woman who can only be Delilah's mother. The resemblance is clear, though her mom has an expression I've never seen on Delilah's face. It's a pleased, haughty sort of look, like she's just walked into a dinner being held in her honor. Or maybe like she's just finished drinking the blood of her enemies. One of those two.

I don't even have time to plan a response when Abby swoops in, giving me and Delilah a sloppy joint hug.

"You guys," she slurs, slapping my cheek a little harder than necessary before kissing Delilah. "The best. You're the best. The very, very, very, very best."

Abby sways, almost pulling us down with her. She kisses Delilah on the cheek again and then tries for me. She's too short and ends up rubbing her face on my shoulder like a cat. I swear, she even makes a purring sound.

I try to remove her from us, but she's all arms. "Uh, hey, Abs. Good kitty. Now maybe isn't the best time."

Mom and Delilah's mother are still approaching but have gotten caught up with Mr. Abramson. I need to talk to Delilah before they get over here, to ask if she's okay or how to handle this. Delilah didn't want her mother here. There has to be good reason for that. If I have to, I'll throw her out myself.

Too bad my mom didn't seem to get that memo. I can smell an Elizabeth Walker surprise from a mile away. She probably sent the plane to pick her up, thinking of this as a sort of wedding present.

I try again but can't seem to get Abby off. She's like a starfish, suctioned onto our bodies with a million arms.

"Um, Abs? Have you been into the liquor, sugar?" Delilah asks.

Abby tries to step back, looking up with wide eyes. "No! I mean, not really."

She hiccups, then giggles, lurching to the side, and it takes both me and Delilah to keep her on her feet. I swear, twenty minutes ago on the roof, she seemed sober. Or, at least, more in control of her motor functions. Maybe I just didn't notice? But I think I would have noticed. Everyone in the room now certainly has.

"I had wine!" Abby whispers. She puts a finger to her lips. "Shh! Don't tell Zane!"

Zane appears as though she conjured him. Shaking his head, he helps peel Abby off. "Zane knows, Abs."

Abby whips around so fast she almost falls. Zane scoops her up in his arms, and she plants a sloppy kiss on his mouth, then wipes her lipstick off with her hand.

"Zane! I love you! I want to get married!" she shouts.

"I know, Abs. We will, okay?" He gives us a sheepish look over her shoulder as she tries to scale his body like a climbing wall.

"We're getting married!" Abby shouts, throwing her head back.

"I'm so sorry," Zane says. "I'll calm her down."

"It's fine," Delilah and I say at the same time. Honestly, I think we're both glad for the distraction. I pull her into my arms, wanting her to know that whatever happens, I'm here.

"Hold still. I want to sit on your shoulders, see what the view is like. You're so tall! What's tall like?"

"Abby, now is not the time." But Zane grins as he tries to keep her still.

"You tall. Me small." She laughs, her head tipping all the way back. "'S fine. I've got bike shorts on under this. Learned it from D. Yo, D! Check it!"

Abby yanks the bottom of her dress up, thankfully revealing medium-length black bike shorts. Both Zane and I take deep breaths of relief.

"Abs? Are you okay, darlin'? Is this the medication?"

I can still hear the tension and worry etched in Delilah's voice as she glances at Abby, then over her shoulder where my mom and Delilah's mom have almost reached us. Her whole body tenses and I tighten my arm around her.

Zane sighs. "They said not to mix it with alcohol, a warning she clearly ignored. I had to go to the bathroom. I was gone for three minutes. Three minutes, Abs."

Abby giggles. "I can get into a lot of trouble in three minutes."

He glares down at her, but a smile still plays on his mouth. "Clearly."

"Don't be mad, Zane. I'll be good." She pats his cheek. "Promise."

"Let's get you some water and some food, Abs."

"Food! Ahoy, matey! Onward to the buffet table!"

It's a sit-down dinner, but whatever. Hopefully, one of the staff members will take pity and give Zane some dinner rolls or something.

"Sorry!" Zane calls over his shoulder. Abby has wiggled her way to the side and is trying to smack Zane on the butt. I'd laugh, but now, standing in front of us, are our mothers. I think I'd like starfish Abby back as a shield.

"Surprise!" Mom beams, giving Delilah's mother a gentle nudge forward. "I know you said she couldn't come, but I just couldn't let you get married without your mom here."

"Darling daughter," the woman says. She pulls Delilah into a hug, and I reluctantly let her go, but pull her back as quickly as I can. Delilah manages a sort of smile that's more of a grimace. "And you must be Thayden. Charmed to meet you. I'm Verity."

What kind of name is that? "You as well," I say, shaking her hand quickly.

She studies me with cool calculation. I'm surprised by how different her accent is from Delilah's. It sounds slightly British, very posh and highbrow. She's dressed similar to my mother as well. I thought Delilah had grown up struggling financially, but it doesn't appear that way if her mother is any indication.

"Mama," Delilah says, a bit of warning in her tone.

Delilah's mom shakes a finger like she's scolding, and I want to slap it away. "I can't believe you were going to let me miss this. We'll talk about you being naughty later."

No, they most certainly will not. I'm not letting Verity, if that's her real name, anywhere near Delilah again. I squeeze her tighter to me, trying to steady her with my body. That smile I hate is still in place, the one that's fixed and fake.

I'm almost ready to yank her behind me when her mother's eyes meet mine again. They're scary eyes. The same color as Delilah's but with no love or softness. A predatory gleam lights them, and there's some triumph there too, like causing her daughter distress is winning a prize of some kind.

"You're one lucky mark," she says. "I mean, *man*."

"Mama," Delilah whispers. "Don't."

What did her mom mean by *mark*? Like, a con man kind of mark? Whatever Delilah's mother is selling, I'm not buying. Every move of hers is cold and calculated. I know my mom meant well, but I want her gone.

"I think they're about to start serving," my mom says, hooking her arm through Verity's elbow. "I've got our seats together so we can compare notes on our children."

"I'd love that," Verity says, turning those bright, cold eyes on Delilah. "So many things to catch you up on."

"Mama—" Delilah starts, but is interrupted by Zoey, raising her voice over the din in the room.

"Please, take your seats. A lobster dinner is ready to be served, with toasts to follow." Zoey gives Delilah a questioning look, but D just shakes her head.

"Lobster?" Verity asks, sounding horrified, then shooting Delilah an accusatory glance. "I'm allergic to shellfish."

"Don't worry," my mom says, already flagging down a server. "We'll take care of you."

"I didn't think you'd be here, Mama," Delilah says. She sounds like a dog that's been kicked one too many times.

Her voice breaks something in me. I just want to surround her and protect her. I'm relieved we're at the opposite end of the long table from our mothers. As I help guide Delilah to our seats, I lean close.

"I'm sorry. I didn't know," I tell her. "Are you okay? What can I do?"

She shrugs, and despair seems to roll off her. "What's done is done," she says. "Thayden. I need you to know—"

We are interrupted by servers putting plates in front of us. I'm not the least bit hungry, my stomach twisting painfully. I'd love for the lobster on my plate just to crawl away.

Gavin leans in close. "Everything okay?"

I glance over, making sure Delilah is talking with Sam on her other side. "Delilah's mother is here."

Gavin's brow furrows. "And that's a bad thing?"

"Seems to be, yes." I run a hand over my jaw, keeping my eye on Verity. She seems like a ticking time bomb. Like Lindsay Lohan, in mom form.

"Everything else okay?"

It's hard to even remember the events from earlier in the day. I shake my head and smile at Gavin. "Oh, and in other news, I found a loophole that means we don't have to get married."

Gavin jolts. "I didn't think that's why you wanted to get married anymore."

"It isn't. And I quit my job today." I can't help but feel lighter just thinking about it. The Walker Firm has been like an anchor this whole time, tugging me down. I only realized how much when I gave my notice today. Since I'll be gone for the whole two weeks, I'm basically a free man now. Duke was thrilled, and I don't even care.

Gavin grins. "See? There you go. That's a grand gesture."

"Now I just have to tell Delilah about the loophole. Just, you know, in case she doesn't actually want to marry me."

Gavin smacks me on the back of the head. "She's not marrying you for the money or the contract, dummy."

"I still need to tell her. But now ..." My eyes flick to Verity, who is watching Delilah with such open hostility that it unnerves me.

"Could I have your attention?" Zoey interrupts again, standing as she clinks her glass. Servers pass glasses of champagne around the table.

"It's customary to toast the bride and groom," Zoey starts.

"I love toast!" Abby shouts, and there is laughter as Zane wrestles her into her seat, replacing her champagne glass with water.

Zoey only shakes her head, ever unflappable. I take Delilah's hand, and she holds onto mine like it's all that's keeping her sane.

"We'd like to open the floor, starting with—"

"Actually, I'd love to start." Verity stands, dread marches up my spine. "Mother of the bride," she says, cocking a brow as though daring anyone to challenge her.

Zoey glances at Delilah, who is a statue next to me. I consider interrupting Verity, but what would I say? Delilah never filled me in on her past, never said more than a few dismissive words about her mother. I'd love to think that Verity is going to make nice, to bridge what are clearly some canyon-sized gaps between them, but the look on her face has me believing otherwise.

"It's wonderful to be here tonight, and I extend a thank-you to the Walker family for hosting. I've felt very welcome, despite not receiving an invitation."

There's laughter, as her words seem at the surface like the polite ribbing that sometimes takes place during toasts. But there's nothing polite about the cold fire in her eyes, and she's stabbing more than ribbing.

"I don't have much to say, considering my daughter trimmed me out of her life like split ends."

Verity pauses here, and the scattered laughter is less and more forced. My mother's eyes are wide. I give her a look, wishing she could pull out the wooden cane and yank Verity off the stage. Leaning closer, I put my arm around Delilah, who is shaking.

Why wouldn't she open up? Why hasn't she told me about her past so I could be prepared, so I could protect her from whatever attack this is?

I'm about to stand, cutting Verity off, when she raises her glass. The room follows suit, except for me and Delilah.

"Let's raise a toast to my daughter, the entrepreneur. Or, as she might be more accurately labeled, the con artist."

There's a gasp in the room, and Delilah is already standing. I'm right beside her. Fury is burning a hole through the center of my chest. I don't need to hear Delilah's defense. I believe nothing coming out of this woman's mouth.

Verity lifts her glass higher. I wish my mother had a WWE training rather than a debutante one. I'd love to see her body slam Delilah's mom right now.

"To Delilah! Who has clawed her way up from conning people at pageants to a wealthy and legitimate family. Well done, daughter." Her mouth becomes a sneer. "They deserved to know," she hisses, her voice sliding into an accent that's much more like Delilah's.

While I was watching her mother, she slipped away from me. Arms wrapped around herself, she backs toward the door. I catch my toe on a chair, stumbling as I try to reach her. Servers are poised behind us with trays filled with more champagne flutes, and I crash into one, both of us ending up on the floor, the server on top of me, champagne soaking through my suit.

"Boo! Booooooo! Rubbish!"

Abby's voice draws my attention. As I manage to free myself, getting to my feet, I see her, standing on the table— well, *swaying* on the table—pointing toward Verity.

"Queen of Lies! Queen of Slime! Queen of Putrescence!"

I'd know those lines anywhere. Abby mixed them up a little, but she's quoting *The Princess Bride*.

Solid burn, Abs.

And where is Zane? He looks like he's about to jump out of his seat, but his dad holds him back with one palm flat against Zane's chest. Interesting.

"Boooooo!"

When Abby throws the first lobster at Verity, Mr. Abramson let Zane loose. Not soon enough to stop the half-eaten crustacean. It hits the center of Verity's green dress, leaving a buttery streak as it slides to her lap. Verity shrieks, jumping to her feet.

Zane grabs for her, but Abby darts away, spilling champagne and water glasses as she goes. She tosses a second lobster along with a mini carafe of melted butter. The lobster hits Verity's neck, and the butter sends an arc of gold down Chase's shirt. He blinks twice, then turns back to Abby. She has another lobster already, while Zane grabs for her again.

The third lobster solidly thwacks Verity in the cheek.

"I'm allergic!" Verity screeches, jumping to her feet and brushing herself vigorously with a napkin.

Indeed, her skin begins turning an angry red. Though that might be the force of the throw. Abby's got quite the arm.

"Serves you right!" Abby yells.

We're all thankful she's got bike shorts on as Zane bodily drags her kicking and screaming off the table. One of her heels ends up dangling from a water glass, another in the light fixture above.

Somehow Abby manages to snag another lobster on the way down. For someone impaired with a pills-and-wine combo, Abby has deadly accurate aim. This one bounces off Verity's collarbone.

There's definitely an allergic thing going on, with red splotches appearing on Verity's face, arms, and chest. I hope it's not anaphylaxis. The last thing Abby needs is to be arrested for assault with a deadly lobster.

I mean, I also don't want Delilah's mother to die. Hives? Totally fine by me. I'd be okay with boils. That might be too kind. The plague would be fitting. That and banishment.

Apparently, my sense of justice is very Middle Ages.

Abby is still yelling as Zane drags her away. "No one messes with my D!"

"Y'all don't even know who she really is!" Verity screeches. "I'm her blood! Her only family!"

Zoey stands at her full height, a head taller than Verity at least. "No, *we* are her family."

I wholeheartedly agree. So does this small room filled with people, all of whom are now on their feet, angry faces turned toward Verity. Even my mother looks like she's about to go medieval on her.

I turn to see Delilah's reaction, but she's gone.

Delilah! She must have bolted while we were all distracted by Abby's antics.

"Go get her," Gavin says, slapping me on the back. "I'll try to manage this."

"Thanks." I sprint for the door.

I'm halfway down the hotel hallway when two security guys jog toward me. I pause and point toward the doorway behind me.

"It's the woman in the green dress. She's screaming—you can't miss her. She crashed the rehearsal dinner. Definitely arrest her!"

"We can't arrest people, sir," the first man says.

"Can you tase her?"

"Definitely not."

"Well, do whatever you *can* do and get that woman out of there. I'm the one footing this bill and I want her gone."

I peel a hundred-dollar bill out of my wallet and tuck it in the first guy's pocket.

"Yes, sir."

And then I'm off. Down the hall, down the stairs, and out the front doors of the hotel. I arrive just in time to see Delilah stepping into a rideshare at the end of the block.

"Delilah!" I shout.

But she's already gone.

CHAPTER TWENTY-EIGHT

Delilah

I'M NOT sure why I chose Thayden's bathroom for my break-down. The softest thing in the whole room is a bath mat, and I sink down on it, dropping my head between my knees. Maybe all the hard lines and surfaces is my way of punishing myself. Or maybe I like this room because it reminds me of the time Thayden and I fell in the tub, and all the nights we brushed our teeth at the same time. Small things, but they matter so much to me.

Are they over now? Has Mama's little reveal made Thayden rethink our relationship? Or rethink me?

Shame tastes like charcoal and ashes in my mouth. My past, so ugly, so humiliating, has now been dragged right into my present. Part of me knows my friends will love me no matter what. They certainly blew up my phone until I finally turned it off. Thayden also knows me well enough to know

I'm not conning him or marrying him for money. And if he doesn't … well. Maybe we weren't meant to be.

The bathtub against my back is hard. The tiles on my bare feet—cold. Uncomfortable is an understatement.

But I don't want comfort. I want hard, gleaming surfaces, punishing edges, and cold against my skin. Everything in here is white or gray, and I crave the starkness, the purity.

Apollo followed me upstairs, and whines softly outside the door leading to my room. His nose snuffles along the crack below the door.

"It's okay, big guy. I just … need to be alone."

I hear Apollo turn in circles, scratch the floor a few times, and then heave his body down with a groan. I can see his shadow under the door, and it comforts me to know he's there.

"You'd never judge me for my past, would you, big guy?"

I know the answer. I also know that my friends wouldn't. Thayden wouldn't. I shouldn't have run off. But of all the things I imagined might go wrong this weekend, my mama appearing out of the blue hadn't been a thought in my mind. And boy, does she know how to make a scene. To cause a stir. To ruin a life.

Did she lose the art of subtlety over the years? In my memory, she would use a slow-acting poison, not a sawed-off shotgun as her weapon of choice. Maybe she had been storing up punishment for me, letting it grow over the years I've been gone, waiting for a chance like this to strike. Her words had been swift, unexpected, and brutal.

I lift my palms to my cheeks, unsurprised by my tear-slicked skin. They have pooled at my neck, dripped down into my bra.

"Delilah!"

I freeze at the sound of Thayden's voice, his swift feet on

the stairs. Every muscle in my body tenses, locking up tight. So tight that as I pull my knees to my chest, my hamstring suddenly cramps.

"Ow!" I gasp, contorting and trying to shake out the cramp at the back of my leg, which only seems to make it worse. It won't let up, like someone has clamped a vise around the muscle and is squeezing.

"Delilah?" Thayden's panicked voice is right outside the bathroom door on his side. I'm thankful we fixed the lock, though the door rattles as he bangs his fists on it. "Open up! Are you hurt?"

I groan, but the cramp is starting to lessen. I dig my fingers into the back of my leg, massaging through the pain.

"Fine," I grunt through clenched teeth. "Just a cramp."

The banging stops. His throat clears. "Oh. Cramps? You have your period?"

I shake my head, dropping it into my hands as I laugh silently. Thayden talking about periods is about enough to get me out of my funk. He's trying to be casual, but it doesn't fit, coming off like a parent using their teenager's lingo. I wonder if he's ever talked to a woman about periods before. I'm betting on no.

"There's a heating pad in the cabinet. Do you need aspirin?" He pauses. "Maxi pads? Uh, tampons? I could go to the store. Or, do you, use one of those cup things to—"

"I have a LEG cramp!" I have to stop him before he finishes that sentence. How has Thayden even heard of a diva cup? The only way I know about them is from a Facebook group I'm in that's supposed to be a book club but is almost totally just women chatting about life. ALL aspects of life.

I'm crying again, but this time with laughter. Or maybe it's just an overflow of all the emotions.

"A *leg* cramp?" Thayden sounds relieved and also mysti-
fied. "Were you ... exercising?"

"No. It's probably just stress. Or from sitting weird on
the floor."

"Why are you sitting on the floor?"

"It was better than sitting on the toilet or in the bathtub."

Thayden says nothing, but I can practically hear his brain
forming questions, like clouds sprouting before a storm.
Probably logical ones like, *why are you in the bathroom to begin
with?* Under the door, I see his shadow. He's pacing.

"Delilah, we need to talk about what happened."

My eyes squeeze shut, loosening a few more tears as they
do. "Can we just not?"

"I think we should."

"Sorry, I'll have to decline."

He blows out a frustrated breath. "If anyone understands,
it's me."

My face feels like it's going to blow off from the heat
suddenly blasting up from underneath my skin. My fists
bunch at my sides, fingernails cutting into my palms.

"You know what it's like to grow up on food stamps? To
have your mama pimp you out to pageants to keep her
pockets lined? Did Elizabeth teach you how to slip a wallet
from someone's back pocket, and how to pass it off as a
mistake if you get caught? Did you learn the art of running a
con before you learned to read? Do you know the shame that
kind of past brings, even after years?"

Underneath the door, I can see his shiny dress shoes.
That's how close he's standing to the door. I inch closer
to him.

My breath feels thick and heavy in Thayden's silence. I
lick my lips, which feel dry and cracked, my lipstick from
earlier totally gone.

"Unless you have a criminal resume I don't know about, one that includes training at your mama and daddy's knee, then I don't think you do understand."

The thing about outbursts is you think you'll feel better after you get them off your chest. And there is something to the act of release, like steam in a high-pressure-plumbing situation. But I don't feel better now. Just scraped out and thin. Just as full of shame and doubt as before.

I watch as Thayden's shoes disappear. He walks away, and I feel each step like a slap.

I've finally been too brutal, hurt him too much. Been too disappointing, both in my past and how I'm reacting, even now. I ran when I should have stayed. I'm locking the door when I should open it. I pushed him and pushed him, and I finally pushed him away.

I know his family situation hasn't been perfect. We wouldn't be in this situation without his father's manipulations. I've seen the defeat in his eyes because of his father, heard the bitterness swirling in his voice. We should be comforting each other about our family wounds. Instead, I just tore his head off.

"I'm sorry," I whisper, knowing he probably can't hear me. He's not close enough anymore.

A soft sound makes my eyes blink open. A pile of envelopes spills underneath the door. My heart leaps, knowing Thayden is still there. He hasn't left me. A tiny sliver of hope unfurls.

"You probably recognize these," Thayden says. His voice sounds closer, like he's crouching now. And I swear I hear a smile in his voice. "You know, from all your snooping around when I'm not here."

Now I'm smiling, even if it's through tears. I hadn't thought of these mystery envelopes in weeks. The man himself is much more interesting than the secrets he harbors behind the Calvin Kleins in his drawer.

"Why, sir, whatever do you mean?" My tone isn't quite as light or flirty as I'd like, but I'm doing my best here.

His chuckle is like a key, turning over some rumbling engine in my chest, starting it up. "Don't tell me your curiosity didn't lead you into my underwear drawer. *I know you.*"

Those are probably the only *other* three words that could strike such a chord with me. Especially because they're true. He does know me. I've hidden so much for so long from so many people. Even—no, *especially*—from my closest friends. But Thayden has seen it all.

I've intentionally unwrapped some of me for him, sharing things that I hadn't planned to share. More than I've shared with my best friends. And tonight, Mama forcefully unwound the last bits of fabric covering all my secrets, all my shame. Thayden knows my worst shame.

And he's. Still. Here. My smile is so big it hurts my cheeks.

"You can't prove a thing," I say, but I'm leaning forward, touching one white envelope, running the corner underneath my fingernail.

"I'd like you to read them," Thayden says. Then, in a teasing tone, "I know you want to."

I do. So badly. In spite of all the emotional overwhelm from tonight, the cat in me wants to lose another of its nine lives to my curiosity, tearing open every single envelope with my claws and teeth, digging out the secrets inside.

I hesitate, scooping the envelopes into a pile, counting them out. There are eleven now. My interest sharpens into a blade. Eleven?

I run my tongue over my teeth, then my lips. "Are these ... letters?"

There's a soft thump and a sigh on the other side of the door. I imagine Thayden sitting with his back against the wall next, loosening his tie and toeing off his shoes.

"Yes. I wrote them to myself. Mostly at big events or celebrations. Milestones like high school graduation, getting my first internship, being accepted into law school, passing the bar." He pauses. "They're the things I wish my father would have said to me, but never did."

I rub a hand over my sternum, trying to ease the ache I feel for Thayden. "Thayden ..." It's all I can say.

"Read them," he says. "I want you to."

I gather the letters up, almost weightless in my palms, yet heavy as an anchor. "I'm not sure I can. Right now, anyway. I will," I promise.

There's no way I could keep myself from tearing them open now that I've been granted permission. But at this moment everything is too raw. Too real.

I stand up, clutching the letters in one hand and pressing my other palm flat to the door. I hear Thayden shift on the other side, then the shadow moves under the door as his feet line up with mine. I swear I can feel him through the door when he leans up against it, a soft groan of wood and a faint vibration. We're so close, but so far.

He's there. Right ... *there*. I push my palm and forehead harder against the door.

"I need to tell you something," Thayden says, making my heart flinch. No good conversations start with that opener.

"Okay."

"It's more than one thing, actually." He sighs, and I wish I could feel it feathering over my skin.

"Please, just say whatever it is. Don't make me wait."

311

"I found a loophole in my father's contract. I don't have to get married to keep the company."

The room is suddenly so cold, like all the tiles and metal surfaces have frozen over. I feel the ice rising up from where my feet touch the cold tile, the frost skimming up my legs, past my hips, encasing my heart and spreading outward to the tips of my fingers.

I bite my lip. "Okay, then. We can just—"

"I wasn't going to tell you. I didn't want to."

These words roll around in my mind for a moment. I'm trying to make them sit still so I can examine them. "Why?"

"I was nervous you wouldn't still marry me if you didn't have to."

When I don't speak, mostly because an ache in my chest has stolen my ability to do so, Thayden keeps going.

"Then, I decided it was stupid not to trust you. We both said we want this to be real. Which is why ..." He pauses. "I'm leaving the firm."

Of all the things he's said, this one shouldn't jolt me to attention, but it does.

"You *what?*"

"I need you to know I'm not marrying you because I have to. I'm not doing it because of my father, and I'm also not *avoiding* it because of my father. I don't trust my own motivations where he's involved, so I'm just taking him out of the equation. I've stepped out of his game. I'm not playing anymore."

"Thayden, you didn't have to give up your firm!"

"I did," he says firmly. "For me as much as for you. And I feel so much better. I feel *free*. I've already let the board know, and it's official, as soon as I get back from our honeymoon."

Honeymoon?

"Oh yeah." I can hear the smile in his voice now, like it's

just starting its wind-up. "While I'm confessing, might as well tell you everything. I booked us a honeymoon. You told me you've never gotten to go on a real vacation. You're going to love it. As soon as you're done being mad that I did it when you told me not to."

"Were you planning to drug and kidnap me?"

He chuckles. "I was hoping you'd go willingly, but ..."

"I don't know what to say."

Thayden takes a deep breath, loudly enough that I can hear it as I imagine his shoulders rising with the inhale.

"Delilah, I know I'm a mess. I'm not the best man. I'm not what you probably envisioned in a husband. I know I drive you crazy sometimes. But I want to spend the rest of my life figuring out how to be a man who deserves you, even if I'm doing so one mistake at a time."

Everything in me feels too sensitive, too aware. The white of the door is whiter than white, it's a brilliant, painful glow. I have to close my eyes against it. The sound of the AC kicking on is too loud, the air frigid as it whispers over my arms and bare neck. I imagine Thayden's handsome face, slumped against the other side of this door, biting his lip as he waits for me to answer.

I know what I have to say, what I *want* to say, and yet actually getting my lips to move takes effort.

"I love you."

My voice is strong and clear, and I know Thayden has to have heard me, but before he can respond, I say it again to make sure he knows. And then again. Each time, it gets easier, my chest feels lighter.

"I love you. I *love* you."

There's a quick inhalation of breath, and the door creaks and groans, as though Thayden is trying to push his way through it.

"You ... love me?" He speaks on an exhalation, and there's awe in it, like he's standing at the edge of a cliff, admiring a breathtaking view.

I speak through a smile. "I tried not to."

Then he chuckles again, and I'm pretty sure it's my favorite sound in the world. "I love you too, Delilah Hart. But I wanted to say it first," he whines playfully.

I'm grinning, squirming against the door a little. "You already did. Everything that you said just now—it was I love you. Everything you've been doing for me, even the things I complained about and said I didn't want—you've been telling me this whole time, haven't you?"

"Yes. In a coward's way."

"You're not a coward."

"I could have just said it."

I'm shaking my head. "No. You couldn't have. I wouldn't have heard you, wouldn't have believed you. Not until now."

"Why now?"

I glance down at the letters. I'm doing my best to keep them pristine, but they're wrinkling a little from being clutched in my fist, pressed against my body.

"You've seen my ugly," I tell him, picturing Mama's smug face. "All of it. And you're still here."

"There is not one thing ugly about you, Delilah."

I scoff, and he thumps the door lightly, maybe with the heel of his hand. I feel it in all the parts of my body touching the door.

"Abby threw lobsters at your mother," he says.

"What?" I'm struggling to follow this leap in conversation. "She—what? Mama's allergic."

"She'll probably be okay. Whatever. She deserves it."

"But she didn't lie, Thayden."

"You can't tell me you blame yourself for what your

314

mother forced you to do as a girl. That was abuse, Delilah. Manipulation. It's not *you*."

I know this. I've *known* this. But hearing Thayden confirm it makes my heart feel lighter. I feel … absolved.

"Everyone stood up for you," Thayden says, and now my eyes are burning again. "They said they were your family."

"Really?" My voice is an embarrassing squeak.

"Really. Abby was up on the tables, slinging lobsters while Zane chased her down. It was a thing of glory."

My smile is huge, and I can feel tears dripping into the corners. I don't even mind a bit.

"I know she wants to tell you herself, but my mother is so sorry. She wanted to do something nice."

"I know she did. I'm not mad at your mama. Is mine gone?"

"Yep. Made sure we paid for a bus ticket and I got Mr. Abramson to make sure she got on it."

"Delilah?"

"Yes?"

"I have to ask you something, because I really never did." Thayden thumps the door again, more gently this time. "Delilah Hart, will you marry me?"

I'm grinning like a fool. "Hm. I need to consult my day planner. When were you thinkin' about doing this?"

"Maybe tomorrow? After lunch, if you're free."

"I could probably clear my schedule. Sure, that could work."

"*Sure*, you'll marry me?"

"Uh-huh."

"*Uh-huh*? Maybe I should hold out for a woman that would say yes. Or Absolutely. Definitely."

"Oh no, you don't, Thayden Walker. There are no take-backs, mister. You proposed. I answered. This is happening. Tomorrow. After lunch."

"Fine."

"Fine."

I have a sudden mental image, Thayden and me with gray hair, a bit stooped. Maybe there's even a walker involved, the kind with tennis balls on the bottom. We're shuffling side by side, arguing about whether the sky is blue. He says something snappy, flashing that dang dimple. I jab him with a wrinkled finger, and we both laugh.

I want that future *so* bad that sweat begins to bead on my lower back.

I touch the doorknob, flicking the lock open. My heart bangs around behind my ribs, seeking release. I need to see him, to feel his arms around me, to cement all this talk with action.

But when I go to turn the knob, there's resistance. I give it a little shake.

"No." Thayden's voice is a hiss.

"And why not?" I'm outraged and sound like a toddler throwing a tantrum.

"Why not? Because I'm about ready to crash through this door, pick you up, and toss you onto my bed."

Oh my. I don't hate the sound of that at all. I only hate the door between us, and his resistance.

"Thayden," I whine.

He's right there, so close, and my skin feels alive and achy. I need his hands on my waist or in my hair, his lips on mine. I need to smell him, to feel his whispers on my skin. I want to see the love in his eyes, a look I already know, and recognize it finally for what it is.

"Not gonna happen," Thayden says.

I give the handle an angry shake, grinning when he makes a growling sound.

"Stop it," he says.

"Why? Why can't we just … kiss?" I'm almost breathless at the memory of our few kisses, and that achy feeling in my skin intensifies. "I need to *see* you."

"No."

"Just a hug?"

"Delilah, in twenty-four hours, *yes*. To all of it. Right now? I want to save everything until after we say very real I dos. I want the very first time I toss you on my bed—the first of many times thereafter—to be when you share my last name."

I'm so overcome by the words. They make me want to grab a sledgehammer and take it to the door. With the adrenaline coursing through me, I think I could throw *him* on the bed. But he's right, and as much as I want to blast through the door, I can wait.

"Technically, I won't share your last name until I file the paperwork," I tell him.

"Delilah," he growls.

I giggle. "You sound like the big, bad wolf. Why don't you do a little huffing and puffing and see what you can do about this here door."

"Why don't I say my goodbye right now instead? I'm staying with my mom tonight."

"Too much temptation at home?" I tease, biting my lip.

"That's exactly right," he says, completely serious.

I rattle the handle again, unable to keep myself from messing with the man. He makes a frustrated sound somewhere between a growl and a groan. It's a *groal*, a sound that's all Thayden. I should apply for a trademark, then gift him the paperwork on his birthday.

"When's your birthday?" I blurt.

"What?"

"I … can't marry you if I don't know the important information."

He laughs softly. "February eleventh."

I wait for a moment. "Don't you want to know mine?"

"November seventh. You're a Scorpio. And yes, I already have your present."

"Thayden Walker, you're such a stalker."

"I am. And you better believe if you don't show up tomorrow on time, I will stalk you until the day you die."

I'm smiling as I turn, putting my back against the door, wishing he was curling an arm around me and pulling me close. "I can't decide if that's the creepiest or most romantic thing I've ever heard." I pause, still smiling. "Promise?"

He waits a beat, then says with a throaty groal, "I do."

CHAPTER TWENTY-NINE

Delilah

I STARE in shock at the dress. THE dress.

Elizabeth beams, holding it out to me on the padded hanger. "Take it. It's yours."

I want to protest. I don't know exactly how much this cost, but I don't want to know. "Elizabeth! You shouldn't have! No, really. I mean it. But I'm so glad you did."

"You looked too beautiful in it for me not to. I hope you don't mind."

"Mind? I'm overwhelmed. Thank you."

I hang the dress on the clothing rack next to the distant runner-up dress I bought at some strip mall bridal mart. It seems to shrink in on itself, as though embarrassed to be seen next to its couture counterpart.

I shake my head. "You and your son—you're cut from the same cloth. When did you do this?"

"The day you tried it on."

My head snaps up. "Are you serious?"

Elizabeth's eyes soften. "I had to. It was *the* dress for you. Like magic. I knew the moment I saw it. I also knew you didn't want to accept it, so I sneaked."

I want to turn away the too-expensive gift. But I can't. I remember the feel of the dress sliding over my body and how it looked in the mirror. It is my dream dress. And though the one I bought at the big wedding chain store would have been just fine, this will be perfection.

I wrap my arms around Elizabeth, and we stand that way for a few seconds. I know she's as choked up as I am, because I can feel her breath shuddering. I squeeze her tighter.

"I hope you know that I consider you as a daughter. And today, we make that official. For *real.*"

Her words are too much. I try to keep in the tears. Not happening. I'm like a dam—one leak and the whole thing is toast. I'm wearing waterproof everything, but still.

"And, Delilah? I'm so sorry about that woman. *Verity.*" She says the name with so much venom. It's oddly validating.

I pat her shoulder. "Her real name is Trixie."

Elizabeth pulls back, already laughing. She covers her mouth. "Trixie? Short for …?"

"Trixie." I bite my lip as Elizabeth laughs.

I should feel something, talking about Mama. But after talking with Thayden last night and knowing how the people in my life stood up for me, I've been able to let go. I wish I had some kind of happy, normal childhood experience. But I don't. Instead, I have a group of amazing friends, a fiancé I can't wait to marry, and his mom, who has already shown me more love in six weeks than Mama showed my whole life.

Elizabeth gives me a kiss on the cheek and a quick squeeze. "I'll get out of here. I think when you put this dress on, I should be far away. Just, considering the last time." She winks.

I laugh. "Guess you ended up buying a dress that day after all."

She coughs, her eyes shifting away. "Yes. I did buy *a* dress."

"Elizabeth." I grab her arm. "You bought *a* dress, as in one dress? Please don't tell me you had to buy the one we ripped."

Laughing, and waving a hand, she slips away from me. "Okay, I won't tell you!"

"Elizabeth!"

"It's just money, dear! Get used to being spoiled." And then she's gone.

I shake my head, blowing out a breath and trying not to think about how much money she dropped in that bridal salon. Now, I've had three wedding dresses bought for me. Ridiculous.

Abby appears out of nowhere, gasping at my new dress. "That dress is gorgeous!" She circles the rack, eyeing every bit of the fabric with something like lust.

"Just think—you might be next," I tell her. "And if you want one that's already paid for, you can have my other one."

"Thanks, no, thanks," Abby says. Her eyebrows shoot up. "Sorry! It's just … this other one is butt-ugly."

I roll my eyes, choosing not to be offended because she's right. And I can admit that now that I have the right dress. "How are you feeling today? After your big night?"

The night before, all the girls but Abby showed up at Thayden's after he left. Apparently, she conked out moments after her big show, and had been snoring before they got her home.

Abby looks horrified. "I'm so sorry. I didn't think that

warning about no alcohol medication was serious. Are you mad?"

I laugh. "Mad? No. Thank you. I just wish I could have seen it."

"Sam filmed the whole thing," she whispers, as the door to the suite flies open as Zoey, Harper, and Sam pile in with more garment bags. Abby darts away, and I make a mental note to borrow Sam's phone later.

"I've got our dresses," Sam singsongs. The girls start unzipping garment bags.

"Yo, D. What do you think?" Abby asks.

I turn, blinking in surprise at my friends, who have all donned matching gowns in shades of pink, Abby in the brightest and Harper's dress a faint blush.

"Hey! What is this?"

Zoey winds an arm around my waist, resting her head on mine. She's tall enough that her cheek rests on the very top of my head. "I know you said you didn't want to have brides-maids, but we weren't about to let you stand up there alone. We're always going to stand with you."

I fan my eyes with my hands, like that's going to keep the tears in. "I didn't want to cry today, y'all!"

Zoey shakes her head. "And you really thought you wouldn't?"

"Well, no." I laugh and sniff, wiping my nose in a most inglorious way. Harper throws a box of tissues at me, which I'm lucky to catch. "I just didn't think it would be so *much*."

Sam touches my arm. "Are you okay that we did this? I mean, we all brought other dresses. Just in case. It's *your* day."

I'm shaking my head before she's even done. "No. I love it. I love y'all."

This, as I knew it would, precipitated a group hug that

had Harper rolling her eyes. But she still wraps an arm around me, sighing heavily. I think the fact that we've made her don two bridesmaid dresses in as many months is starting to wear her thin. She pats me twice on the butt as our group breaks apart. Which to athletes means good game, so I think for Harpy, it's a best-wishes kind of thing.

Zoey claps her hands. "You're going to be late if we don't get you in your dress, D. Let's move."

"Bossy, bossy," Abby says, clucking her tongue. "That's the Gavin influence."

"I don't mind being bossed, darlin'. Today, I need all the bossing you can give me. I feel like I'm walking in a dream."

"You look like a dream," Sam says.

The magic dress settles fully and perfectly around my curves as Zoey zips it up. I've got my hair done, half up with loose waves over my back, and my makeup's finished. I just need the veil, and I'll be complete.

Scratch that, I think, as Sam helps pin the veil in place. I'll be complete when I make it down the aisle and am standing next to my not-any-longer-fake fiancé.

———

Thayden

I'm pacing the suite, ready to get on with this already when Mom knocks and pokes her head inside the room. I'm relieved, at the least for a little distraction. I hate waiting. Especially today. We should have planned a morning wedding.

If anyone had told me two months ago that I'd be impatient to walk down the aisle, I would've laughed my way into an aneurysm.

And yet, here I am. Faster than I'd suggest anyone get married. But I *know* it's right.

"You look beautiful, Mom," I say, giving her a hug. She really does, and for a moment, I'm sad, thinking about her alone, missing out on my dad. Why she loved him, I can't say, but she did, and I hate that she's alone now.

Gavin and Chase wave while Scott smiles from the couch, still looking a little shocked that I asked him to be here. Almost as shocked as when I asked him to leave the Walker Firm and start over with me. But he was overly eager to do both.

Mom's eyes shine as she gives me the once-over. "I really and truly didn't know if I'd live to see this day, Thayden Walker. I'm so glad I did. She looks incredible. Prepare yourself." She calls to Gavin and Chase. "Be ready to pick him up off the floor, fellas."

"Yes, ma'am," Gavin says with a knowing smile.

Mom's smile grows. "I have something for you. I've been keeping it for a while."

Digging into her purse, she pulls out an envelope. I recognize my father's handwriting on the outside, and my stomach lurches. The feeling is brief, and then I'm steady again.

"What is this?"

Mom is fighting her tears, a losing battle. "He made me promise to give you this on your wedding day." She presses the envelope against my chest.

A letter from my father. I think of all the envelopes I shoved under the door last night, the letters I wish he had written.

Here's a real one, from him, and I don't feel what I imagined I might. I'm curious, but my feelings are largely underwhelming. Mostly, I ache for Mom, for how much she invested in him.

She kisses me on the cheek. "I'll leave you to it. See you in a few minutes, boys!"

I'm still standing there, a few minutes later, when Gavin claps a hand on my shoulder. "It's almost time. Do you need to read that?"

"Not sure I want to."

"Then don't," Gavin says. "If it's from him, will it make today better or worse?"

I think about that for a moment, then realize something that startles me.

"It won't matter." I tuck the envelope into one of my bags. "It doesn't matter at all."

My father either penned a heartfelt letter of love and regret or a big I-told-you-so. My money would be on the second. And for the first time in my life, I don't care about his rejection or need his approval. Whatever my father has said can wait.

I'm going to marry the love of my life. That's all that matters.

And suddenly, the slow hours before the wedding turn into speedy moments. The time comes to ride the elevator up to the roof, and I take my place up front, today with Gavin standing with me. I'm not sure why we made the change, and frankly, I don't care. I just need Delilah.

Gavin leans in from behind me. "Breathe. Just breathe, buddy."

Am I not breathing? I feel like I'm breathing. Maybe I should—

All thoughts vanish. Delilah is at the end of the aisle, so beautiful that it takes all my self-control not to run down the aisle to her. I can't tear my gaze away as she glides toward me like some kind of dream.

Her smile cracks off a piece of my heart. I'm holding it out for her, unsure why she'd want such a poor offering, but she's still coming toward me. And then she's here, standing before me, smiling.

"You're supposed to take my hand, tiger." Her grin is the kind I love best, the one where she's giving me a hard time.

"Oh!" I step closer, and Mr. Abramson, her stand-in dad, shakes my hand, leaning close before letting go.

"She may not be my daughter but hurt her and I'll make sure you get acquainted with my shotgun."

Gavin chokes out a laugh behind me. I bet he got a similar threat when he married Zoey.

I take Delilah's hand, feeling forever slide into place. Words are spoken, vows are exchanged, and through it all, I keep my eyes on hers. In the sunlight, while wearing a wedding dress and holding my hand, her eyes are the most brilliant blue of all.

I don't want to wish away a moment of this, and I hope each second stays in my memory forever. And yet, I'm eager and anxious for the almost final moment when I get to kiss her.

The minister smiles at my eagerness. "You may now kiss your bride."

There is no hesitation. No holding back. Okay, fine, a little tiny bit of holding back, only because we have an audience. Cupping Delilah's head, I tip her back slightly, my other hand sliding back to hold her waist. She's mine. And as I vowed, I will love and cherish and honor her, from this moment until my last breath.

My lips move against hers, broadcasting my feelings as

much as I can without embarrassing myself in front of our guests. My *mother* is watching.

She's also the one whistling through her fingers when I finally break the kiss. From his spot beside her, even Mr. Abramson cracks a smile.

Our friends whoop and cheer, and even as we're smiling, I go for broke to kiss her again.

"I love you, Mrs. Walker," I say between kisses.

"And I love you, Mr. Walker. Now, let's get out of here. The sooner we get done with this wedding, the sooner I can have my way with you."

I'm still laughing as we walk back down the aisle, our friends and family cheering as we go. I don't loosen my grip on her one bit, and I don't plan to anytime soon. I have everything I never knew I wanted, and all that I need. Right here. With *her*.

EPILOGUE

Delilah

THE MOMENT we reach our hotel room, we drop our towels and beach bag and Thayden slides his arms around my waist. His chest and arms are still damp, and he smells like the ocean. I feel the grit of sand brushing against my skin. He kisses the spot right in below my ear, and I shiver.

"Hello, wife," he says in his signature groal. Every time, it has the same impact, making my nerves do their own version of a body roll.

"Yes, husband?"

"I love you."

"I love *you.*"

When he spins me around, his grass-green eyes are dark, yet lit with amusement. "I need to shower. I have sand in my unmentionables."

I giggle as his lips close in on mine. "Are they still unmentionables if you mention them by calling them unmentionables?"

"Hmm," he says against my lips, kissing me again and again until my legs are wobbly. "A question worth considering." His eyes spark. "Wait! I have to give you your birthday present!"

"Thayden," I call as he rummages through his suitcase in the large suite closet. "You didn't need to do that! This trip was present enough."

"Quiet, you," he says, returning not with a gift bag, but a manila envelope and a wide smile. "It's not a traditional gift." He clutches it to his chest, like he's not going to give it to me.

I hold out a hand. "Gimme."

"I thought you said I didn't need to do this," he teases.

"Thayden Freaking Walker!" He loves it when I act like *freaking* is his middle name. Especially after I told him about all the names I used to use in my head for him. Though he wasn't too fond of Lucifer.

Thayden laughs, which was my intent, because I snatch the folder from his hands, already working the clasp. I pull out a stack of paperwork and groan.

"I thought we said no more contracts!"

Slowly, he shakes his head, now suddenly looking nervous. "Take a closer look."

I do, and the breath leaves my lungs in a long exhale. "They're applications," I whisper.

"To all the schools I thought you might want to apply to for your PhD."

I glance up at him, my eyes wide in shock. "But, all of these aren't in Austin. Or even Texas!"

Thayden rocks back on his heels, somehow looking both nervous and pleased with himself. "I'll go where you want to go, D. I can lawyer anywhere. As long as I'm with you."

The applications flutter to the ground as I wrap my arms around him, squeezing him in a bone-crushing hug. "Thank you," I whisper against his neck. "Thank you. Best birthday present ever."

Thayden pries me off his body and presses a last kiss to my cheek "Now, call your friends! You've got a ten-minute window until things might get too interesting for their eyes and ears," he teases.

I giggle and toss a flip-flop at him, but he only darts inside the bathroom. I hear the shower turn on.

Stacking the applications neatly, I slide them back in the envelope, feeling a warmth that reaches from the ends of my hair all the way down to the soles of my feet. Thayden Freaking Walker *loves* me. So much. I am the luckiest girl alive!

I dial Sam. The girls are having lunch today at the new apartment where Sam, Abby, and Harper live. It's my birthday, and I promised them before I left that I would call.

Am I ridiculous for missing my besties enough to video chat on my honeymoon? Maybe. But I don't care. One thing I realized at the wedding—they aren't just friends. They're *family*.

"Happy birthday!" They shout in unison as soon as the video call connects.

Abby shoves her way in front of the camera, giving me an up close and personal view of her nostrils. "How's your first ever real vacation? Is Thayden properly spoiling you? If not, lemme know and I'll come do some damage."

"I'm being more than properly spoiled. Y'all! They serve

us drinks on the beach! In pineapples! I had a massage in a cabana!"

"I bet that's not all you had in a cabana!" Abby yells. Even out of sight, she's somehow the biggest presence in any room.

"I will neither confirm nor deny such allegations," I say, hoping the blush isn't evident in my cheeks.

"Confirmed!" Thayden yells from the shower.

"THAYDEN!" I shout.

The girls are dying with laughter and I have to set down the phone to fan my cheeks. When I pick it back up, I send them my fiercest glare. I may come in third behind Zoey and Harper when it comes to nasty looks, but mine does its job.

"This phone call will be over if y'all don't promise me you'll quit it. Now, how's Apollo?"

Though Elizabeth is keeping him, Harper and a few others volunteered to take him on walks or to the dog park.

"Your firstborn son is fine!" Harper calls. "I'm not sure he misses you. He might need to come live with me."

"Not a chance." I hear the shower turning off, which means it's my turn. We wanted to get to a happy hour in twenty minutes.

"I've got to run, ladies. Just want to thank y'all again for everything. Miss and love you!"

Sam blows me a kiss, Zoey waves, and Harper reappears just before I set down the phone.

Just in time too, as Thayden calls, "Hey, D? What's this duct tape thing—oh! It has a bunny tail! Ohhhh, Delilah!" His voice takes on a singsong tone.

I guess we can forget about happy hour. At least, the happy hour in public. Giggling, I dart for the shower. Because I need to get the sand out of my own unmentionables.

Harper

It takes us a little too long to realize that Delilah didn't disconnect her end of the video call. Thayden's voice comes through the phone.

"Hey, D? What's this duct tape thing—oh! It has a bunny tail! Ohhhh, Delilah!"

Sam drops the phone and squeals. "She didn't hang up! She didn't hang up!"

Zoey snags the phone and ends the call as Abby cheers. "Yay! She's wearing my duct tape lingerie! Maybe I should start a duct tape fashion line."

I groan. "No more lingerie talk."

"Duct tape sportswear?"

"Do you have any idea how sweaty that would be?" I ask. "Hard pass. Duct tape had its day with the wallets and stuff. Let it go, Abs."

"Everything comes back around," Abby argues. "Bell bottoms became bootcut jeans. Leggings were big in the early '90s and now again. Chokers! Overalls!"

I let Zoey pick up the pieces of this argument while I start fixing a salad. I need to get back to the gym for a session in half an hour. I open the door next to the microwave, still expecting to see plates and bowls. But this is the coffee mug cabinet. I can't get used to this stupid new apartment.

And soon, it will just be me. One by one, my friends have fallen in love like human dominoes.

I'll be the last woman standing. It's not something I question or even something I mourn anymore. Nah, I've been resigned to my own lonely fate, since elementary school. It's not going to change anytime soon.

My phone buzzes, and I pulled it out of the side pocket of my workout pants.

Chase: im bored
Harper: what's new?
Chase: whatcha doing?
Harper: Just finished video calling D.
Chase: she's calling from her honeymoon??? Guess it's not going well.

"Harpy! What are you doing?" Sam asks.

Abby makes a kissing sound. "Texting with her *boyfriend*."

"He's not my boyfriend." The answer is automatic. Ingrained. An involuntary muscle response.

Lately though, there's a bitterness that comes with it. Like every time I say it, some new part of me shrivels up and dies.

It's true though. I need to hold to that. Chase is not, and can never be, my boyfriend. The sooner my various body parts get that memo, the better. But it seems like lately they're all mutinying against my cerebral cortex and the very real knowledge that it can't and won't happen.

Harper: She looks tan and happy. And accidentally left the video chat on ... trust me. It's going well. There was duct tape involved.
Chase: TMI
Harper: LOL
Chase: TFS
Harper: VIP
Chase: I've run out of three letter thingies

Harper: BRB
Harper: G2G
Harper: FYI
Harper: IMO
Harper: AMA
Chase: okay, I will ask you anything. Want to go to dinner?

I pause, the phone suddenly feeling heavy in my hands. The answer should be easy. I'm already eating dinner. It's girls' night, a rarer and rarer occasion these days.

But I can't help myself from thinking... what if?

What if Chase was asking me not just to dinner but on a date?

What if I said yes?

Harper: Can't. Work.
Chase: You work too much.
Harper: I know. You can drop by?
Chase: Maybe I will.

And just like that, my mood improves. It should. I can't hope for Chase or want him. He needs to find a great girl who can settle down and have the kind of life I know he wants. I am not that girl. It will kill me when he does find someone, but Chase deserves it. Then I'll back off and just be that girl he used to hang out with. My phone buzzes again.

Chase: Maybe we could get dinner after?

I stare at my phone, remembering the conversation with Delilah before her date with Thayden. The one she kept calling a dinner. Is this a dinner? Or a date?

What do I want it to be?

Before I can honestly answer the question, I send a text back, my heart thumping as I do. Just one word, but it feels bigger.

Harper: Yes.

THE END

———

ALSO BY EMMA ST. CLAIR

Love Clichés

Falling for Your Best Friend's Twin

Falling for Your Boss

Falling for Your Fake Fiancé

The Twelve Holidates

Hometown Heartthrob Series

Marrying Her Dream Groom

Forgiving Her First Love

Loving Her Cowboy

Trusting Her Cowboy Poet

Managing the Rock Star

The Billionaire Surprise Series

The Billionaire Love Match

The Billionaire Benefactor

The Billionaire Land Baron

The Billionaire's Masquerade Ball

The Billionaire's Secret Heir

Sandover Island Sweet Romance Series

Sandover Beach Memories

Sandover Beach Week

Sandover Beach Memories

Sandover Beach Christmas

Sandover Beach Series

Secrets Whispered from the Sea

ABOUT EMMA

Emma St. Clair is a *USA Today* bestselling author of over twenty books. She loves sweet love stories and characters with a lot of sass. Her stories range from rom-com to women's fiction and all will have humor, heart, and nothing that's going to make you need to hide your Kindle from the kids. ;)

You can find out more at:
http://emmastclair.com
Join her email list:
https://emmastclair.com/romcomemail
Or join her reader group at:
https://www.facebook.com/groups/emmastclair/

OTHER SERIES BY EMMA

- The Hometown Heartthrobs
- Sandover Island Sweet Romance
- Sandover Beach Books
- The Billionaire Surprise Series

facebook.com/thesaintemma
instagram.com/kikimojo

A NOTE FROM EMMA

Every book I write is a joy and a struggle. What makes it worth all the work is YOU.

I really do mean it. Without readers showing up, messaging me about the books, leaving reviews—this would be a very empty profession.

DON'T GET ME WRONG! I love writing in and of itself. But it only feels complete because of you.

This book... well. It was hard-fought. I have NEVER written a fake romance. *(Though I had one at summer camp before 8th grade that, just like the books, turned real... for a week. Hats off to you, John Smithdeal. You had GAME.)* I struggled more than I thought with making the whole faking setup and the push-pull of it much more than I thought I would.

I LOVE Delilah and Thayden, and if you haven't read how they met in *Falling for Your Boss*, it's a pretty great meet cute.

I also love Apollo, who is largely based on our Great Dane, Vader. He was the cover model, though my illustrator (@simplydylandesigns on Instagram) changed his color to gray for me because a giant black dog doesn't show up. Even in photos sometimes he looks like a big blob.

For my readers who have been with me a long time and read my other books, I wanted to make a note and a promise. My books have always (and will be) without sex on the page or language. It's the line I have drawn for myself in writing for my own personal reasons.

That said... **comedy pushes boundaries**. Always. Different boundaries depending on the comedy, but that's one of the things that makes it effective. In my romcoms, I might push some boundaries.

I'll always stick to what I feel comfortable with and will

keep the things off the page that are across my personal line. I do keep YOU, my readers, in mind.

But I also tend to feel like some things can be (and maybe should) be discussed frankly or used to lighten things up. Things like periods, our bodies, and sometimes even sex.

I really debated about the scene here with the Reverend Billy Blanks and had other people read for feedback. One reason I wanted to keep it *(besides the fact that it all made ME laugh)* was because I DO think it is important for couples to discuss those things frankly. That's HUGE! Especially for women. Maybe NOT with a weird internet reverend. And probably NOT with coloring pages.

So, while that scene may have pushed past some of the boundaries for readers used to my books or other books in the bookstore's clean & wholesome category, I was very intentional about including it.

I don't want to offend in my books, and I'm always going to think hard about what goes on the page. Our lines might not be the same *(and some of you might have lines that go wayyyyyy past mine and I'm glad you're reading too!)* but I just wanted to assure you that though we might have a one-boobed wonder, discuss periods, or have an adult coloring page, I'm not going to be graphic. I'm not aiming for shock. I'll always be intentional about what goes in my books with YOU in mind, even if we don't have the exact same lines.

Thank you so much for reading and I hope you finish out this series with me! *The Twelve Holidates* is a slight detour, following Sam's assistant, but you'll get to know Chase better toward the end, and the timeline will match up with *Falling for Your Best Friend*, Harper and Chase's book.

A few true-ish things from the book:

- I once got stuck in a dress in a fitting room alone. I

did get out without ripping it, but I was a stressed out, sweaty mess.

- I also got my leg caught in a high boot in a shoe store. (#widecalfproblems) A blushing 16-year-old employee had to help me, the fetching older college woman. A manager ended up having to come and they literally had to rip the leather boot off my leg with some kind of pliers. Thankfully, the zipper had gotten stuck, so I didn't have to buy them.
- My bestie made me duct-tape lingerie for my wedding. No bunny tail. I will decline to answer how my husband liked it. Shout out to Ginny!

Also, many of the Dear Dr. Love ideas come from readers in my Facebook group. If you aren't in there, you should join! (https://www.facebook.com/groups/emmastclair) Thanks so much to Patty, Jaclyn, Brittany, Kathy, and Dayna for some of the ones in this book!

Oh, and you'll see more of Grandpa Gosling in a future book...

Happy reading and thank you for being here!

-e

ACKNOWLEDGEMENTS

A MASSIVE thank you to the best ARC team and typo-catchers ever! (Also, it's kind of awesome that I have a paid proofer named Judy and two ARCs named Judy.)

Thank you to Ruth, Lisa, Vivian, Lissa, Marsha, Rita, Judy, Jillian, Priscilla, Judy, Devon, Lyn, Sandra, and Patty (who has provided so much support in so many ways!).

I always feel like my books stink until y'all read them. And you have the best feedback ever!

A big thanks to my second cousin once removed (did I get that right?), Walter Yates Boyd, for talking me through the lawyering stuff with regards to the will and stipulation. It convinced me NOT to get too deep in the weeds with that whole thing. I've also appreciated all the conversations about the work you're doing with movies and theater! Total inspiration.

Thanks to Aspen, Gigi, Rachel, Patty, Laura, and Summer for reading my Reverend Billy Blanks scene and helping me keep it fun and over the top without being over the line.

Thanks also to my husband, Rob, for letting me constantly scandalize you. :)

Thanks to Judy of Judy's Proofreading for my last line of defense against typos! Except when I add on whole chapters after you've checked it... lol.

Love you all!

-Emma

Made in the USA
Las Vegas, NV
07 May 2022

48531700R00208